"I'm not sure this is wise," Alex murmured, setting Fiona away from him.

His breath was coming fast and hard. His eyes were dark with hunger.

But Fiona was tired of wise. Tired of safe. Tired of watching life from the sidelines and living to regret it. "I want to feel alive," she pleaded. "Just for tonight. Just for this once."

"Tomorrow's the operation," Alex said gently. "You'll be giving your daughter life again. Then you'll be going home the day after."

Fiona let her fingers brush Alex's cheek. "Then this seems a good way to say goodbye."

"Oh, Fiona," Alex said on a sigh.

But, as if he no longer had the strength to keep her away, he pulled her back into his arms....

Dear Reader,

Weddings, wives, fathers—and, of course, Moms—are in store this May from Silhouette Special Edition!

As popular author Susan Mallery demonstrates, Jill Bradford may be a *Part-Time Wife*, but she's also May's THAT SPECIAL WOMAN! She has quite a job ahead of her trying to tame a HOMETOWN HEARTBREAKER.

Also this month Leanne Banks tells a wonderful tale of an *Expectant Father*. In fact, this hero's instant fatherhood is anything but expected—as is finding his true love! Two new miniseries get under way this month. First up is the new series by Andrea Edwards, GREAT EXPECTATIONS. Three sisters and three promises of love—and it begins this month with *On Mother's Day*. Sweet Hope is the name of the town, and bells are ringing for some SWEET HOPE WEDDINGS in this new series by Amy Frazier. Don't miss book one, *New Bride in Town*. Rounding out the month is *Rainsinger* by Ruth Wind and Allison Hayes's debut book for Special Edition, *Marry Me, Now!*

I know you won't want to miss a minute of the month of May from Silhouette Special Edition. It's sure to put a spring in your step this springtime!

Sincerely,

Tara Gavin
Senior Editor

Please address questions and book requests to:
Silhouette Reader Service
U.S.: 3010 Walden Ave., P.O. Box 1325, Buffalo, NY 14269
Canadian: P.O. Box 609, Fort Erie, Ont. L2A 5X3

ANDREA EDWARDS

ON MOTHER'S DAY

Published by Silhouette Books
America's Publisher of Contemporary Romance

For Megan—At last, an operation!
Thanks for healing the heart.

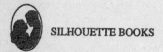 SILHOUETTE BOOKS

ISBN 0-373-24029-5

ON MOTHER'S DAY

Books by Andrea Edwards

ANDREA EDWARDS

is the pseudonym of Anne and Ed Kolaczyk, a husband-and-wife writing team that has been spinning romantic yarns for more than twenty years. Anne is a former elementary schoolteacher while Ed is a refugee from corporate America. After many years in the Chicago area, they now live in a small town in northern Indiana where they are avid students of local history, family legends and ethnic myths. Recently they have both been bitten by the gardening bug, but only time will tell how serious the affliction is. Their four children are grown; the youngest attends college while the eldest is a college professor. Remaining at home with Anne and Ed are two dogs, four cats and one bird—not the same ones that first walked through their stories but carrying on the same tradition of chaotic rule of the household nonetheless.

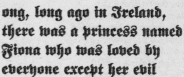

Long, long ago in Ireland, there was a princess named Fiona who was loved by everyone except her evil stepmother. She was jealous of Fiona's goodness and beauty and put a curse on the princess and her three younger brothers, turning them into swans.

For years and years, Princess Fiona and her brothers flew over the land. She tried hard to keep them all together and safe. After almost a thousand years, the spell broke and they turned back into people. But they were so ancient, they died almost immediately. The townspeople buried them together so Fiona could always watch over her brothers.

Prologue

July—Twenty years ago

"Fiona Fogarty, what are you doing here?" Mrs. Warner asked. "You're supposed to be down at the kickball tournament."

Fiona edged closer to the picnic table covered with art supplies. She was doomed. "I was helping Miss Kerns clean up," she explained.

Mrs. Warner wasn't impressed. "You're not at camp to clean up after people. Now get down to the athletic field. You're on Cassie's team."

The girl's heart sank clear down to her ankles. They might as well throw her off a cliff now—ten years was as old as she was going to get. "I don't feel good." And she didn't. She was allergic to kickball, and to being on her sister's teams.

"Fiona." Mrs. Warner's tone said she didn't care if Fiona threw up or broke out in hives or turned purple.

Fiona looked at Miss Kerns, but the art teacher just gave her a helpless smile. No one bucked Mrs. Warner. Sighing, Fiona put down the paintbrushes she'd been cleaning and started trudging through the trees, carefully keeping her new white canvas shoes in the middle of the path.

There was no hurry, in spite of what Mrs. Warner had said. Cassie wouldn't care if Fiona ever got there.

It wasn't fair. Cassie was nine—a year younger than Fiona—but was prettier and thinner and better. She could be really nice when she wanted, but since their parents had died three years ago, she mostly just fought with everybody. And Samantha was so cute everyone loved her. That left Fiona trying to make sure they weren't too much trouble for anybody.

Not that Fiona really believed what Mrs. Cochran had said at their parents' funeral. Still, the accident had happened in Minnesota, when Mom had said they were going to Milwaukee. Sometimes at night when Fiona couldn't sleep, she tried to remember things that would prove their parents hadn't been leaving them, but all she'd get was a stomachache and then nightmares when she finally went to sleep.

"Fiona. Hey, Fiona." Cassie was running along the path, with a look in her eyes that meant trouble. She stopped in front of Fiona. "Juliet's missing."

"Missing?" Fiona caught her breath. The pair of tame swans were the only good thing about this place. They were so beautiful, like something out of a fairy tale. "Maybe she and Romeo are on the other side of the lake."

"Romeo's over here. And you know he never leaves her." Cassie grabbed Fiona's hand. "Come on, we gotta go look for her."

But Fiona's feet wouldn't move. The lake was so big and the woods were even bigger. She didn't have any idea where to look. "We should tell Mrs. Warner," she said. "She'll know what to do."

"Don't be silly," Cassie snapped. "Grown-ups don't care about birds or kids or anybody small."

Fiona hated agreeing with Cassie, but she was right. Sometimes she and Cassie and their little sister Samantha were put in a foster home together, but sometimes they were separated. And no one bothered asking them which they wanted. "Miss Kerns likes kids. She'd help us find Juliet."

But Cassie just rolled her eyes. "I'm going to look. You do what you want."

Fiona stood there a moment, watching her sister stomp off toward the lake. The trees were thicker around the water and Cassie soon disappeared. From behind her, Fiona heard the kickball game starting.

Kids always thought Cassie was so cool because she'd just go off and do whatever she wanted. But what people didn't realize was that she usually got them all in trouble. And trouble was one thing they didn't need right now, not with the Scotts talking about adopting them. It was probably just talk—they already had three kids of their own—but Fiona couldn't let Cassie screw up the little chance they had. She hurried down the path to the lake and caught up with Cassie near the narrow beach.

"Aren't we supposed to be playing kickball?" Fiona asked.

"I said I had a stomachache. Jeff told me to go see the nurse."

Cassie got the nurse for her stomachache; Fiona got kickball. That figured.

"Where are you guys going?" a voice behind them called.

Fiona turned to find their little sister had followed them. "Go back to camp," Fiona told her. "They're gonna notice you're missing and get us all in trouble."

"Little kids don't get in trouble," Samantha said, circling around Fiona to chase after Cassie. "They only yell at the big kids."

"There she is!" Cassie called out, rushing into the weeds at the far end of the beach. "There's Juliet. And look, Romeo's with her!"

Fiona and Samantha followed. Once into the weeds, they could see the swan. She was about five feet from the shore, in among fallen branches at the edge of the water and listlessly struggling. Cassie began to wade out toward her.

"Cassie, you can't go in the water!" Fiona cried. "There's no lifeguard around."

Cassie gave her a look and waded in farther, keeping the branch in between her and the swan. The closer she got, the more frantic the swan seemed to be. She flapped her wings but couldn't rise out of the water.

"She's trapped!" Cassie shouted.

Juliet fell back, exhausted. Her head hung down and her wings drooped. Romeo swam closer, making worried sounds as Cassie continued to peer into the water.

"Her foot's caught in one of those plastic ring things from pop cans," Cassie called out. "All we have to do is cut the plastic and she'll be okay."

Fiona had been down this road with Cassie before. Everything was always easy—until disaster struck. "We need to tell Mrs. Warner."

"She won't do anything," Cassie said as she came back to the shore. "You know how she went on and on that first day about swans being mean. She won't let anybody near them. She'll just call somebody and Juliet will die before they get here."

"She might not."

"Come on," Cassie said, pulling on Fiona's hand. "We can help her. We just need something to cut the plastic."

Fiona was scared. She hated having to make these decisions. She never knew what to do. Should she listen to Cassie or to that little voice inside?

Juliet's eyes seemed to plead with her. "All right." Even as Fiona said the words, Cassie was running off. Fiona turned to Samantha. "You stay here and keep Juliet company."

"Me?" Samantha cried. "What am I supposed to do?"

"I don't know, Sam. Sing to her. Read her a story. Show her what's in your knapsack. Just stay out of the water."

She had a quick glimpse of Samantha slipping her precious knapsack off her shoulders before she hurried off after Cassie. She chased her across the beach, catching up with her at the beginning of the wooded path. Up ahead through the trees, Fiona could see Mrs. Warner and Miss Kerns were still at the arts-and-crafts table.

"I could ask Miss Kerns for a scissors," Fiona said.

"No," Cassie hissed. "She'll just ask you what you want them for. I'll go talk to Mrs. Warner. When they're looking the other way, you take one."

She couldn't steal something! "Why can't I talk to them and you get the scissors?"

"Because you're not cool," Cassie replied.

Fiona just sighed. Cassie was right. She was the most uncool kid in the whole world. She was chubby; her hair always curled wrong; and she couldn't tell a joke to save her life. She'd never be able to distract anyone. But to steal a pair of scissors!

"Fiona," Cassie hissed. They had gotten to the bend in the path. Mrs. Warner and Miss Kerns would notice them in about a second.

"All right. All right, already."

Before Fiona could warn Cassie not to get them caught, her sister was walking over to the counselors. Soon they were laughing like old friends, leaving Fiona to wish she could just find a hole to hide in. But Juliet was in trouble and Samantha was all alone down by the lake. She had to be brave like the Princess Fiona her mother used to tell her about.

Dropping down to the ground, Fiona crept around the tables and up behind the counselors. She snatched a pair of scissors and crawled toward a clump of bushes over by the dining tent, where she dropped to the ground. She was a thief. She'd thrown away all those years of trying to make everybody like her and had turned to a life of crime. By the time Cassie arrived, Fiona was shaking so hard she hurt.

"Let's go," Cassie said, striding right past her.

Groaning, Fiona struggled to her feet and hurried after her sister. "What if they call the police?"

"Why would they do that?" Cassie asked. "They've got so many scissors, they'll never know one is missing."

Fiona ran along behind Cassie, not knowing which she should feel worse about—that she was now a common thief, or that her sister had a criminal mind.

They raced along the path and across the beach, then through the weeds. Samantha was kneeling in the water, reading a story to Juliet through the fallen branch.

"Samantha!" Fiona shouted. "I told you to stay out of the water."

"I had to show her the pictures," Samantha explained as she tramped out of the water. "You always show me the pictures when you read to me."

Fiona just flopped down on the shore. God was punishing her for being a thief by giving her the dopiest sisters in the world. Trying to catch her breath, she watched Cassie wade over toward Juliet. The bird panicked, flapping her wings and trying to pull backward.

"Stop it, you stupid old bird!" Cassie screamed, tears filling the cracks in her voice. "We're just trying to help you."

She tried again but, even though the branch was between her and the bird, every time Cassie got close, Juliet would set her powerful wings to flapping, trying to lift herself from the water.

"Fiona," Cassie finally wailed. "I can't cut the plastic away unless she holds still. You've got to come over here and help."

"In there?" Fiona stood, looking down at the new sneakers their foster mother had just bought her and at the muddy lake they had been told never to go in without a lifeguard.

But then she saw Cassie—who never cried—in tears in the water and Samantha clutching a picture book to her chest. Her heart-shaped paper name-tag was wet and ripping from her shirt, like a heart ready to break in two.

Suddenly Fiona was so tired of nothing ever going right. She was tired of not having parents to look out for them. She was tired of being good and trying to be liked, only to have the three of them sent on to another home anyway. Keeping her shoes clean wasn't going to make the Scotts adopt them, and neither was staying out of the lake. They might never be adopted. And she couldn't do anything about it.

But she could save Juliet. She could make sure Romeo was never as lonely as she sometimes was.

Fiona stepped into the lake, walking gingerly through the mud and circling around the branch until nothing was between her and Juliet. "When she's looking at me, you cut her free," Fiona told Cassie.

Juliet did turn to watch Fiona as the girl waded farther out into the water, the bird's dark eyes pleading somehow. Fiona found a strength in being free of all her hopes.

"Hi, Juliet," she said softly. "You remember me. I'm Fiona."

Cassie was easing in closer, almost close enough to reach under the branch and get at the plastic, and Juliet flicked a worried glance her way. Fiona took a step farther into the water, dragging Juliet's gaze back.

"Did you know there was once a swan named Fiona?" she asked the bird. "My mommy told me about her. She was a regular girl first, a princess with three little brothers. Then an evil old witch got mad at her. She turned Fiona and her brothers into swans."

Cassie was right up to the bird and Fiona hurried on: "The four of them flew all over Ireland for hundreds and hundreds of years," she said. "And the princess always watched out for her brothers and kept them safe. After almost a thousand years, the spell was broken and they became people again, but really, really old people.''

Cassie's hands were working under the water, her face scrunched up in concentration. Back onshore, Samantha had both hands over her mouth as if keeping her fear in. Fiona looked back at Juliet.

''I was named after that Fiona,'' she told the bird. ''And I try to look out for Cassie and Samantha just like the princess looked out for her brothers. But sometimes it's hard.''

The bird's dark eyes seemed to understand and out here amid the branches and mud, Fiona felt her fears rising to the surface like sticks in the water. ''Sometimes I think nobody'll ever come along and love us again,'' she whispered. ''I mean, really love us. Like Romeo loves you.''

Cassie stood suddenly and Juliet jerked away from her and away from Fiona. She was free! With a burst of strength, the bird turned and half flew toward Romeo. As Fiona watched, the swans swam away from the shore, their bodies rubbing and their necks intertwined.

''Look at this stupid junk,'' Cassie fumed, waving the plastic ringed strip in the air as she went back to the shore. ''People who throw this stuff in the lake ought to be hung by their necks with it.''

Fiona walked slowly back, glancing over her shoulder at the swans. Their joy at being together again touched her, made her eyes tear. Love was worth any price.

''Come on,'' she said, as she climbed out of the water and took Samantha's hand. ''We'll go back to camp around past the nurse's office. We can say we went there with you.''

How they'd explain the fact that the three of them were soaking wet, she didn't know. But for once, she wasn't trying to think up explanations just in case they were needed. The three of them walked along the shore, and were just about to start up through the trees when an old woman came toward them.

''I saw what you did,'' she said to them.

Fiona grabbed Cassie's and Samantha's hands and pulled them close. She'd known they would get caught; she wasn't any better at being a criminal than she was at kickball. The woman looked too old to be a counselor, but she was probably going to tell on them.

Fiona took a step forward although her heart had climbed into her throat. Mommy had told her to take care of Cassie and Sam and she would. "It was my fault," she said. "I'm the oldest and I should have known better."

"Boy, Fi—"

But the old woman's laughter cut Cassie's words off. "The gods will smile on you," the old woman said. "You fought so love might live. Someday, the spirits will return to fight for your love."

As Fiona stared at her, the woman turned and disappeared among the tall weeds. Spirits fighting for her love? That sounded about as likely as making a home run in kickball.

Chapter One

"I'll pick you up in a half hour," Samantha said. "We'll go to the drugstore, then the bakery. After that we'll go back to your place and—"

"And everyone'll jump out at me and yell, 'Surprise!'" Fiona closed her eyes and leaned against the wall, mashing the phone up against her ear. "I really don't want to do this," she said. "I hate these birthday parties."

Fiona could feel her sister's hurt feelings vibrating over the phone lines. "Look," she said wearily. "It's not like it's a surprise. Why can't we do it tomorrow night? I'm beat. Fourth-graders are exhausting the day before spring break."

"Come on, Fiona. Be a good sport. Today's your birthday and you know Dad. With Mom gone, he already thinks he's the only one who cares about the family traditions."

Fiona never ceased to be amazed at how easy the words "Mom" and "Dad" rolled off her sister's tongue. The Scotts had adopted the three of them almost twenty years ago. They were wonderful people and Fiona loved them dearly, but at ten it had been a little hard to put aside memories of her biological parents.

It probably had been easier on Samantha; she'd only been six when they'd come to live with the Scotts. Although she'd always been more adaptable than either Fiona or Cassie. Maybe that came with being the baby of the family. Fiona and Cassie had always taken care of her and that hadn't changed once they'd been adopted. In fact, Sam had just gained three more siblings to care for her; Fiona and Cassie had gained extra sparring partners.

"You don't have to go shopping if you don't want to," Sam said. "But you're getting out of your apartment so it can be fixed up for your party. I don't care if I have to tie you up and drag you around like a sack of potatoes."

"Oh, all right," Fiona replied. "It's not like I have anything else in my life." She straightened up from the wall, wondering if she had time for a shower.

"Sounds like you're deep into the big three-O blues."

"My kids have more exciting lives than I have," Fiona grumbled.

"Yeah," Sam said. "I hear those fourth-graders can be pretty wild."

"More than I've ever been. Or ever will be." Except for that one night eleven years ago.

"I agree with the *been* part," Sam said. "But that doesn't mean you have stay that way the rest of your life."

But she'd learned her lesson. "Oh, Sam. I wear sensible shoes. And I like them."

"Will you cheer up if I promise you two pieces of cake?" Sam said.

Fiona gave in to Sam's pleading with a laugh. "Sure."

Sam had always been the one who wanted everybody to be happy. Cassie was the one you called on if you needed some muscle. And what was she? Fiona asked herself.

The one who watched to see that the rules were all followed. The boring one. The unexciting one. The one with no life. Her students truly did have more exciting lives.

Fiona sighed. It had been her choice, after all. "We were cleaning up the classroom this afternoon and I found this questionnaire that the girls had worked up. They were voting on who was the sexiest boy in the class."

"And who won?"

Fiona couldn't help laughing. "For heaven's sake, Sam, why should you care? We're talking about fourth-grade boys."

"Hey, they have older brothers, cousins, uncles, whatever."

Fiona just sighed again.

"Don't be such a fuddy-duddy, Fiona," Sam said. "One never knows where her prince will come from."

Before Fiona could reply, her front-door buzzer sounded.

"Like through your front door," Sam said.

"Yeah, right," Fiona replied. "That's about as likely to be my prince as me—"

"Making a home run in kickball," Sam finished for her. "We know. We've all heard it a million times."

The buzzer sounded again, this time more impatiently. "Well, it's true," Fiona said. "That's either going to be the paperboy or Mr. Kaminsky from upstairs. Both nice people, but neither a prince."

"Fiona, you gotta believe."

The buzzer grew even more impatient, sounding almost continuously. "Mr. Kaminsky," Fiona decreed. "No one else expects me to be there immediately."

"Well, I'll let you go. See you in a half hour. Remember not to have dinner," Sam said.

The dial tone joined the buzzing of Fiona's doorbell. Shaking her head, she hung up and hurried to the door. "I'm coming," she shouted as she unlocked the door. "Hold your horses."

She was all set to give Mr. Kaminsky a scolding, but instead of looking into her short, squat neighbor's faded blue eyes, Fiona found herself looking at gray dolphins leaping about on a red tie. Her eyes crept up until they were looking into the darkest eyes she'd ever seen, eyes with merry little lights dancing in their shadows.

"I don't have any horses," he said. "But I'd be glad to hold you."

Fiona felt the warmth crawl up her neck and into her cheeks and ears. Men didn't look at her the way this man was looking. She wasn't the chubby little girl she used to be, but no one would mistake her for a skinny little waiflike model, either.

"What is it you wish?" she asked, summoning up her best no-nonsense teacher's tone.

"Fiona Scott?"

She just stared at him. There was no reason to give a stranger information.

"I'm Alex Rhinehart." He flashed an official-looking ID that said he was a private detective from Chicago. "We need to talk. May I come in, please?"

"We can talk out here," Fiona replied, implying that any funny business on his part and she'd bring down a passel of neighbors on his head. She watched as he took a moment to check the area around him.

"It's about your daughter," he said quietly.

In the blink of an eye the warmth in Fiona's face was replaced by a painful cold in her heart. Her daughter! For a moment, Fiona thought she was going to faint. There was no air to breathe, or strength in her body to pull it in. But then she steadied herself against the doorframe and looked into the private detective's eyes. They were no longer laughing.

"What do you want?" she whispered.

He looked around again, at the still-empty entryway and porch. "I'd really rather talk inside."

"I was told the records would be sealed forever."

"Yeah, well." He shrugged. "The courts use old-fashioned wax seals. You know the kind. They break real easy."

Fiona continued staring at him. It had been a baby girl. The result of that one night of excitement eleven years ago. Fiona had given her up to a better life and then had buried the secret deep in her heart.

"I don't think this is anything to joke about."

"I'm sorry, Miss Scott." He looked around again. "But I'd really prefer to discuss my business inside. Please."

Moving as if in a dream, Fiona stepped back from the door. The detective came in, closed the door softly behind him and walked straight into her living room. He sat down in the recliner by the front window. Forcing her leaden feet to move, she followed him.

"What do you want?" Fiona suddenly felt so frightened. Was this some sort of blackmail attempt? It took every bit of strength she could muster to speak. "Why are you here?"

"It's a long story," he said. "Why don't you sit down?"

"I don't have long. I . . . I have things to do."

"Sit down, please." His face was stern; his voice was firm.

And she had no strength to resist. Fiona sat down.

"Ten years ago on July 16, in Los Angeles, you gave birth to a daughter at County-USC, correct?"

The day came back to surround her. The pain of labor was nothing compared to the pain of holding that tiny life in her arms, knowing that she'd never see her again.

"Miss Scott?"

Fiona nodded, unable to say anything.

"Well, your birth child needs your help."

Fiona could feel her heart stop. "Oh, God." She could barely push out the words. "What's wrong?"

"She has leukemia," the detective replied.

The whole world froze in horror. "Oh, no." It had to be some sick joke, this whole thing.

"Her parents commissioned me to find you. They're hoping that you could be a donor."

But Fiona barely heard him. "Leukemia?" She shook her head. "But I was so careful. I didn't smoke or drink or even take aspirin."

"No one's blaming you," Alex said. "I don't think the doctors have any idea what caused it. Right now, they're just looking for a donor."

Fiona looked up at him, his words starting to make some sort of sense. "They think I might be one?"

"Siblings are the first choice."

He looked around the living room, obviously looking for signs of other children, but Fiona knew all he saw was the sterile decor. He must think she was some boring, stuffy old maid. Her two cats were both sleeping in the bedroom and out of sight, but they'd only add to the image. As would the quilted pillows on the sofa, even though she'd researched the patterns and made them herself. She doubted he'd care that she'd refinished that desk herself or that she'd read all the books on the shelves around the television.

His eyes came back to hers. "I take it that you and the child's father had no other children."

She shook her head. "No." That would have been hard since she'd only seen the jerk once after becoming pregnant. He'd denied knowing her then, denied having met her at that frat party and denied being the one to coax her to stay when she'd been about to flee back to her dorm.

Alex nodded. "From what the doctors told me, the matching process is complex and a sibling with the same parents would have the best chance of being a good match, but any blood relative is a possibility."

"I see. Well, of course, I'm willing. What do I do?"

"Submit to a blood test. If you don't match, the parents would like to test other relatives of yours, and the child's father."

Fiona's senses froze slightly. She couldn't care less about disrupting the father's life, although she wasn't at all sure she could give this detective enough information to find him. She'd been a stupid, lonely college freshman who'd drunk too many California Sunshines. All she'd wanted to hear was how special she was, not his last name or hometown or even his major.

Telling her family would be the real agony. Years ago, she'd wanted to spare them the hurt and disappointment, so she hadn't told them about the child. But she would break her silence, and in a second, if need be.

"So where do we go from here?" she asked.

"Chicago."

Fiona blinked at him. "Right now?" She wasn't good at impromptu, improvisational kinds of things. She liked to plan things out, then follow the plan. Especially when it came to something new.

"Is that a problem?"

"No. No, not at all." Fiona stood. She'd need to have someone come in to care for the cats, and take in her mail. "I guess I should pack a few things."

"Oh, Miss Scott."

Fiona paused and turned to face him, noticing that a shadow had filled his eyes.

"It's the parents' wish that this be treated as if you were an anonymous donor."

She stared at him as sudden pain jabbed at her heart. Then she looked away. What the heck? Anonymous mother, anonymous donor. She did anonymous real good. It was one of her better features.

After a quick nod, she turned toward her bedroom, but before she'd taken a step, her front-door buzzer sounded. Now who—?

Samantha.

"Oh, Lordy. I forgot." Fiona turned toward Alex. "My family's throwing a surprise party for my birthday. Here. In about an hour."

Alex watched as Fiona opened the door and a short, bubbly woman bounced inside. The family resemblance to Fiona was strong but the younger woman lacked the quiet maturity that made Fiona seem so easy to be around. And she wouldn't have made nearly as comfortable a handful.

Alex pushed the thought away sharply. Where had those thoughts come from? Fiona was just somebody his client wanted found. He'd made some calls, pulled some strings and told this kid's story to a file clerk at the hospital. It had worked; he'd found Fiona. End of story.

"Uh, Sam—" Fiona was talking to the young woman.

But the woman spotted Alex and her face lit up. "Well, hello there," she said. "You're not the sexiest boy in fourth grade, are you?"

"Huh?" It was not his most clever response, but it wasn't a question he'd been asked before.

"I mean, you'd have my vote, but you do look a little big."

"Mr. Rhinehart." Fiona took the young woman's arm firmly. "This is my sister Samantha. Sam, this is Alex Rhinehart."

"Hello, again," Sam said, shaking his hand firmly. Her eyes kept dancing back and forth between himself and Fiona and it was obvious she was dying of curiosity.

"Mr. Rhinehart is from Chicago," Fiona said.

"Oh, how nice."

"He's...ah..." Fiona looked at him and Alex reached into his pocket for his ID. "He's with a hospital in Chicago," she quickly finished.

Alex paused, his hand still in his pocket.

"I thought I told you." Fiona was concentrating on Samantha and seemed to be avoiding Alex's eyes. "Months ago I signed up as a volunteer bone-marrow donor. And I might be a match for a young child in Chicago." She glanced quickly at Alex, then looked away again. "And that's why Mr. Rhinehart is here."

"Oh, that's wonderful, Fiona," Sam said.

Alex let his hand slip out of his pocket. Okay. So Fiona had never told her sister about that little baby in L.A. Oh, well. It was her choice. No big deal. Sympathy tweaked his heart momentarily at the flicker of fear in her eyes, and that concerned him more than her obvious hedging. He never got involved. Never.

"Does this change our plans?" Sam asked her sister. "Is the party still on?"

Fiona looked over at Alex. He shrugged; he could come back later. "A few hours more won't matter. They wouldn't run the tests tonight anyway."

"Great," Sam said as she moved over to Alex's side. "Drive Fiona around the block for a while, will you?"

He stopped. This wasn't what he had planned. He looked quizzically at Fiona.

"It's so they can set up for my surprise party," she explained.

"How can it be a surprise if you know about it?"

"It's a family thing," Sam replied, as she pushed them out the door.

The next thing Alex knew, he and Fiona were standing outside the door of her small apartment building. He wasn't sure what he was supposed to do or say. He couldn't exactly leave her on the doorstep, but he was definitely not into birthday parties.

"My car's the green Ford down the block," he said as he led her down to it.

She frowned at him as he unlocked the door. "This is a Mercury. Don't you know what kind of car you own?"

"Actually, this isn't my car," he said. "I've got a friend who owns a used-car lot and when I need a car, I just rent one from him."

"Isn't that inconvenient?"

"Not really." He opened her door. She got in, reaching over to unlock his door. "You don't need a car in the city. There're a lot of stores within walking distance of my apartment and I can take a cab or a bus most other places. So it saves me the trouble of parking and insurance."

"But you never know what you're going to get," she told him.

"No, I get just what I need. It's a hell of a lot better than picking one kind of car and thinking it's going to be exactly what I need for the next five years."

He started up the motor. A car was unloading just as they pulled away from the curb, its occupants waving wildly to Fiona. She waved back, but halfheartedly at best. She didn't appear to be too enthused about this party business. Maybe it was just the news about her kid, or maybe she just wasn't crazy about parties.

If that was it, he could sympathize; he wasn't into them, either. The last birthday party he'd been involved with was Jenny Lipton's sixteenth when he was seventeen. He'd gotten her the wrong present, had worn the wrong clothes and hadn't stayed glued to her side like she'd wanted. Rescuing her from that jerk that had been hitting on her had been a hell of a lot easier than everything that had followed.

Then there'd been Louisa Turner when he'd been in the army. Seven months pregnant, she'd been dumped by her recruit boyfriend. Alex had found her living hand-to-mouth and had steered her through the proper channels to get help only to have her dump him and return to her old boyfriend at the first chance. But there'd been no birthday there.

Or with Karen Lipinski about five years back. He'd still been a cop then and she'd had her purse snatched. Nothing major, but still a trauma. She'd leaned on him through the aftermath and for a while after that. But then he'd reached the end of his fuse when one more perp had walked because the rules had been more important than justice and he'd traded in his uniform for his P.I. license. He wouldn't be busting the bad guys as a P.I., but justice would be within reach. He could keep some woman and her kids from being cheated in a divorce settlement. He could find some deadbeat who'd walked out on a debt. He could find a possible donor to help save a kid's life. Karen hadn't shared his excitement, though, and had gone. It hadn't been him she'd been leaning on, but what he'd been.

"Go straight down this street," Fiona said, bringing him back to the present with a thud. "Then take a right at the light. We're not far from Clements Woods. I thought we could go down and walk along the lake."

"Okay." He'd sworn off relationships after Karen, finally coming to accept that some people didn't belong in relationships, and he was one of them.

He followed Fiona's directions through town and eventually came to the entrance to a county park. A gravel drive wove through trees, after a time leading them into a small parking lot ringed by logs. Down a slope ahead of them, through the budding branches of the trees, he could see the bright glints of sunlight on water. No one else seemed to be around.

"Quiet here," he noted.

"Not too much happening in early April," she said. "Winters, the whole world comes here to go cross-country skiing. Summers, it's packed with day campers. My sisters and I went to day camp here when we were kids."

They got out of his car and followed a path down to the lake. The day had been pleasant, warm almost, but it was damp and chilly here amid the trees. Alex was tempted to pull his suit coat closer around him, but Fiona in her lightweight jacket seemed unbothered, so he'd be damned if he'd show he was.

"I went to a summer camp once," he said.

"This remind you of it?" she asked.

He shook his head. "Mine was at a field house in the city." He thought that sounded almost pitiful and hurried on. "It was good fun, just not woodsy."

"Ah."

They'd come to the edge of the lake and it was slightly warmer here. She turned to walk across a narrow beach and he trailed after her. They'd only gone a few yards beyond the beach, along a less worn path, when he noticed two swans gliding toward them across the glittering water.

"There're swans here?"

"Yep." She pulled a bag from her purse that turned out to have bread crusts in it. "Want some?"

He frowned at her and then at the huge birds bearing down on them. "You think those measly little pieces are going to pacify those beasts?"

She just laughed and it sounded almost as if the woods had come alive. "They're tame," she said, then turned to the birds who were now just a few feet offshore. "Hi, Romeo. Hi, Juliet. How're you guys doing?"

"Romeo and Juliet?" He didn't like his reaction to her laughter. Clients never touched him and she was less than that. He forced joviality into his voice. "Are they star-crossed teenage lovers?"

She tossed a piece of bread to each of them. "I don't know about star-crossed, but they aren't teenagers," she said. "They were here twenty years ago when my sisters and I came to camp. Swans mate for life. And they can live into their thirties and even forties."

"Jeez. Thirty years." He thought of his mother's frequent and short-lived marriages. "That's longer than most of the marriages I've seen."

But Fiona didn't laugh. She just tossed another piece of bread to each swan. "Isn't that sad? That real faithfulness and loyalty can only be found among animals?"

It was indeed, but he just let the question hang in the air until it fell silently into the water. This whole situation was making him uneasy. Fiona was making him uneasy. It should have been a simple job—find her and bring her to Chicago. Yet it was feeling anything but.

She tossed the last crusts to the swans, then sat down on a fallen log to stare out over the water. Alex felt somehow that the silence was more than just silence. He sat down at Fiona's side. There was a peacefulness here that began to ease the knots in his soul.

"What's her name?" she asked suddenly, and turned toward him. "My daughter, I mean."

The question wasn't exactly hard, but it started a battle brewing in his brain. Anonymously, that was how the Andrewses wanted this whole thing to be handled. They wanted Fiona to come to save the girl's life, but they didn't want to admit she had any rights. But, hell, it wasn't like she couldn't find out the kid's name on her own. Or that it would hurt anything if she knew.

"Kate," he said. "I don't know if that's short for anything."

She nodded and looked away. "Has she been sick long?"

"I don't know. I guess she's been getting worse lately." He was sorry he'd started this whole thing—not because he didn't want to answer these questions, but because he didn't know the answers. And under that calm, quiet exterior, Fiona must have real fears that needed calming. "They said that she's got a real curable kind of leukemia, though."

"With the right donor," Fiona added.

He nodded. "Yeah. With the right donor."

The silence came back but he had to stretch to find the peacefulness. The damp in the air must have pushed it away.

"Isn't it nice here?" she asked. "I've been coming here to think for years."

"Oh, yeah?" He did his best thinking while stuck in traffic.

"I used to think there was magic here, somehow," she said. "Good things seemed to happen right after I'd leave. Like the time I got a new bike or got asked to my prom. I even found one of my cats abandoned up in the parking lot."

"It's your lucky place, huh?"

She shrugged. "It seems pretty silly, now that there's a real problem needing fixing." She got to her feet as the swans were turning to glide away as regally as they had come. "Either I can help Kate or I can't. Nothing here is going to change that."

He got to his feet also. "My mother believes in magic," he said. It was what she was always looking for in her relationships. He doubted she ever found it, though.

"Maybe magic's just hoping for something so much, you make it come true," she said.

"Maybe."

She started back toward the car, then stopped at the water's edge. "Look, a swan feather."

She seemed more excited about it than seemed reasonable. "Must be molting season," he said.

She was too busy getting a stick to push the feather to the shore to respond. Once it was close, she reached down to pick it up, shaking it slightly to get the water off it.

"It'll bring me luck," she said and put it in her pocket.

They traveled back to the apartment in silence. He was relieved to leave the park. Their conversation there had been getting just a bit unnerving. Although Fiona didn't seem all that glad to be getting back to her "surprise" party. Why didn't she just put a stop to them if she didn't like them?

But then there was a lot he didn't know about families. His mother had gone through four husbands before he was sixteen and two since then. A couple of them had brought kids along—maybe part of the guy's appeal, since his mother had been warned not to have more kids after Alex had been born—but none of them had ever been together long enough to get past the annoyance stage.

The street in front of Fiona's apartment was filled with cars and they had to park over in the next block.

"Looks like somebody's having a party," he said, as they walked back to her place.

"Ha-ha," she murmured.

Fiona's family certainly did things up right. Quiet reigned in the building until she opened her apartment door, then the whole world exploded into sound. People were yelling "Happy Birthday!" streamers filled the air, and little kids were blowing horns. Fiona smiled bravely through the whole thing. She didn't become flustered until the initial wave of noise died down.

"Hey, look!" somebody yelled. "Fiona brought a date."

"Nice-looking fella."

"Maybe he's one of those mail-order dates."

"Yeah, I hear you can get anything from a catalog these days."

"All right, that's enough." Fiona held her hands up and had turned on her sternest schoolmarm tone. "This is Alex Rhinehart from Chicago."

Everyone quieted down for a moment and Fiona gave the explanation she had given Samantha. It was fairly obvious that nobody in this group knew about her child.

As Fiona came to the end of the story, the noise started up again. Maybe a little more subdued, but partying nonetheless and it pulled her into the flow. Alex drifted toward a quiet side of the living room.

His first impression of Fiona's apartment had been of quiet comfort and now, left to his own devices, he could see that he was right. Everything seemed to fit together—the inviting pillows on the sofa, the occasional shelf of figurines in among her books, even the family pictures on the wall.

Maybe once this thing was over he should hire her to redo his place. He didn't know if it needed a woman's touch, but he did know his touch hadn't done anything positive to it. He picked up a glass swan from a shelf.

"That's Aunt Fiona's."

"Yeah, you drop it and you're dead meat."

He slowly put the figurine back before turning to look at a group of kids watching him. "Hi, guys," he said.

"We ain't all guys," the bigger of the girls said.

"I'm sorry," Alex replied. "Hi, guys and gals."

They stared unblinkingly at him.

"Is that better?" he asked.

They continued staring.

Alex cleared his throat. "Those glass swans are real pretty."

"She got them 'cause she rescued a real live swan," the bigger girl, apparently a spokesperson, said.

"Oh, yeah?" He looked at the figurines again. "Who gave them to her, the Royal Order of Swans?"

They reverted to their unblinking stare. Alex didn't know much about little kids but, from what he could see with this group, they didn't have much of a sense of humor.

"You know," he said. "Like maybe the king swan had them made and—"

"Swans can't make things."

"Okay." Alex nodded. "So they bought them at the glass-thing store."

"Swans don't got no money."

Their frowns were starting to deepen and Alex wondered if kids became dangerous when irritated. "All right," he said. "So how did Fiona rescue this swan?"

"The swan was stuck in the water."

"No, it was stuck in some garbage."

"But the garbage was in the water, so that makes it stuck in the water."

"Aunt Cassie and Aunt Sam helped."

"They cut it loose."

"And Aunt Sam says that because of it, they're going to be lucky in love."

Alex blinked at the solemn little faces surrounding him. Lucky in love? He knew that Fiona was single. And judging from the reception he got from her relatives, there wasn't a whole passel of leading men pursuing her.

He was also single but quite happy with that. Maybe being lucky in love meant that you weren't caught in a suffocating relationship.

"Hey." Alex pointed toward the pictures on the wall. "Who are all these people?"

The bigger girl pointed to a photo of a couple standing next to a car. "Those are Aunt Fiona's other mom and dad."

Other mom and dad?

"And this is Grandma Scott."

"That's Aunt Cassie and Auntie Sam when they were little."

They were racing ahead, pointing out pictures and throwing names at him. Alex stopped trying to keep it all straight. They skipped one picture, though—an old one that looked like a reproduction of a newspaper photo. "Who's this old guy?"

"Aunt Fiona's great-great-grandfather."

"Not great 'cause he was swell."

"No, great like really, really old."

"What's so great about being old?"

The last question brought quiet to the group as they all pondered the pros and cons of growing old. But Samantha took that moment to announce the lasagna was out of the oven, causing the kids to charge toward the kitchen.

Once he was alone again, Alex turned to study the picture. The man looked familiar. Alex moved closer and found a name in tiny letters beneath the picture—Horace Waldo Fogarty. Good Lord. He was Fiona's ancestor?

Horace Fogarty had been a well-known newspaper editor at the turn of the century and one of Alex's guiding lights once he discovered Fogarty's works while in high school. His major thesis was that a man's honesty defined his worth, not how much money he had or to whom he was born. Alex even had a signed copy of one of his editorials in his autograph collection.

And to think he now knew a relative of the great man.

Although he wasn't sure that Fogarty would have agreed with Fiona's keeping her pregnancy a secret.

"They reminded me of a swarm of army ants," Alex said.

"Army ants?" Fiona closed her suitcase and looked up,

desperately struggling to close the latch and put her mind in order. It was more than four hours since Alex had appeared at her door, turning her life upside down. The shock was only starting to wear off. "Who?"

"Your family," he replied. "They swoop in, set things up, and party hardy. Then they clean up and disappear. Unless you were here yourself, you'd never guess that only minutes ago, a gang of people had occupied these premises."

"They're quite efficient," Fiona said as she wiped her palms on her jeans and looked around the room. She could feel Alex's eyes on her but that was just one more thing bombarding her. At the moment she wished she were a little mouse with a hidey-hole to run to.

"Nervous?"

She nodded.

"I've never been a donor," he said. "But as I understand it, the procedure isn't too bad."

Fiona gave him a quick glance, a half smile twisting her face, before she turned away. "I haven't seen her in ten years."

There was a long pause before Alex spoke. "She won't know who you are."

"But I'll know who she is," she replied, so quietly that she almost didn't hear herself.

If she was a basket case now, how would she be once she got to Chicago? Once she was in the same room with her daughter and the adoptive parents? But was it right to consider the girl her daughter?

No. Her only two babies were right here—Elvis and Prissy. They were the only ones she had a right to love and to spoil. She went to the cabinet and took out a small handful of cat treats, leaving a few in each of the cat dishes. Sam would come by and feed them, and even play with them. For all Fiona knew, they wouldn't miss her at all. She hadn't let a whole lot get attached to her.

"Take your bags, ma'am? My bellhop uniform is at the cleaners," Alex said. "But my lifting muscles are just fine."

Fiona shook her head. "I can't go yet. I need to check on somebody first. I look after some of my neighbors. They're old and there are no relatives that live close by."

"Oh."

"Sam and Cassie will look in on them while I'm gone," Fiona said. "And Mrs. Callan and Mr. Kaminsky will be fine. But I want to look in on Mrs. Torcini before I go. She gets confused easily and I want to tell her about the arrangement myself."

"Okay," Alex replied.

Fiona let him take her arm as they exited her apartment. Not that it meant anything—they both knew it didn't—but it was nice nonetheless. She pressed her neighbor's buzzer.

"She doesn't hear too well," Fiona explained, turning away from the door.

"Hello."

Fiona almost jumped through the roof. Her neighbor always spoke loudly.

"Hello, Mrs. Torcini," Fiona said. "I just came by to tell you that I'd be gone for a little while."

The elderly woman's hair was as white as newly fallen snow, but her eyes were black as coal. She stood there staring at Alex. Fiona hoped that the old dear understood her.

"Samantha and Cassie will drop in and see how you are."

"You're getting married?"

Fiona looked at Alex, whose face now wore a crooked grin, and then back to Mrs. Torcini. "No!" she shouted. "We're not getting married."

"You're going to live together?"

Fiona found herself sputtering, unable to utter anything that made sense.

"Young people do that a lot nowadays. I don't know why." The old woman shook her head. "It's like a pair of shoes. You wanna buy a pair of shoes after someone else's worn them?"

"We're just going to Chicago." Fiona, her cheeks burning, felt her agitation grow as she tried to get some eye contact with her neighbor, who was still checking Alex out. "He's driving me."

"Make sure it's to Chicago he's driving you. Men can drive a woman to distraction."

Fiona stared at her neighbor. Was she making a joke? Her words said yes but her face said nothing.

"I got a light bulb burned out in my bathroom," Mrs. Torcini said. "How about you put in a new one?"

"Light bulb?"

"They're sort of round things with a tail that has screw threads at the end," Alex whispered in Fiona's ear.

She glared at him before turning back toward Mrs. Torcini. "Of course," she said. "I'd be happy to."

Her neighbor stood back and let them enter. After closing the door she shuffled off to find a new bulb, leaving Fiona alone with Alex in the foyer.

"How many schoolteachers does it take to screw in a light bulb?" Alex asked.

Her nervousness evaporated as she turned her best schoolmarm stare on Alex. The one that told every little boy from six to sixty to go ahead and "make my day."

"One," he said, as a little smile, full of devilish innocence, danced on his lips. "Because they're so smart."

Fiona frowned. A little voice inside her was shouting out, *Be careful.* If anyone was going to drive her to distraction, she had a feeling it could be this man.

Chapter Two

"You have a nice family," Alex said.

Not that he strictly knew that was true. His years as a cop and then a P.I. had taught him not to judge anything by what he saw on the surface. But Fiona was sitting in the dark over by her car door, quiet as a church mouse. She looked so forlorn he had to say something. Otherwise this drive to Chicago would feel twice as long as it actually was.

"Yeah," she murmured. "They're fine."

She was staring at the night-shrouded rolling countryside that lined the Indiana Toll Road. There was nothing to see but an occasional light here and there, yet it was holding her attention like she was watching a thriller.

"Your mother must have had some hard times for a while."

He could feel her blink. Then, like Lazarus, she slowly turned and came to life. "I beg your pardon?"

It was good to see that she wasn't totally comatose. "Well, except for Samantha, you guys all seem clustered around thirty. There must have been a time when she was drowning in diapers.''

"Oh.'' Fiona almost smiled, but she'd turned back to the window before he could be absolutely sure. "We're one of those blended families.''

"Your parents married and each brought kids with them?''

Fiona turned toward him. "I thought that as a private detective you'd know a lot more about us. I mean, you found me out of the blue.''

"I was just supposed to find Kate's biological mother,'' Alex replied. "There wasn't any need for me, or any other stranger, to know all the personal details about you and your family.''

"That's very kind of you.'' Her voice was sincere.

Alex gripped the steering wheel and squirmed in his seat. Kindness had nothing to do with it. Jeez, she was making him sound like some knight in shining armor. "I couldn't really afford the time,'' he said gruffly.

He could feel her looking at him, could feel his shirt collar tighten around his neck. "Data gathering takes time,'' he explained. "And time is money.'' He paused a moment and checked out the traffic before him. "Besides, I'm congenitally lazy.''

She murmured something and a quick glance confirmed that she was back to staring out her window. He couldn't figure out what she could see, but maybe it didn't matter. Most likely Fiona wouldn't see any more in the middle of a sunny day than she did now.

A sign surfaced on the horizon. An oasis was coming up in two miles. "Care to stop?'' he asked. "Get something to drink? Stretch your legs? Roll around naked in the grass?''

"No, thank you.''

He nodded and suppressed a sigh. Little Fiona didn't want to talk. It was going to be a long ride, but then she had a right to her privacy and her thoughts. They sped by the oasis.

"We were adopted."

His mind had gone into automatic pilot and, although he heard her words, he didn't quite catch the sense of them. "Pardon?"

"The three of us were adopted," Fiona said. "Myself, Cassie, and Samantha. We're biological sisters."

"Oh." He shrugged. "I was thinking that was another possibility."

"Yeah, right."

His own spirits perked up at the snicker in her tone and he turned to smile at her. They soared even higher when she returned it. It wasn't like he was coming on to her or anything; he just hated to see her wallowing in the depths of a blue mood.

"Our biological parents died when I was eight. We went through a bunch of foster homes in the eighteen months after that, then we landed with the Scotts. We seemed to get along, and they adopted us."

Alex's mind returned to Fiona's birthday party. To the joking and feeling of camaraderie that was so much a part of that gathering. "Looks like things worked out good."

"Yes, it did." She turned toward him and shrugged. "All kids have to work at figuring out who they are. It's just harder when you're adopted."

"You were old enough to remember your biological parents."

"Yeah, and I went through a long period when I felt I didn't belong to anybody. Not the Scotts. Not my biological family. Not anybody."

Alex thought back to his own childhood, to the procession of husbands that had paraded through his mother's house. To his own feelings of wandering lost in this world. "Well, you certainly didn't let those concerns drag you down."

"Everybody needs to feel a part of something," Fiona said. "They need a connection to their past before they know who they are in the present."

"I suppose." He had his life reasonably under control and he didn't see any need for testing the solidity of his base.

"It's true." Suddenly her tone turned passionate. "I was well on my way to lost. And then I remembered my dad talking about his Great-grandpa Horace."

She shifted in her seat to face him. "I really had nothing left of my parents except a few photographs. After they died in a car crash, me and my sisters were carted off to a foster home with barely half of our clothes. And none of our toys or any mementos of our parents. We never had much to start with—it's not like we had a legacy coming to us or anything—but I would have liked more of the photos and my mom's cookbooks and her diaries." She paused and took a ragged breath. "God, yes, her diaries."

"What'd they do with the stuff?"

Fiona shrugged. "Threw it all out, I guess. They said there wasn't enough space in foster homes for us to have a lot of stuff."

"Yeah, but..." His voice died away. The cruelty of it all shouldn't surprise him, but it did make him sad.

"Anyway." Fiona's voice sounded brighter, but with a forced cheerfulness. "When I was in a junior-high history class, we read about Horace Fogarty and I realized that had to be the Great-grandpa Horace Dad talked about and suddenly everything changed. I had a relative. I don't know if you've heard of him—"

"Heard of him?" Alex said. "I'm a big fan. I even have an autographed copy of one of his editorials."

"Really?" Her voice radiated her excitement, filling the crevices of the car with her joy. "Most people only vaguely remember him from school."

"Maybe because I didn't just read him. I agreed with him. Everyone in the world seemed to think honesty was a subjective value, except for me. You can't imagine how excited I was when I found someone who not only agreed, but thought it was the basis for who you were as a person."

"I didn't care so much about his philosophies," Fiona said. "I had always loved to write, so when I found him again, it was like finding my way back home. It was where my writing talent had come from. And that was a connection that I needed badly."

Alex felt a distant twinge of jealousy, like the remembered ache of an old pain. He'd once longed for a connection to the past, thought that he'd needed it as an anchor to keep him from drifting into darkness.

But then, finding out your father wasn't your father tended to unsettle a kid. Especially when you were also told he didn't want to be your father, either.

"Of course, growing up still wasn't easy," Fiona went on, her voice still surging with energy. "I didn't really mature until after my daughter was born."

He pushed all that anger into the past where it belonged. "I'm guessing your family doesn't know about this child."

"No," she said slowly, carefully. "I couldn't tell them."

He sensed her turning back to the window, to the blackness that she could lose herself in.

"I've never been a very brave person," she admitted, then added a short laugh. "Just ask Cassie. I used to drive her crazy when we were growing up. I was so afraid to get in trouble, so afraid of people being mad at me."

"But your family seemed so—"

"I know. They are nice. And they probably would have been very supportive, but I just couldn't tell them. I was a freshman in college, alone in L.A. and incredibly scared. It was my secret."

"And you never shared it."

"Mr. Rhinehart." The temperature in the car suddenly plunged down toward freezing. "I have spent every day of my life wondering how my child is. I was not going to subject those I love to that kind of pain."

It was on the tip of his tongue to point out to Fiona that there was no reason for her, or anybody else, to carry that kind of pain. Sealed records or no sealed records, the world was filled with people like himself. People who could find the key to any strongbox.

"And I don't think it would have been right for me to go barging into her life just to satisfy my curiosity."

Alex started slightly, throwing an uneasy glance her way, but her gaze was straight ahead. He sighed and concentrated on the road.

Back in the third grade, he'd had a teacher who supposedly could read your mind. Since then, Alex had been uncomfortable around teachers, afraid that they could read the thoughts buried in the most secret recesses of his soul. Although he knew that was nonsense. He shifted in his seat, trying to ease the strain on his back. He was sure it was nonsense.

They exited the tollway, continuing to Chicago along the Borman Expressway. The traffic was heavier on this road and they fell into a silence, giving Alex more time to concentrate on his driving. And he did. He had to. Once he delivered Fiona, that was it. He'd never see her again. There would be no need to.

They reached the Dan Ryan Expressway and the lights from Chicago's Loop flickered in the distance. Fiona hadn't said anything for forty-five minutes now. Sighing, he stirred in his seat.

"I wonder if it's Kate for Katherine," she said suddenly.

Her words had cracked his trance and he took a moment to gather his thoughts. "I don't know," he said. Great thoughts to gather. Maybe he should have left them ungathered. "They haven't talked to me about her much. You know, not that kind of personal family stuff."

"It was my mother's name," Fiona said.

Alex looked at her then, drawn by a stillness in her voice. The streetlights bathed her with a gentle glow that he felt almost came from within. He wanted to reach over and take her hand, to feel that warm glow seep into his heart.

A horn sounded to his left and Alex shot his gaze back to the road. What was the matter with him? The Dan Ryan was a diabolical mixture of entrances and exits on the right, then on the left, of drivers weaving wildly from one lane to another. You could have an accident on the road without half-trying.

"Did you name the baby?" he asked.

Fiona laughed. "Of course not."

Man, this was spooky. He forced himself to watch the road as he took the right fork, the one that would take him to Lake Shore Drive. He wasn't a statistician, but the odds of an adopted kid getting the name of her biological grandmother had to be a long shot.

"I bet the lake looks beautiful during the day," Fiona said.

Alex grunted an answer.

"We always came to Chicago for our back-to-school shopping," she said. "We'd go to the stores in the Loop, have some lunch, and then walk along the lakefront."

He grunted again.

"We did it until into high school," Fiona said. "Even though a lot of the stores had moved out to the suburbs."

"You're staying at the Water Tower Inn." He was having a hard time getting that name thing out of his mind. "It's just down the street from the hospital."

"That's nice," she replied.

As they passed by the museums on Lake Shore Drive and headed into the S-curve, Alex began feeling his weariness. This had been a long, long day. He'd drop off Fiona, let her get some rest; then head for the barn and hit the sack himself. This hadn't been a hard case but it seemed to be taking a lot out of him.

"I don't think I'll be able to sleep at all," Fiona said.

Jeez, it was as if she was reading his mind again. "I've been told that the procedure isn't that—"

"Oh, I'm not worried about that." Fiona gave a short laugh. "Well, maybe a little bit. What's really scaring me is the thought of meeting my daughter."

"Oh, hell," he muttered tiredly. Had he forgotten to tell her or had she just misunderstood? "Ah—" he cleared his throat "—you're not going to actually meet your . . . Kate."

Alex could feel her looking at him and he studied the line of cars ahead of them. "I thought I told you," he murmured as he pressed his foot to the gas.

"I'm sure you did. I must have misunderstood." The reply came too quickly, the way it would from someone who'd spent her entire life worrying about the feelings of others. "And it makes sense."

Why did it make sense? What harm would it do for Fiona to meet the kid? No one had to spill the beans or anything. As far as the kid knew, she'd just be meeting a person who was donating some bone marrow. A wonderful, generous woman.

Alex clenched the steering wheel and took a deep breath. Damn it. He was violating Alex Rhinehart's rules numbers one, two and three. All of which said to never get involved.

"It's a very stressful time for Kate and her parents right now," Fiona said. "They don't need anything to add to it."

It was obvious that Fiona was a caring woman, the kind that everyone took advantage off. Like now. His inner soul was screaming a warning, but he ignored it.

Kate's parents were willing to take her bone marrow, but they didn't want their daughter exchanging a handshake with her donor. Damn it all to hell and back. He took a left at Chicago Avenue and could feel his aggravation growing.

"Is that the hospital?" Fiona asked, indicating a complex of buildings to their left.

"Yeah." A cab stopped to pick up a fare and Alex stopped behind it. "And your hotel is just up there on the right."

"Oh, good. It's close enough to walk."

Alex had the feeling that anything within five miles would be close enough for Fiona. Some people just left themselves open to exploitation. It was a good thing that he was done with this assignment. He didn't need this kind of aggravation.

The cab's customer was slow getting into the vehicle. "Damn it," he muttered. "I don't have all day." Alex backed up, then gunned forward, his tires squealing as he laid rubber in an arc around the cab. They were pulling up to the hotel entrance in a matter of moments.

"You in a hurry to get rid of me?" Fiona asked.

"No," Alex replied. "I just thought the quicker we got you settled, the more time we'd have on the town."

She shook her head. "I don't think so."

"Aw, come on," he said. "I got us some tickets to clown mud-wrestling. Front row, center."

Fiona just shook her head slightly and opened her door. A doorman, dressed like a Third World general, was standing there waiting. "You folks checking in?"

"I am," Fiona replied. "He's checking out."

Alex stepped out himself, walking around back to the trunk. Without saying anything, he gave the doorman her bag, closed the trunk lid, and leaned on it, watching the man take the case into the lobby. He could feel Fiona slowly approach him.

"Well," Fiona said, "I guess this is it."

He closed his eyes briefly against the sight of her. She looked so vulnerable, like a princess imprisoned in a tower. But closing his eyes didn't work. He didn't need to be looking at her to feel it.

"I'm sorry about my little remark," she said.

When he was a kid, he'd always imagined himself as a swashbuckling knight, rescuing the weak from the clutches of evil. By the time he'd reached high school, he'd learned that women wanted more than a rescue. They wanted more than he could give.

"Forget it," he said. "I have a tendency to wear on people."

"No, it's my fault."

She smiled, a nice, comfortable smile that reminded him of cozy rooms, a crackling fire, and a winter's storm blowing outside. It left an ache deep inside him.

"But I do have some good points," he said.

"I'm sure you do."

"Let me take you to dinner. Give you a demonstration."

"Not tonight." She shook her head. "I ate more than I needed to at my party. What I do need is my instructions for tomorrow. Like times and where I should go."

He looked into her face, friendly but looking a bit wan right now. Her eyes had a touch of concern in the corners. He'd brought her up here and now he was supposed to disappear, leaving her to the so-called mercies of the medical bureaucracy.

"I'll meet you at seven-thirty in the restaurant here." He nodded at the hotel. "We'll go for a swim in the lake, do some hang gliding, have breakfast, then I'll take you down to the hospital."

Her forehead wrinkled. "I thought you were just supposed to find me."

"Oh, no." He forced a smile to his lips. "I'm a full-service kind of guy. You see a puddle and I'll be right there to throw my coat over it."

"But I thought you said—"

"Hey." He put his hands on her shoulders. "Like you said, this has been a tension-filled day and you could have misunderstood any number of things. That's why I'm supposed to stick with you."

"Lucky me." Her eyes had brightened; a touch of color had come to her cheeks. Her head was turned up to look at him, her lips slightly parted.

For the fleetest of moments, he was seized with a fierce desire to drink fully from those lips. He took a step back so that he had room to breathe, but not so far that he had to let go of her shoulders.

"It's just until things are settled," he said.

"I appreciate it."

"And well you should."

Her left eyebrow arched upward as she gave him one of her no-nonsense teacher looks, the one that said, I've seen every trick there is, buddy. He dropped his hands to his sides.

"I mean, how many women wind up with an escort like myself? You know—handsome, witty, smart, and an all-around good-time guy."

"Very few, I'm sure," she said.

They fell into a silence, during which she stared at him and he searched her eyes to see how seriously she was taking him.

"It'll be like having your own personal slave," he said.

She continued looking at him, without even a hint of a smile cracking her face. Finally she said, "That could prove interesting."

Her voice had a low, husky tone that made his hands grow suddenly moist. "I guess I'd better get a lot of rest, then," he said, before hurrying into the car.

Except that he didn't think he'd get much at all tonight.

The next morning, Fiona stood on the corner with Alex, a stiff breeze at their backs, as they waited for the light to change. Michigan Avenue was such a fantastic street and it was a beautiful spring day. She took a deep breath of the crisp air. There was no reason for butterflies to be dancing in the pit of her stomach.

Except that she was on her way to hopefully give her child life again.

"Better hold on to me." Alex took her arm and wrapped it around his own. "We don't want to lose you. Not after all the work I put into getting you here."

She turned toward him, her hopes and fears mashing her mind into mush. "How am I going to get lost?" she asked. "I can see the hospital from here."

"I'm not worried about you getting lost," he replied. "I just don't want you to get blown away."

Her feelings took a sudden dive like a candy wrapper falling with the death of the wind. Memories of mockery danced in her mind and put an edge in her voice. "I've worried about lots of things in my life, Mr. Rhinehart, but never about blowing away."

The grin slipped off his face, his eyes going from sparkling to hurt, and Fiona was swamped with guilt. When they'd first met, she'd been put off by his sarcasm, but the more she got to know him, the more she saw it was only a shield.

"I'm sorry," she said. "I'm a little touchy about my weight."

"Why?"

His non-understanding seemed genuine and Fiona just turned to look at the buildings towering over them. And then at the people, with eyes all shuttered and distant, who were rushing past them.

How did one explain it? She'd lost a lot of weight after Kate was born, but in her mind, she'd always be that chubby little girl who was afraid no one liked her. The thin fashion models that dominated the magazine covers didn't help. And neither did the bombardment of ads saying you had to exercise, not eat, and take pills to be a beautiful—another word for thin—woman.

"You wouldn't be beautiful if you were skinny."

She looked at him, searching his face for the hint of laughter that had to be there. But she found none. His dark eyes seemed warm and gentle. They made her uneasy and she forced a laugh.

"Well, I'm not thin," she said. "So I guess that makes me beautiful."

She laughed again, just to show that she knew this was all a joke, that neither of them was serious. But something in his eyes made the laughter die on her lips.

"You are beautiful," he said. "You're just what a woman should be."

Everything retreated to the far edge of her world—the honking horns, the noise of the city street, the gusting winds. No man had ever called her beautiful. That warmth in his eyes seemed hotter, ready to burn her if she wasn't careful.

"I'm going to be late," she murmured.

Alex shrugged. "So what?"

"I'm never late for my appointments," she said, a nervous laugh bobbing in her throat.

"Maybe you should be."

Fiona shook her head. "Maybe some other time. Not today."

He took her arm and led her across the street. Fiona thought he'd release her once they reached the other side, but he didn't. He kept his mouth shut and her arm in his all the way to the hospital complex, not letting go until they were standing in front of a bank of elevators inside the lobby.

"We're going to meet the parents first." He made a little face as if he'd tasted something just a bit sour. "I mean, the adoptive parents."

"They raised her, Alex. They are her parents."

He looked away, seeming ill at ease.

"Hey," Fiona said, shaking his arm. "Some kids have no parents. This kid's lucky, she's got three who care about her."

The elevator arrived and they stepped inside. The doors slid closed silently, meeting with a quiet kiss as the elevator began its race upward. Despite that, Fiona's stomach climbed into her throat. Her mouth went so dry, the Sahara would be a rain forest in comparison. She'd come so far in the last eleven years, and now she was back at square one— terrified for this child she'd given life to.

Then suddenly Alex was taking her hand, offering her his strength to draw from. She dared not look at him, letting her eyes watch the floor lights above the door, but she was able to take a slow breath and then another. The slow steady beat of Alex's heart forced hers to match so that when they got off, she was able to flash him a small smile. It would be all right.

Alex led her down a long hallway lined with doors, then stopped and opened one. Fiona took a deep breath and stepped into the waiting room. A scattering of people sat reading magazines and only the receptionist looked up.

"Alex Rhinehart and Fiona Scott," Alex said. "We have an appointment with Dr. Sears."

"Oh, yes." The receptionist looked at Fiona, her eyes both curious and sympathetic. "We were expecting you."

She led them to an inner office, standing back to let them enter. A couple was in the room—the woman staring out the window, the man at her side, his arm around her shoulder. Their sloping shoulders said worry and fear; but the arm around the shoulder said they were in it together. They turned from the window as the door closed behind Fiona and Alex.

"Miss Scott?"

The man was tall, balding, and wore glasses. His eyes said nothing but weary. The woman was also tall. Her brown hair was cut short, sprinkled with gray, and Fiona liked the fact that she didn't feel the need to color it.

"I'm Claire Andrews," the woman said. "This is my husband, Don. We're so grateful that you were willing to come."

Fiona nodded at the husband, but had no idea what to say. How could she not come? Kate was still her child, no matter who was raising her. No matter if Fiona never got to see her. Fiona had given her life.

And would again, God willing.

"I hope that I can help," Fiona said.

As if working from some unseen cue, they all sat down— the Andrewses on the sofa, Alex and Fiona in the chairs.

"How is Kate doing?" Alex asked.

"Fine," Mr. Andrews said.

"Yes," Mrs. Andrews agreed. But their hands reached out for each other, clinging with obvious need.

Fiona bit her lip. This was so hard on them. They'd adopted a baby and expected to be a real family. Now circumstances were forcing them to beg for her help.

"Has she been sick long?" Fiona asked.

Mrs. Andrews shook her head. "Even now, you'd hardly know she was sick. She tries so hard to..." The woman stopped as tears threatened to overcome her.

Fiona turned to Mr. Andrews. "Do you have any other children?"

"No. We were older when...when we adopted Kate." He looked away for a long moment. The words came out slowly and painfully, like teeth being pulled. "Claire had two miscarriages before that."

"She's all we have," Mrs. Andrews said, her voice trembling.

Fiona said nothing, but let her eyes wander over the Andrewses. She didn't know much about suits and shoes and jewelry, but everything about the Andrewses said wealth. Money and the assuredness that came with it. Yet she didn't for a moment doubt Mrs. Andrews's words.

"Fiona has an appointment with Dr. Sears after this," Alex said. "Then she'll have blood taken for the test."

"Yes," Mr. Andrews said. "I guess it'll take about three days before we'll know."

"So long?" Fiona wanted the answers right away, wanted to be able to save Kate's life now.

"But we'd like you to stay here in town until we know," Mr. Andrews said. "If you are a match, they'll need to set up the time for the transplant."

"That's fine," Fiona replied. "It's spring break now. I didn't have much of anything planned."

"Kate's kind of illness responds well to a bone-marrow transplant," Mrs. Andrews said quickly. "The doctor said that she'll be good as new with the right donor."

"Then we'll have to find the right one," Fiona said.

Mrs. Andrews nodded, then they all slipped back into the pit of silence lying before them. There were so many things Fiona wanted to ask. What did Kate look like? Was she cursed with Fiona's "chubby" genes? Did she like school? Was she good at sports like Cassie? Did she love chocolate like Samantha? Did she like to write? Fortunately she was rescued by a gentle knock on the door.

A thin man in a gray hospital coat entered. "Hello." He nodded at the Andrewses before turning to Fiona, his hand out. "I'm Dr. Sears."

Fiona stood and took his hand. "I'm Fiona Scott."

"I'm sure you must have a million questions," the doctor said.

Fiona shrugged. "A few."

"The first step is a blood test. From your end, no different than others you've had, but we'll be comparing characteristics of your blood with those in Kate's blood. We need a certain number of them to match to even consider the transplant."

"What are the chances I'll be a good match?" she asked.

He got the same look she'd seen on dozens of kids' faces when they didn't want to answer a question. "Better than finding a donor through the donor banks," he said and moved toward the door. "If you're ready, we'll go down to my office where I can explain the procedures better. Then, if you're still willing, we'll need to give you a physical. If everything looks good, then we'll draw the blood for the test."

Fiona took a deep breath. "Okay, let's do it."

He opened the door and she started after him. At the door she turned. The Andrewses were watching, all their hopes written on their faces for the world to see. Alex was at her side.

"Might as well walk you down," he said. "Full service, remember?"

Fiona nodded at the Andrewses, then slipped into the hall. By the time the door closed behind her, the doctor was already disappearing into a room down the short hallway.

"Thank you," she said to Alex, although the words seemed so inadequate for the strength he was giving her.

"What for?"

"For being here."

He pulled her into his arms for one blessed sweet moment and she felt her heart relax. She was so lucky to have had him here with her.

"I'll be here when you're done," he told her.

She was glad. Everything seemed just a bit less overwhelming.

Alex was back at the corner of Chicago and Michigan, glaring at the traffic. This area never had a rush hour; the traffic was congested all the time.

The traffic light said to walk but Alex just stood there. He should get back to his office, but his feet just didn't want to take him there. Hell, with his economical life-style, he could easily take a few years off.

The light went to red again and he glanced at his watch. Maybe he should just give his answering service a call. Somebody might be looking for him.

"The hell with it," he muttered. Since he didn't want to work, it was best not to call in.

The traffic going north eased and, going against the traffic light, he dashed to the traffic island in the middle of Michigan Avenue. He paused there a moment before completing his dash to the west side of the street.

Dr. Sears had said that Fiona would be tied up for a couple of hours. Alex decided to walk around the city until that time. The exercise would be good for him.

As he walked south on Michigan, he glanced into the shop windows. Shoe stores, bookstores, clothing stores. The images came into his mind, then passed right on through, leaving no impression. His thoughts were on a good-looking lady he'd just left.

He couldn't believe how selfless she was. Not that self-ishness was a virtue. But sometimes it was necessary for a person's self-preservation. And right now, Fiona needed a good strong dose of "selfish" if she wasn't going to get eaten alive.

Well, if there was anyone around who could inject the necessary selfishness into the proceedings, it was him. He had enough "selfish" in his bones to furnish an army. That's how things developed when you were a loner all your life. Maybe he should stick around a little longer, keep an eye on Fiona and make sure she wasn't taken advantage of.

He had no destination in mind but his feet kept him on the near north side of Chicago. Years ago this had been the city's nightclub district. A few bars and clubs were still left but rising rents and gentrification had driven a lot of them out.

Suddenly his eyes caught a sign up ahead. The French Pastry Shop. His stomach gave a rousing cheer and directed his feet into the bakery.

It was getting late in the morning, but the noon rush was still an hour away. A number of clerks milled about behind the counters but they let him peruse in peace.

He picked out a couple of double-chocolate doughnuts for himself pretty fast, but he had a harder time deciding on something for Fiona. He didn't know what she liked, if anything. Maybe she hated sweets.

He was about to give up when he saw some swan-shaped cookies. That was it. There was no way she'd turn them down.

His certainty waned, though, as he hurried back to the hospital. He'd never been good at predicting a woman's mood, and for some reason he really wanted to this time. He wanted to give her something she'd like. Something that would be special to her. He ate his doughnuts to settle his nerves.

His stomach was still growling for more when he reached the hospital complex. He tried to ignore it as he rode the elevator up to the ninth floor and was surprised to see Fiona waiting when he stepped into the office.

"I didn't know you'd be done this soon," he said. "Have you been waiting long?"

"No." She gave him a soft smile as she laid her magazine down. "Just a few minutes."

"I'm sorry."

"Don't be," she said, standing. "You're not my nanny."

Her courtesy annoyed him and he shoved the package at her. "I brought you a present." He held his breath as she opened the package.

"Oh, they're wonderful!" she cried, and held one of the swan cookies up as if for everyone in the whole stupid world to see. "It's like Romeo and Juliet wishing me good luck."

Before he could do or say anything, Fiona kissed him on the cheek. It was just a quick peck, no big deal, but suddenly he felt a little shaky. Like he was coming down with the flu. But he didn't think he needed to see the doctor. Maybe he ought to get his head examined, though, for staying around.

"It's just a couple of cookies," Alex said with a gruffness that wasn't in his heart. He took her arm. "Glad I didn't buy you a cake."

Chapter Three

Fiona took a deep breath to steady her nerves as Alex led her out of the hospital. She felt like a bungee jumper bouncing between tired, scared and hopeful. Or maybe she felt like the cord, wound tight and ready to spring. So much was happening, she barely could register half of it. Doctors, labs, diagrams of cross sections of bones, videos of doctors harvesting bone marrow from a donor's hipbone, charts of bone marrow production. Fears, hopes and desperate prayers. And always someone asking if she was sure she wanted to go ahead with it, followed by an offer to say she wasn't a good match if she wanted to back out.

But how could she not give her child life, if the chance was offered to her?

Alex seemed the only rock around to cling to, but that seemed hardly fair to him. This wasn't his fight; it was just a job. Yet, when he brought her those swan cookies, she felt that he knew her, really knew her, and could see the dreams that were hiding deep in her heart—the dreams that the swans were magic and were somehow promising her love. Which was about as silly as dreams could get. Swans were just swans; big birds, nothing more.

When Alex wanted to take her to lunch, she agreed, not because she wanted any, but because he was trying so hard to take care of her. So, clutching her little bag of swan cookies, she let him take her to a coffee shop down the street from the hospital. It was a noisy place, between the conversation of the patrons and the servers calling orders back to the cooks.

"So how'd it go?" he asked, once the waitress had taken their orders.

"All right."

She rubbed the inside of her elbow, but not because the spot hurt. In a way she was sorry—afraid—that the blood had been drawn. The die had been cast. There was nothing she could do now to make it right for Kate—an absolutely crazy thought. She couldn't change her potential as a marrow donor by eating a different breakfast or wearing different clothes.

"Waiting's always hard," Alex said.

She just nodded and let the silence come back. Except that there was no such thing as silence in this place. Everyone seemed to be shouting and clanking and slurping and laughing.

Three days until the results! That seemed like forever.

Alex didn't push her to talk and in a short while their meals came. Once they had eaten, he suggested a stroll around the neighborhood and she readily agreed. Anything to keep from thinking too much!

The afternoon didn't exactly race by, though. The stores along Michigan Avenue were wonderful—so much to look at—yet Fiona couldn't forget for a moment why she was there.

Alex tried hard; he was a wonderful guide. He took her into the Water Tower Place shopping center and showed her all the best spots from the glass elevator, then walked her through the specialty stores. She saw dinosaur wind socks in the nature store and socks of every imaginable style and color in the sock store. He bought her a cup of sweet cinnamon coffee, then a pound of it when she said it was good.

"You didn't have to do this," she said as the coffee was wrapped for her. "We have good coffee at home."

"Hey, everybody needs a treat now and then."

What was his? she wondered. When he was feeling down or lonely or confused, how did he bring joy back into his life? But she knew him well enough to know she wouldn't get an answer.

Just as she was wearying of the elegance of the multistoried shopping mall, he took her across the street to a toy store and made her walk across the piano keyboard in the floor. Then he showed her robots of every size, shape and function. Dolls, hundreds and hundreds of them. And stuffed animals so real she expected them to move.

He was trying so hard to distract her thoughts that she forced herself to laugh and marvel and smile, even if no sunshine was reaching her heart. But she was glad when he saw it was almost six o'clock and suggested that they drive to one of the restaurants on the north side of the city for dinner.

"You feel like Italian? Chinese? Mexican?" he asked her.

"Anything is all right," she assured him. She was no more hungry for dinner than she'd been for lunch, but would be glad to sit down for a while.

"How about steaks?"

She really didn't care; she would eat whatever he wanted. But she could see he wanted her to make a decision. "Steaks are fine," she said.

So they went to Bowers—in a red sports car that was Alex's car du jour. The restaurant was embarrassingly expensive and decorated to look like a forest. Between murals on the walls, potted trees, and a babbling brook that wove through the dining room, Fiona felt like she'd wandered into "Little Red Riding Hood." The hushed elegance of the at-

mosphere made her want to whisper. The food was deli-
cious, but she suspected the manners police were hiding out
behind every fake tree here, waiting for her to use the wrong
fork or spill something or talk too loudly. Weariness crept
up on her finally, though, and she sat back from the table,
her meal only half-finished.

"You have a dog?" Fiona asked Alex.

He looked surprised at the question. "No. I don't have
any pets."

"Oh." She made a face at the food left on her plate. "I
thought maybe you'd have a use for a doggy bag."

"Only if dust bunnies eat meat."

"Doesn't it get lonely living alone?" she asked, then
frowned at her stupidity. She felt like a fool. Or worse, like
some lonely old spinster, assuming that everyone was alone
also. "I'm sorry. I don't know where my mind is. Just because you don't have a dog or cat, doesn't mean you live
alone. Or are lonely."

He smiled at her. "Well, I do live alone," he said. "And
no, I don't have any 'significant other' at this time."

She thought he was mocking her, that he thought her
statement had been a pressing for details of his personal life.
"I wasn't asking that," she said. Her voice sounded stiff and
that troubled her. He'd been so kind to her, she shouldn't
repay it with rudeness. "I just have had pets for so long, I
can't imagine not having them."

He looked away. "I didn't have any pets as a kid," he
said. "I think that's what sets you up to have them later."

"I guess."

He looked at her plate. "You done?"

She shrugged. "It seems a waste of good money, but..."

"It's the Andrewses' money," Alex replied and waved the
waiter over. "And, believe me, we could spend ten times as
much and they still wouldn't miss it."

She suspected that was true, but it still wasn't in her to
waste things. "I have a refrigerator in my hotel room," she
said. "I could take it with me and have it for breakfast."

"Cold chicken Cordon Bleu for breakfast?"

"You've never had cold pizza for breakfast?"

"Yeah, but—"

The waiter was there, looking like a disapproving father. "Was something wrong with your dinner, ma'am?" he asked.

"No, nothing," Fiona said quickly, almost afraid she was going to be sent to her room. "I'm just a touch under the weather."

"Want to pack those leftovers up?" Alex asked him.

"Oh, it's all right," Fiona replied. "I don't want to be a bother."

"It's his job to let us bother him," Alex told her, and glanced up at the man. "Right?"

"Absolutely," the waiter said as he took Fiona's plate. "No problem."

"See?" Alex smiled at her. "Nothing to worry about except how you're going to manage to eat that for breakfast."

Fiona smiled at him and at the waiter, but knew they both must think she was an idiot. Maybe she was. She just waited in silence for the waiter to return with her leftovers and Alex's change, then went with Alex out to the car.

He opened the door and tenderly put her into the passenger seat, holding and guiding her as if he were laying a fragile egg in its nest. Then, while he hurried around to the driver's side, she dropped her head back and watched her mind collapse.

She was such a fraud. She was stronger than this. She didn't need a sitter. She just needed to pull herself together and take charge.

"What do you want to do now?" he asked, once he was settled in the driver's seat. "Want to go to a movie?"

"Look, I—"

"Of course, you wouldn't." He thumped the side of his head with his open hand. "Dumb. You don't have to come to a big city to see a movie."

"There's nothing wrong with the idea, it's just that—"

"How about a play?" Alex asked. "You don't have many of them in South Bend, do you?"

"We have a lot of theater productions," she informed him. "There are four colleges in the area. It's not like we're some hick burg. But you don't have to entertain me."

"Why don't I buy a paper and we can check out the entertainment scene? There's got to be something you'd like to do or see."

Didn't he know how to listen? "I'd like to go back to my room."

"The evening's barely started," he replied, glancing at his watch.

"Don't worry," Fiona said. "I won't tell Mr. Andrews that you quit early. It'll be our secret."

Alex just stared at her, his lips tight and straight. No fast quips. "What's that supposed to mean?"

"I know you're looking after me because Mr. Andrews has hired you to," she said. "And you've been really sweet about it, but—"

"You're going to ruin my reputation with talk like that."

Fiona looked more closely at him. Was he laughing at her? She was sure that there was a definite smirk on his face.

"Good," she snapped.

There was a long moment of silence that didn't feel all that quiet, somehow. Then Alex's arm came around her shoulder. She wanted to push it off, to tell him that she didn't need his sympathy or his strength or his support. But it was so nice to have someone to lean on.

"This whole thing just getting to you?" he said gently.

Oh, heck. She let her body lean against his.

"I hate to admit it," she said. "But yes, it is."

"Let's go over and look at the lake."

Fiona just sat there. Going back to her room would be a better idea. It would be like running into a deep, dark cave and hiding from the world.

"I go down to the lake whenever my own load gets heavy," Alex said. "You look at that wide expanse of water and space, and whatever's bothering you shrinks down to a manageable size."

She didn't say anything, but the idea sounded tempting.

"Just for a little while." Alex's soft voice gently massaged her ear. "Just until you feel better. Then I'll take you to your room."

A lump had risen in her throat. All Fiona could do was nod. Silently, Alex turned on the ignition and drove the car out of the parking lot.

They went quickly from gritty streets to luxurious avenues lined with mansions. Once past those brownstones they came to a large parking lot and the lake was before them. It had been a windy day and the surface of the water was active, but even that seemed restful. It was as if the waves were washing away her cares.

They got out of the car and walked slowly over the sand to sit on a low wall about thirty feet from the water. Fiona took a deep breath of the evening air—damp, chilly, smelling like fish and water, but wonderful.

"Is it working?" he asked as he took her hand in his.

"Yes," she said. She was becoming a little more relaxed. It wasn't like a peace descending on her; it was more like an acceptance. "You know, I had pretty much come to terms with never knowing anything about my child."

"But now things have changed."

"What if I can't help her?" she said. "I don't have very many blood relatives. Just Samantha and Cassie."

"Would you ask them to be tested?"

Was he joking? She looked at him, but couldn't read his eyes in the fading light. "Of course. Just because I never told, it doesn't mean I wouldn't."

"The longer the silence, the harder it is to break."

"Maybe," she said. "But there was no reason to tell them before."

"Except that it was the truth," he said. "An awful lot of pain could be avoided if people just told the truth up front."

Fiona frowned at him then. A bitterness in his voice said he was elsewhere, that some ghost from the past had come back to claim him. She wished she could reach her hand out to him as he'd been doing for her, but he didn't seem the type to accept solace.

"Why hurt someone unnecessarily?" she asked.

"Because the hurt is always there. It's just not so mean if it doesn't have to smash down a bunch of walls to get out."

She said nothing, but just clutched his hand as they gazed out at the water. What kind of hurts did he come here to ease?

Alex led Fiona through the midday sunshine along the paved park path. He'd picked her up just a little before noon, telling her that he had a special surprise for her. From the shadows under her eyes he doubted that she'd taken advantage of the chance to sleep late, but he didn't mention it.

To be honest, he hadn't slept all that much himself. And he didn't have the excuse that Fiona had. No, it was just thoughts of her and all she was going through that haunted him. And that in turn annoyed him. What was happening to his professionalism? He thought he'd outgrown his need to rescue damsels in distress. Around four in the morning, he'd given up his self-analysis and just tried to figure out what they could do that day. The answer came to him about the same time that the early sun filtered through his blinds.

So he'd picked Fiona up and they'd taken a cab to Lincoln Park. Just outside the aviary, he blindfolded her, much to her irritation.

"Alex, I don't like this." She raised her hand and pulled at the blindfold. "I like to see where I'm going."

"Don't worry. I'm watching out for you."

He guided Fiona around a cluster of benches in the middle of the walkway and past flower beds with some little purple flowers just starting to bloom. Somehow she reminded him of those little blossoms, poking their heads out into the cold and trying to be brave enough to bloom.

"I prefer to watch out for myself."

He knew that. "You're going to spoil the surprise."

He also knew she didn't like surprises, but he'd decided this morning, while eating some stale toast for breakfast, that this certain surprise was just what she needed. It would show her that Chicago wasn't so foreign a land as she thought.

"How much farther do we have to go?"

"Just a little bit," Alex replied.

They rounded a curve and Alex led her to a three-rail wooden fence. All around them the park was just starting to come alive with spring. This couldn't help but make her feel good.

"Okay." He put her hands on the top rail of the fence and took off the blindfold. "Here we are."

"This is the surprise?" Her expression was quizzical as she looked around the pond. "You wanted to show me the Chicago duck pond?"

"Hey, what's wrong with it?" He pointed over the expanse of water. "We got lots of swell ducks and over there are some great geese."

"And it's certainly bigger than ours back home."

"Actually this is the Lincoln Park duck pond." He looked all around the lagoon. Ducks and geese were fine, but not why he'd brought her here. Where the hell were the damn things?

"Boy, now you're really showing off. Not only do you have bigger duck ponds than South Bend but you have more of them. I've always envied the cultural amenities of the big city."

Out from behind some low-hanging branches glided two regal figures. About time! "Pipe down for a minute," Alex said. "And look over there."

She did as she was told, then gasped.

"Oh, Alex!" she exclaimed. "Swans."

His heart lifted with the excitement in her voice as the two white birds glided out into more open water, but rather than watch them, he turned to look at Fiona. The light dancing in her eyes was as bright as the sun, the laughter flowing from her lips was more lilting than the songs of the birds around them. He felt a tightening in his loins, a hunger to bury himself in that warmth and sweetness.

"What are their names?" she demanded.

His smile faded. "I don't know. Mutt and Jeff?"

She frowned at him and the hunger in him grew. He wanted to see if that frown would taste any sweeter than her laughter. He wanted to bring that laughter back into her eyes.

"Those aren't swan names. They have to be something special like Adam and Eve. Anthony and Cleopatra. Pocahontas and John Alden."

He leaned on the fence, his back to the swans. "You're a romantic," he said. "I never would have guessed it, but you're a romantic."

"I'm about the most unromantic person around," she countered, her voice sounding slightly dejected. "I lead a very practical life."

"And look for romance everywhere," he added.

"I do not," she protested.

"Sure, you do. I can see you getting all sentimental around Valentine's Day. You probably love weepy movies and think that there's one true love for everybody."

"I wish that there was," she said. "But I'm not always sure."

He laughed, hoping to extinguish those sparks of sympathy. That was the last thing he needed. Or wanted. "You want proof there isn't?" he said. "Just look at my mother. She was married four times before I was sixteen and twice since then. Not one lasted more than a couple of years, though most were finished long before that."

"Poor woman," Fiona murmured.

"What?" That was just like Fiona. She would feel sorry for anyone, no matter whether they needed it or deserved it. "My mother just always goes out with jerks."

Fiona put a soft finger to his lips, holding them closed. "Shush," she said. "You shouldn't say anything bad about your mother."

Alex felt a twinge of exasperation. Fiona could only say that because she'd never met his mother. Even his mother agreed she would be better off taking up needlepoint as a hobby.

"She must desperately need love," Fiona said.

Alex frowned at Fiona. He'd never seen his mother painted in that kind of light before, not by himself nor by anyone who knew them. People had always mocked her, laughed about how she would wear a man out in a matter of days. Now he felt a little sorry for her, and that made him uncomfortable.

He looked off over the lagoon, at the two swans swimming together as if they were the only ones that existed. It made Alex feel almost lonely, like he was missing out on something by not even looking. It wasn't a feeling he liked, and he kicked it aside like a branch fallen across his path. He had looked and found himself lacking.

"Hey, you're sort of a swan expert," he said to Fiona. "What secret do you think they have? Do they date a lot before settling down? Or is it just a first come, first served thing?"

She just gave him a look that said she wasn't fooled by his attempt at humor. "I don't think swans are all that different from us. I think there's something deep down inside them that calls to the other."

He laughed. "Guess I wasn't home when my call came in. I never got it."

"Or else you purposely weren't listening."

"Me? How can you say that?" He didn't have to pretend surprise at her remark. But the surprise was that he was that transparent. Or was she reading his mind again?

"Because you obviously avoid involvement." She stretched up and kissed him on the cheek. "Come on. Show me the rest of the zoo."

But his feet stayed rooted in place as fears warred with hungers in his heart. Fear that he would always be alone struck out at his fear of letting anyone close to him. But they both weakened in the face of his hungers. He had never met someone trying so hard to be strong who needed so badly just to be held. And he wanted to be the one to hold her, to taste her sweetness and drown in the caring in those eyes. He wanted to be strong and fight her battles, slay her dragons and teach her that she deserved to be happy.

His arms pulled her to himself, pulling her into his needs and fears, but mostly into his arms. For a quick moment, as his lips danced across hers, she belonged to him and he to her. While her mouth whispered magic into his heart, he was whole. There were no doubts, no long empty hours before dawn. No silences that stretched out for days on end as fear nibbled at his soul.

They pulled apart as if scorched by the sudden contact, but his arms didn't want to let go. His body ached with a curious mixture of tenderness and savagery. Of possessiveness and protectiveness. Feelings that he'd thought would never be a part of him.

"They got big cats here?" she asked, as she slipped her arm through his. "I like cats."

Never in his life had he stepped into a quagmire like this before. Not in college. Not in the army. Not on the police force. Not as a private detective. Never in his whole miserable life was he so torn. Stay and hurt her; leave and feel the pain himself. It was time for him to run. Run as if the devil were after him.

"Yeah," he replied huskily. "They're down this way."

They turned from the lagoon and moved down the path, arm in arm. He couldn't stay around Fiona. She'd already taken enough hits in her life.

He'd never known his real father, so he'd always thought he must take after his mother. And the years had proved him right. He couldn't remember a relationship of his that had lasted longer than six months.

"I'm going to have to get back to work," he said suddenly. He wasn't sure where the words had come from but he knew they were right.

"I figured you would," she replied. "You wouldn't last long as a private detective with just one client."

The irritation fluttered in his stomach again. Fiona was taking the news of their impending separation well, but she took everything well.

And why should he be surprised? Women were always pushing him out of their lives. He'd lay his cloak down over a puddle and once they'd walked over it, they'd pick it up and take it with them.

But Fiona hadn't.

He just shook his head, not wanting to analyze and push deeper. It was time to move on. Time to bury himself in another case.

And he wasn't abandoning Fiona. He'd found that beneath that tender exterior was a backbone of steel. She didn't need him.

Fiona hadn't expected Alex to baby-sit her the whole time she was in Chicago. She had known that she wasn't the only thing in his life. She was only a job, for goodness' sake; not someone that he cared about.

But still, it was awfully lonely sitting around the hotel that evening. He had offered to take her out to dinner, but she had pleaded exhaustion. His job was over, after all; she should let the poor man get on with things. He told her to order something from room service and had even made sure she had a menu in her room before leaving. But she was not ordering anything that way, not at those prices!

So she went to a coffee shop down the street and then came back to her room to work on an essay she was writing. It was going nowhere, though, and didn't change direction with her efforts. She wished she had taken Alex up on his offer to spend the evening with her, but that was just selfish. And proof that she had been growing too dependent on him.

Finally, she put her notebook away and turned off the lights, sitting by the window to watch the city below her. So many people and all rushing off somewhere. She used to have a dream that she was on some city street, surrounded by people hurrying away, but she had no one and no place to go. Maybe that was why her writing was so important to her; it was proof that once she had had someone. She and Cassie and Sam had nothing of their parents save a few photographs. They didn't even resemble them—not in identifiable ways.

Would Kate?

Fiona turned away from the window and climbed into bed. If she had wanted, Alex would have taken her to a movie. Or a play. Or just for a walk. He was good at keeping her thoughts at bay. Except that was her job. She should manage her own self better, rather than being weak and relying on someone else.

Fiona rolled over and closed her eyes. Tomorrow would be better. Sam and their father were bringing her some more clothes and would stay for a visit. She would be stronger tomorrow.

And she was. By the time Sam knocked at the hotel-room door just before lunch, Fiona had her heart under control. No missing Alex. No wishing he was here to distract her, to lend her his strength.

"Hi, sis," Samantha said, giving Fiona a quick kiss on the cheek before squeezing by her into the suite.

"Hello, honey." Daddy Scott gave her a big hug. "How you doing?"

"Fine, Dad." His eyes still showed concern and Fiona boosted the perkiness in her voice up a few points. "Just fine."

"Wow!" Samantha was gaping around at the sitting room. "Is this like pure luxury or what? This is the kind of hotel you should run, Dad."

"Oh, I don't think so," he said slowly as he looked around. "It seems a bit too ritzy for me. I think I'm more of a little-country-inn type of person." It had been their parents' dream to open their own inn, although it had gotten sidetracked a bit by their mother's death six years ago.

"It is nice here," Fiona agreed. "But I wouldn't want to live here."

"Nice." Her sister snickered. "This is from my sister who said the econorooms on our vacations were nice."

Sam sometimes had too good a memory. "It's a little fancier, but the basics are the same," Fiona said. "Bed, bathroom, and a lock on the door."

"Yeah, right," Samantha jeered. "I bet you got gold fixtures in the bathroom."

"I do not."

Her sister scampered off to check out the bathroom.

"You look tired, honey," her father said. "This been hard on you?"

"It was just a blood test."

"When do you find out the results?"

"Tomorrow sometime."

He put his arm around her shoulder. "I never got a chance to tell you how proud I am of you. This is a very special thing you're doing."

She felt such a fraud. She didn't deserve accolades; she was doing what any mother would do. "It's not that special," she said. She could almost feel Alex there behind her, telling her she could tell her father the truth. And for a moment, she let herself lean again. "There's something I never—"

"No gold in the bathroom," Samantha said, stepping back into the sitting room. "But darn close."

Fiona felt a mixture of relief and annoyance. Alex would probably say it didn't matter if Sam was in the room, too, but it did to Fiona. She had to do things her own way.

She picked up her jacket. It was strange, though, how much Alex affected her. She'd only known him for a few days. If he had such a strong effect on her after such a short time, it was more than enough reason to let him get back to his work.

She turned to her family. "Are you guys hungry? There's a nice coffee shop down the block."

"We had breakfast before we hit the road," Samantha said.

"Yeah, we're fine," their father agreed.

"How about a walk?" Fiona suggested. "It's so beautiful outside that I can't imagine staying in."

"Hey, great," Samantha said. "Let's go to the Water Tower Place. I know it's not outside, but we'd still be walking."

"Do me good to stretch my legs," their father said.

They went down to the street and joined the throngs of people milling about. Fiona didn't feel alone or lost this time, but she did feel like something was missing. She refused to let Alex into her thoughts again and wrapped her arm around her father's.

"It's so good of you two to come up and visit. I was getting lonesome."

"You could have come home while you waited for the results."

"I know." She couldn't explain it, though. It was like she suddenly lived in two worlds and being here to help Kate was part of that other world.

"Don't any of these people have jobs?" their father asked, waving at the people around them.

Fiona just laughed. "Most of them do. Or they don't need one."

He just shook his head. "Where's that young man that brought you here?"

"You mean Alex?" She acted as if he wasn't in the front of her mind, haunting her thoughts.

"I thought he was supposed to be looking after you," he said. "Chicago is a big place and cities like this can be dangerous."

"I'm a big girl, Daddy. And any place can be dangerous. Our little town isn't exactly crime-free, you know."

He looked like he was about to say something else, so Fiona stopped at a shop window. "Aren't those purses beautiful?"

"I bet they're expensive," Samantha said.

"I went in the other day," Fiona said. "You know, just to look around."

"And?" Sam prompted.

"The cheapest ones start at five hundred dollars."

"Wow."

They moved on down the street, with Fiona breathing a sigh of relief. Her father wasn't asking any more about Alex.

She didn't want to talk about him. She didn't want to think about him. He had come briefly into her life and was now out of it. All her mooning around was going to make her forget reality—he'd just been doing his job. If she needed to lean on anybody, it had better be herself.

Chapter Four

Alex leaned back in his chair and rubbed his eyes. That's what he got for being so damn efficient. He'd finished the preliminaries of some background checks for an insurance company and had nothing to do now until he received the credit reports. It was dull but profitable work.

When he opened his eyes, his gaze landed on his full in-basket. Of course, he did have other things he could do. He could tackle that pile and fill his day with filing, answering letters, and paying bills. Wowsers.

Instead he turned to look out the window. He lived on the ground floor of an old brownstone just a few blocks west of the Lincoln Park Zoo. Actually, it was more of a slightly below-ground floor, since the apartment was down a half-dozen steps or so. Looking out his front window gave him a view of a tiny patio, surrounded by chest-high walls; then, above them, feet walking by on the sidewalk. His back windows showed a slightly larger tiny patio, with some bushes above those walls. But he was used to it.

Things had been tough when he'd first started his P.I. gig, and this had been all that he could afford. He could do better now, but felt no compunction to move. He was comfortable here and easily earned enough to pay his expenses.

Focusing his eyes proved that the scene outside hadn't changed from yesterday or last week—not that he could tell much by looking at his patio. The dirty snow was gone so winter had passed, but until fallen leaves were blown into the corners, time might very well be standing still.

Alex turned back to his desk and forced himself to look at the overloaded in-basket. No, time wasn't standing still. He should really take care of this junk. Get on top of things for a change. And who knew? That pile might contain the offer of an interesting assignment—his gaze slid away from the pile of mail—like giving a gentle lady the chance to help out her kid.

Fiona seemed to hover in front of him, smiling that soft smile of hers, and suddenly he found it hard to breathe. His mouth was dry and his heart was racing. He wanted to hear her laughter, see that shadow of worry ease from her eyes.

Damn, he'd been right to bid her adieu. She was becoming an obsession and that wasn't part of his job. His job had been to find her, that was all.

"Oh, hell." Alex stood and stretched. Maybe he should get himself a cat. It would give him someone to talk to.

But what the hell would he talk about? Would he tell the cat about Fiona? How she was constantly in his mind?

And what would the cat tell him? Most likely, he'd say forget about her. He'd point out that Alex was a loner and always would be. And had never brought any good to a relationship yet.

Shaking his head, Alex walked into the hall, took his windbreaker off the hook, and went outside. He'd stroll over to the zoo. Why bother getting a cat when the zoo had so many? They'd listen to him, yet he wouldn't have to feed or care for them. He shut his door behind him, double-checked that it was locked, and hurried up the steps to the sidewalk.

It was pleasant outside but a tad cool. Just right for a brisk walk. He quickly arrived at the zoo, but instead of heading toward the lion house, his feet took him toward the duck pond. The one that was bigger than South Bend's.

It was even greener here today than it had been a couple of days back. When spring finally decided to arrive in Chicago, it came full force. He had a new bounce in his step, a lightness in his heart.

Alex rounded the curve in the walk and came to a dead stop. Fiona was sitting on a bench right where one would have expected her to be. Up near the swans.

Dread froze his feet while joy filled his heart. He wanted to run. Run forward. Run back home. Damn it, he should have known better than to come here.

Alex swallowed hard, then forced himself to move forward. There was no reason to run. He wasn't afraid of Fiona. She wasn't exactly the violent type.

"Hi," he said.

She slowly turned to look up at him, her eyes open wide in innocence and a smile curving her lips. That had to be her small-town upbringing. A city gal would have jumped out of her shoes, then smacked him in the mouth when she came down, telling him that if he ever snuck up behind her again she'd rip his guts out.

"Hi," she replied.

Fiona really had a beautiful smile. It somehow slipped behind all his defenses and weakened his resolve, not to mention his knees. He looked away.

"Beautiful day," he said.

"Yes, it is."

"Too damn nice to stay inside."

"That's why I came out here."

"Did you take a cab?" he asked.

"No, I walked."

Alex frowned for a moment. Overall the area was fine, but a couple of spots between the zoo and her hotel were a tad gritty. He guessed walking was all right, although a cab would have been safer.

"It's supposed to get even warmer by this afternoon," he said.

She just nodded; but then what did he expect her to do, given his sparkling and witty repartee. He took a deep breath and looked around the area. His eyes drifted out over the pond.

The swan couple was there, of course, but so were the ducks and geese. Most of them pairing off like the swans. In the spring a young man's fancy turned to thoughts of—

"Do you like baseball?" he asked.

Still smiling, she shook her head. "Not really."

"Oh."

"Sometimes I take my nieces and nephews to see the Silver Hawks, though." She glanced at him, then went on. "It's the minor-league team back home."

He nodded and checked out the lagoon again.

"Want to sit down?" she asked.

His gaze dropped to the empty spaces on either side of her. "Oh, sure." He felt like some dippy high-school sophomore, but he sat down anyway. "Yeah, sure."

The silence seized them again. He looked out over the lagoon and guessed she was doing the same thing. It wasn't exactly comfortable but it wasn't bad, either. Being around Fiona was pretty comfortable, no matter what.

"Writing something?" he asked, seeing the notebook in her lap.

She made a face. "I've been working on an essay about the lack of courtesy in our society for the last few weeks, but it's not going very well."

"I never pictured you writing essays," he said.

"Why not? It's what my great-great-grandfather wrote."

"Yeah, but you're not him. I somehow thought you'd be more into children's stories or something."

"Well, I'm not." She shut her notebook, though, and stared out at the swans. "I'm very like old Horace. I told you that. Finding him was like finding out who I was."

He wanted to tell her she was nothing like the old guy. She was a hell of a lot easier on the eyes than the old curmudgeon had been and wasn't as stiff and unyielding as stories had him. Neither did she follow his philosophy of honesty above all else. But it seemed so important to her to be his true descendant, Alex couldn't point any of that out.

"Did you keep busy yesterday?" he asked instead.

"Oh, yes." Her smile came back, peeking through the clouds like the sun after a storm. "Samantha and my father came to visit. We walked around Michigan Avenue, then checked out the stores near the hotel."

"Where did you eat?"

"A sandwich shop in Water Tower Place. I forget the name."

He nodded and they took another spin in the pool of silence.

"It was a nice visit," Fiona said. "But I felt kind of uncomfortable. There are so many secrets between us right now."

"There's just one," he softly reminded.

"I guess." Fiona made a slight face and shrugged. "Maybe it just seems like a lot."

He wanted to put his arm around her, pull her in to his heart, but he realized how idiotic that was and kept his hands to himself.

"Right now, you know more about me than anyone in my family."

He shrugged.

"That makes it so easy to talk to you. I don't have to worry about spilling the beans and hurting you."

"Then just tell them the truth," he said, and thought he saw a film of tears cover her eyes before she looked away. "They won't hate you."

"I know." Her voice was choked up. "And I did try at one point, but..." Unable to finish, she just shrugged.

His hand took hers. It wasn't like he was pushing himself on her. He was just offering a little comfort. Just giving her somebody to lean on.

"Aren't the test results due today?" he asked.

She looked away and it took a while before she answered. "Dr. Sears said they'd be in late this morning."

"Want me to go with you?"

The words were out of his mouth before he'd really given them any thought. But he wasn't being some jerk of a knight in shining armor. He was just one of the few people that she knew in the city. And just about the only one who knew all about her. He was someone she didn't have to pretend with.

"I'm sure you have more important things to do."

"Not really."

"You have your own job."

"Why be your own boss if you can't play hooky once in a while?"

Her smile returned.

"Come on." He stood and pulled her up by her hand. "We'll check out the results, then I know this great place we can go for lunch."

"And this time I'd better eat, huh?"

"You damn betcha," he replied and put her arm in his.

It wasn't like he was going to hang around all the time. He was just giving her a little support. Just enough to get her through the day. A little boost until her own natural strength kicked in. Then, once she was solidly on her feet, he'd just fade away. Like an old soldier.

"Man!" Fiona exclaimed. "How can you find your way around this maze? Did you grow up in here?"

"I was a scout for the army in another life," Alex said.

The doctor had left word to meet him on the oncology floor, but it was obvious when the nurse gave them directions that Fiona was quickly lost. It was a good thing he was there, Alex thought.

Fiona squeezed his hand a bit tighter. "I'm indeed fortunate to have someone of your caliber leading me."

"I should warn you." They came to the south elevator bank and he pressed the button for up. "My last job was leading Custer into the Little Big Horn."

She laughed and made his heart dance. He wished he could keep her laughing forever. The elevator door opened and he guided her inside before pressing the button for the seventh floor.

"She didn't even give us a hint," Fiona said as the door closed. "I couldn't read anything in her face."

"Maybe the doctor didn't tell her," Alex replied.

"I doubt he has to. She probably sees the reports before he does."

"Yeah, I guess." The elevator stopped and opened for their floor. "But it is the doctor's responsibility to tell you the results."

"I know," she grumbled. "But I wouldn't mind a teeny tiny hint."

This time it was his turn to laugh as he took her arm in his.

Dr. Sears was just down the hall and came over to greet them, then nodded toward a conference room. "We can talk in here, Miss Scott."

Alex was about to head for the waiting room, but Fiona's hand slipped around his. "Can Alex come too?" she asked.

The doctor shrugged. "Whatever you're comfortable with."

They preceded the doctor into the room. He closed the door, then dropped into a chair, watching Fiona in silence for a long moment.

"Your test results were good," he said. "You matched on more than the minimum number of counts."

Fiona's hand clutched Alex's even tighter. "So I can donate?"

The doctor nodded. "If you want to."

"Oh, thank goodness," Fiona said as she threw her arms around Alex.

He just held her. For a few minutes there, he'd wondered why she'd wanted him in here. He wasn't involved in this; he wasn't needed. But now, with her head buried in his chest, he could see that he'd been wrong. He was needed. And, based on the tension that filled her body, very much so.

He could do this. He could let her lean on him. He'd just have to be really careful not to let their emotions get too entangled. Fiona pulled away from him and he slowly let her go, moving carefully like she was just learning to walk on her own.

Fiona turned to the doctor. "What do you mean, if I want to?" she asked. "I didn't think the procedure was dangerous. Certainly not for the donor."

"Not significantly," Dr. Sears replied. "Although there's always a risk when going under a general anesthetic."

"Life isn't zero risk," she said.

"No, but things can happen. That's why you need to think about this carefully. If you have any doubts or hesitations, we'll just say you weren't a good enough match. Kate's situation isn't critical yet. We could still find another donor."

"We don't need another donor. I want to do it."

The doctor got to his feet. "Then you'll need to come with me. You have to sign forms and I should go over some procedures with you."

"That sounds like a lot of boring stuff," she said to Alex.

"I can wait for you," he told her.

"You don't have to."

"I will," he said. "I'll wait in the lounge up here."

"Thank you," she whispered. Then she left with the doctor, leaving behind an empty silence and a hint of her perfume.

Alex walked over to the window and leaned his forehead against the pane. Although seven stories wasn't all that high, he felt like a bird sitting on a cliff. Down below was the tiny Lakeshore Park. And off to his right was the wide empty expanse of Lake Michigan. The rest of the space was filled with other tall buildings.

Things were getting deep. He was getting into waters that he couldn't swim. But he couldn't get out. Not now. He just had to be sure he didn't go down and never come up. Or worse, took somebody down with him.

He went to the lounge down the hall and flicked on the television. After the midday news, he got an apple from a vending machine to tide him over until Fiona was ready for lunch, then sat through a complete cycle of news on cable television. The Andrewses arrived just as he was sitting through the reading of the last night's basketball scores for the second time.

"Mr. Rhinehart," Mr. Andrews said. "Dr. Sears told us Miss Scott is a good match."

Alex nodded. Why couldn't they call her Fiona? Hell, she was the kid's biological mother. And here she was, giving the girl a second gift of life. Or at least a good chance at it. Why did they have to be so damn formal?

But then they stepped farther into the room and he saw how drawn and tired they looked. He felt a sudden burst of sympathy for them. Maybe they had to keep their relations with Fiona formal. Their daughter's illness was probably enough for them to handle at the moment.

"I hope it all works out," Alex said. When the silence settled back down, he added, "I figured I'd take Fiona back to South Bend tonight."

Mr. Andrews cleared his throat. "Ah, we wanted to talk to you about that."

He looked at them. What were they going to say—let Fiona find her own way back home? Alex found that hard to believe. They had been more than generous with him.

"We really don't want Miss Scott to leave," Mrs. Andrews said.

Alex shook his head. "I thought they needed about two weeks to get Kate ready for the transplant."

"Ten days to two weeks," Mrs. Andrews confirmed.

"But we'd really like her to stay here in Chicago," Mr. Andrews said.

"We're just so worried about this," Mrs. Andrews went on. "Once they start Kate's chemotherapy, she'll be so vulnerable. She won't have any of her own bone marrow left. She'll have to have a transplant, but if something should happen to Miss Scott—"

Mr. Andrews took his wife's hand. "We'd like Miss Scott here, and cared for, so that nothing happens to her."

"Things happen to people no matter where they are," Alex said. "A small town might be safer than a big city like Chicago."

Mrs. Andrews brushed a nervous hand through her short, straight hair. "We know we're asking a lot."

"We've talked to the principal at Miss Scott's school about the possibility that she might miss a week or so," Mr. Andrews said. "And she was very supportive. We offered to pay for the substitute but she said that wasn't necessary."

Alex thought they really should have talked all this over with Fiona first. It was her decision to make—not his, not her principal's. "This is something for you to work out with Fiona." He got to his feet.

"We'd like you to take care of her," Mrs. Andrews said.

That stopped his trek to the door. "Me?"

"I have access to a corporate apartment," her husband said. "It's just a block or two from here. Right on Lake Shore Drive."

"Why me?"

"You two get along so well." Mrs. Andrews shrugged. "It's obvious she trusts you."

He was usually good on his feet, but Alex felt himself groping. "You want me to stay in the apartment with her?" There was a sudden tightening of his breath and a hunger seeping into his blood.

"It has two bedrooms," Mr. Andrews said. "And two baths."

He looked from one to the other. They were serious.

"And you want me to keep her in the apartment?"

"Oh, no," Mrs. Andrews replied.

"We don't want to make Miss Scott a prisoner," Mr. Andrews assured him. "In fact, we would want you to take her out, see some plays, go to the finest restaurants, anything. We'll pay for it all."

"We would just hope that you don't do anything dangerous," Mrs. Andrews said.

"How about skydiving?" But they suddenly looked so stricken that Alex hastened to calm the couple. "It was a joke."

"Then you'll do it," Mr. Andrews said.

He looked away for a moment. A little voice in the back of his mind tried to scream a warning but Alex shut it out. It was just a job. He turned back to the couple. "That's up to Fiona. If she agrees with you, that's fine. If not—" he shrugged "—then I'm out."

The couple exchanged looks again. Now what? Then suddenly Alex saw the light. "No," he said, shaking his head. "It's your idea. It's your responsibility to talk to Fiona."

"But she trusts you," Mrs. Andrews said.

And he was expected to use that trust to manipulate her? Just what kind of man did they think he was?

"Mr. Rhinehart—" Mrs. Andrews laid a hand on his arm "—we're really thinking of Miss Scott."

"Oh, yeah."

"Yes," she replied. "How do you think it will be for Miss Scott? Trying to carry on with her life while carrying a burden of worry? She could easily have an accident."

He hated to agree with the woman but there was some truth to her words. People who were preoccupied were more likely to have accidents.

"I don't know where I'd be if I didn't have Don to lean on," Mrs. Andrews said.

Fiona had a big family back in South Bend, lots of people she could lean on, but in this case that could be more of a problem than a help. Hiding Fiona from all distractions might be the best thing for her.

"All right," he said with a sigh. "I'll talk to her."

"Oh, thank you, Mr. Rhinehart," Mrs. Andrews said.

They shook his hand and started for the door.

"Mr. Rhinehart," Mrs. Andrews said. "Please remember, Miss Scott can do anything she wants while she's here. See things. Maybe sit in on some classes at the universities. Anything. As long as it isn't dangerous."

Then they were gone and Alex flopped down into an overstuffed chair. How about if it might be dangerous for him? They hadn't said anything about that.

Alex leaned his head back and closed his eyes, letting himself go. Feeling as if he were caught in a whirlpool that he was powerless to extricate himself from. What had he gotten himself into now?

"Hey, are you like some kind of doctor?"

His eyes slowly opened. A young girl wearing a sweat suit, thick socks and a baseball cap on her head was standing in the doorway staring at him. It was Kate. Alex had seen her picture in Mr. Andrews's office.

"I was being funny, you know?"

"Hi, Kate," Alex said. "Are you supposed to be out of your room?"

"What are you gonna do?" she asked, flopping down into a chair across from him. "Turn me in?"

"Only if there's a reward."

"I'm bored out of my gourd."

Alex nodded. "Yeah." He straightened in his chair. "I can see that kind of thing happening."

"And then, starting tomorrow, I'm gonna be in isolation for the rest of my life. I like, get chemo for ten days and then I get the BMT. Then who knows?"

"Going to be some rough days," Alex murmured.

"Yeah." Kate took a moment to stare at her feet as she swiveled them back and forth. "You're the one who found my donor, aren't you?"

"Pretty much. But a lot of other people helped."

"Can I meet her?"

Alex paused only a minute. "What makes you think it's a her?"

Kate looked up at him, blinking. "I just thought—" She shrugged her shoulders. "I don't know."

"The donor has to be compatible with you," Alex said. "That means blood type and other stuff. Gender has nothing to do with it."

"I guess." She made a face and looked down at the floor. "But I'd still like to meet her/him/them/it. Whatever."

"They don't like the donor and the recipient to meet for a year or so," Alex said.

"I don't think that's fair. Do you?"

Alex slouched down as if a five-hundred-pound bird sat on his shoulders. Kate would like to meet Fiona. Fiona would like to meet Kate. And he was supposed to explain to each of them why they couldn't.

He didn't like being caught in other people's games, playing by other people's rules. He looked over at Kate and saw the need in her eyes—the exact same look he'd seen in Fiona's eyes.

Damn. He was being sucked in, deeper and deeper.

Fiona jabbed at the floor-selection button and then, as the elevator door closed, glanced quickly at her watch. She'd been gone hours. According to the doctor, she'd just had to sign a couple of forms.

Well, he'd been close on the number. She'd had to sign three forms, but it couldn't be done at the nurses' station. She'd had to go to some administrative area where the hospital's legal counsel could witness it. Then she'd had to visit with a social worker and a minister.

And everywhere she turned, someone was telling her that she didn't have to do it. Showed how much they knew. Of course she had to do it. If she didn't donate the bone marrow, her child could die. There was no choice to it. Not that she had any qualms.

The elevator stopped and the door opened, letting her shoot out like a bullet. She didn't know if Alex would still be waiting for her. He'd said he would, but she wouldn't blame him if he'd left. He had to have better things to do with his day than wait around for her.

She didn't really need any help to check out of the hotel; the room was paid for. All she needed to do was take a cab to the train station. But still, it would be nice to be with him a little longer.

Fiona reached the door to the lounge and saw him there. Her heart gave a skip of happiness as she hurried inside. "Alex, I'm so glad—"

Fiona stopped in her tracks, her heart falling from the sky with a thud. A young girl was sitting across from Alex. A young girl with Sam's smile and Cassie's nose. And Fiona's own blue eyes, except they looked so bright and strong and confident.

"Hi, Fiona," Alex said.

She tried to respond, but nothing worked. Not her tongue, not her brain. Not anything. All she could do was stare at the girl.

Kate got to her feet. "I'm Kate Andrews."

Fiona nodded as her eyes drank up every detail of Kate. She was so beautiful, this child Fiona had given up. She could not believe how perfect the girl was, even in illness. "I'm Fiona Scott," she finally said.

Kate nodded. "You're my donor, aren't you?"

Fiona glanced at Alex, panic filling every inch of her, but he was just watching her blandly, as if they weren't breaking all the rules. She turned back to Kate. "We're not supposed to meet."

"Jeez." Kate made a face. "What are they gonna do? Shoot us?"

Fiona broke into a smile. She was so like Cassie. "I guess they won't."

Kate looked at her thoughtfully. "So how come you're doing this? Isn't it gonna hurt?"

"A little," Fiona replied. "But that doesn't matter if it's going to help you."

"That's what I don't get," Kate said. "I don't think I could do it for some complete stranger."

Of course. That's what they would have told the girl. Dealing with the transplant was hard enough. They wouldn't pile her biological mother on top of it. And they shouldn't. It was enough just to see Kate. The girl didn't have to know everything.

"I bet you would," Fiona said. "You're not so scared of being hurt when you get older." Maybe because life has shown you that there're so many other ways to hurt so much more.

"I guess."

Fiona just smiled at the girl. Looking into her eyes made Fiona feel as if she were looking into a mirror. A mirror that was slowly clouding up. Her smile waned and her throat tightened. Fear squeezed at her heart. The last thing she wanted was to burst into tears, but she wasn't sure that she was going to be able to do anything about it.

"Well, kid," Alex said. "Time to get back to your room."

"Sez who?"

Fiona laughed and the tears retreated.

"Sez the armed guards that prowl these halls," Alex replied. "And if you don't get a move on, I'm going to turn you in."

Kate made a face at Fiona. "I'm gonna be in isolation, like forever."

"But when it's over, it'll be worth it," Fiona said.

"Yeah." Kate just looked at Fiona a long moment. "Well, you know, thanks."

The tears came back without any warning, fast and strong. There was no ducking them this time. "My pleasure, Kate."

Barely able to see, Fiona reached for the girl and hugged her tight. A lifetime of hugs to be given in one short moment. Then she stepped back, trying for a smile.

Kate gave her a short little wave, and left.

Then Alex was there at Fiona's side. Putting his arms around her, he held her close and murmured sweet things into her ears. Warm kisses mingled with the tears flowing down her cheeks. His lips brushed her forehead. Somewhere his heart was telling her she could do it, that she was strong enough. That everything would be great.

She wanted to believe him and would. They pulled apart slowly.

"Are you okay?" Alex asked. He appeared to be breathing as hard as she was.

"Yeah." Fiona pushed gently and his arms fell away. "Enough of this weepiness. I have to pack and get back home."

He ran his hand over the back of his head. "I need to talk to you about that."

"That's okay," Fiona said. "You don't have to give me a ride back. The South Shore train runs between here and South Bend. And I can get someone to pick me up when I get in." She smiled and brushed his cheek. "That's the advantage of a big family. There's always someone around to help when you need it."

"The Andrewses would like you to stay here until Kate is transplanted."

"What?" She was sure she misunderstood. "I can't do that. I've got nothing to do here. And besides, school starts next week."

"They've already talked to your principal about your taking time off."

"They what?" She was angry. Scared. Stunned. She felt like a puppet with some invisible hand pulling her strings. "They had no right to do that."

"No, they didn't," Alex agreed. His voice was calm and took the edge off her. "But they're very worried about Kate. You have to remember that once she's put on chemotherapy, she's really vulnerable. If anything should happen to you, she's sunk. They'd have to find another donor, and fast."

Fiona sighed. She could see his point, but still she felt like she was being shoved around. Couldn't they have asked her themselves?

"All right, I see their fears," she said. "But I have a responsibility to my students, too. If I stay here, I'm leaving them in the lurch."

"How many days would you actually miss?" he asked. "Three or four?"

"Probably."

"Couldn't you work with your substitute to make sure the kids were doing what you wanted?"

"Yes." She knew she was being silly; her kids could do just fine without her for a few days. "I could even request the substitute I want," she admitted.

"But you feel like you should be in class."

"That's a big part of it," she said. "But it's also something to do. I'd go crazy here for another ten days. I need to be busy."

"There are a lot of things we can do to keep you occupied."

"We?"

Alex seemed to be having a hard time meeting her gaze. "Let's go grab a late lunch," he said. "You really should think about this."

Chapter Five

"Wow!"

Alex dropped their bags just inside the apartment and grinned at Fiona as she checked out the parquet floor, the original artwork and sculptures. She looked like a little girl on her first trip to Walt Disney World.

"This is just the foyer," he said. "Save some excitement for the rest of the apartment."

"Too late," she said. "I've already demonstrated the range of my vocabulary."

"That's too bad." He took her by the arm and led her into the living room. "Look at this."

"Oh, Alex. It's breathtaking."

They were up on the twenty-first floor; and the east wall, the one facing the lake, was nothing but glass. Standing on the edge of the living room, back by the foyer, they saw an enormous expanse of sky and lake.

"Come on." He led her to the windows but she hung back as they neared the window wall. "Nervous?"

"Kind of," she replied. "I never had a yen to fly."

Alex had lived in Chicago for most of his life and had become blasé about the city. Hanging around Fiona was like taking a kid to the circus. He was seeing the city in a totally new light—a bright, multicolored light.

"Over to our right is Navy Pier and Olive Park," he said.

"Everything looks so small from up here."

She folded her arms across her chest and looked out at the scene stretching out before them. Alex slipped an arm around her shoulder, letting her lean up against him as she drank in the beauty of the city. This might work out best for her, after all. Hell, all she would have done in South Bend was worry about Kate. At least here, there were all sorts of new things to do. Plus, she wouldn't have to pretend with him.

"I wish Kate could be here instead of me," she said.

"Feeling guilty?" He could feel her shoulder shrug beneath his hand and a sliver of fire shot through him. It was like playing with dynamite, being here like this with her. But it was something he'd have to deal with. Fiona's welfare was what mattered now.

"I guess. She's the one who's sick and all she has is a little hospital room."

"It's not your fault," Alex said. He fought back the urge to take her totally in his arms. "It's not anybody's fault. It's just something that happened."

"And she's going to be in isolation for almost two weeks."

"You're doing everything you can for her," he murmured.

Fiona slipped out of his arms, leaving him with longing tinged with relief, and went toward the small kitchen. He followed her to the doorway. With its space-saving narrow range and a sink about the size of a bucket, it seemed to be designed more for storing drinks and ice cubes than for cooking.

"She's really a feisty little kid," Fiona said as she poked around in the small refrigerator.

"She's more than feisty," Alex said. "Otherwise she wouldn't have made it as far as she has."

Fiona nodded as she stepped past him and went back into the living/dining room. He caught a whiff of her perfume, like a feather slowly tickling his senses. It beckoned him to come hither, but he forced his feet to stay put.

"You're right," she said. "When you really look at things, life has been hard for her. But she still has a sense of humor and a good, ornery attitude. She must have a lot of strength."

"You gave her a good set of genes."

Fiona made a face. "Her parents have done a good job raising her."

"You can't make a silk purse out of a sow's ear," he said. "You have to have good material to work with."

Instead of replying, Fiona walked back to the foyer and looked down the hall. Obviously she'd had enough of the discussion.

"You can have the bedroom to your right," Alex said. "It's the bigger of the two."

Fiona looked around the living room and then frowned back down the hall again. "That's on the same side as the living room, right?"

He nodded.

"And I presume it has just windows, no walls?"

"The windows are walls."

"No, thanks." She shook her head firmly. "You take it."

"It's the nicer one," he said. "And it's also bigger."

"I don't care. I can't see myself getting any sleep in a room where I'd be worrying all night about falling out."

"Out of bed?"

"Out of the building." She snatched up her suitcase. "I'm choosing the door on the left."

He wanted to point out to Fiona that she was perfectly safe here, that the windows didn't even open, but the phone started ringing before he could get the words out. Hell, what difference did it make? Whatever the lady wanted, as long as she was comfortable. Besides, the windows would give him something to stare out on the long, sleepless nights that surely lay ahead.

"Yeah," he snapped into the receiver.

"Mr. Rhinehart. Don Andrews here." The voice sounded especially crisp.

"Everything's fine here," Alex said. "I think Fiona will be quite comfortable."

"I expected that she would be. My reason for calling is to set some things right."

Alex didn't reply. Andrews had the tone of a man who was going to remind Alex who was paying the bills and what was expected of him.

"I understand that Miss Scott met Kate today."

"Yeah, it was an accident. Kate had snuck out of her room and—"

"I don't want that to happen again," Andrews said.

"I don't control the world," Alex replied. "And I sure as hell can't control your kid."

"I want Miss Scott to stay away from Kate."

"Fiona—" Alex stressed her name "—had nothing to do with it. She came into the lounge to meet me and Kate was there. It would have looked a hell of a lot stranger if she'd turned around and walked out."

A silence filled the telephone line and Alex could almost see the man clenching his jaw. Rich, powerful men didn't take well to back talk. Not that Alex cared.

"Look, Mr. Rhinehart." The sudden softness in his employer's voice threw him for a moment. "Kate has a big load to carry right now. She's worried whether she's going to come out of this, and how. She's wondering if she'll ever have a normal young woman's life. I'd rather she didn't have anything else thrown at her right now."

Alex was all set to trade some angry words. But only an idiot could ignore the truth in Don Andrews's words. "I understand all that," Alex said. "But all Kate wanted was to meet her donor. She asked Fiona why she was doing it and said thank-you to her. That was all."

"What did she say?" Mr. Andrews's voice was hoarse. There was no mistaking his fear. "Miss Scott, I mean."

"Nothing you have to worry about," Alex replied. "Nothing to make Kate suspect Fiona's her biological mother."

"Kate knows she's adopted," the man said. "We're not trying to hide it. We just want to concentrate on getting her well."

"Yeah, I know."

Fairy tales divided the world into good guys and bad guys. Unfortunately, the real world was a lot more complex than that. There were no easy dragons for Alex to slay. He was hanging up just as Fiona walked into the room.

"Is something wrong?" she asked.

"Naw." He shook his head but she was still looking at him. He had to come up with something. "It's one of my customers. He's bothered that I had to push his project back a few days."

"I really don't need you to watch over me all the time," she said.

He forced a grin onto his face. "That's what I'm being paid for."

"I'm sorry."

"Hey, it's a dirty job but somebody has to do it."

The laughter in her eyes was like kindling to his already smoldering fire. One step closer, one gentle touch, and he'd go up in flames. Luckily, she stayed her distance.

"I'm hungry," Fiona said. "How about you?"

Alex looked at his watch and was surprised to see that it was almost seven o'clock. They'd had themselves a full day between all the meetings, discussions, and finally moving over here.

"Yeah, I guess. Where do you want to go?"

She made a face. "Do we have to go out? I'd really love to just stay in."

Stay in? Be cooped up here together all evening? Yet he could see the weariness in her eyes and gave in. "I could run out and get us a pizza," he offered.

"That would be wonderful," she said. "And I saw they have a little grocery downstairs. While you're getting dinner, I'll run down and pick up some odds and ends."

"You don't have to," he said. "I could stop there on my way back."

"And let the pizza get cold?" she said with a laugh. "No way. We'll both pitch in and then we'll both be able to relax tonight."

He wasn't too certain about that.

Fiona turned over, pounding the pillow into submission, but it didn't help. Sleep was about a million miles away. It was too quiet here. She missed her cats snuggling up to her legs.

She should never have agreed to stay here in town. It was crazy.

Every time she closed her eyes, she saw Kate. And thought up ten years of questions that she should have asked her. Where had her mind been? She'd been so stupid and tongue-tied.

But then when she opened her eyes, all she knew was that Alex was across the hall in that big room with windows that looked out over the whole world. Ten days with him in this suddenly tiny apartment. Ten days of leaning on him and confiding in him and generally trying to stay out of his arms.

She should have gone home. It would have been so much easier. No distractions, no temptations. No ventures into a world where she wasn't sure what was real and what were her dreams.

She turned over, facing the clock and daring it to flash the passing time in her eyes. It did. Over and over and over until she turned to lie on her back. The ceiling held long streaks of shadows racing from the window into the darkness.

It would be all right if Alex wasn't here. She could handle Kate's illness the way she'd handled Mom and Dad's accident, the foster homes and giving Kate up. By burying everything deep inside and not letting anyone see her fears.

But Alex had. And when he had, he'd been there with his all-too-ready arms to hold her.

And weakling that she was, she'd fallen into them.

She couldn't be strong with him here; not with him reading her every thought, her every fear. And that wasn't good. She had to be strong; she had to stand alone. It was the only way she knew.

But how did she do that?

She had to ignore Alex's strength. She had to pretend he offered nothing to her heart. She had to keep her silly mind from weaving him into her dreams.

All she had to do was put her mind to it.

Fiona set the plates down on the table, one in front of Alex and the other at her place. Then she sat down, tucking her bare feet under her chair as she nibbled at her bagel. She felt really stupid. Her brain must be atrophied from lack of sleep.

"I'm sorry," she said.

"What for?" The words were reasonable enough but Alex's tone was saying, *Now what?*

"We never got dressed up for breakfast at our house," Fiona said.

She was wearing a robe over her nightgown and no slippers, since she'd forgotten to pack them. Alex, on the other hand, was already dressed in his usual knit shirt and slacks with soft brown loafers.

"At home, I wouldn't even wear a robe," she went on. Of course not. At home, there was just Elvis and Prissy. What a stupid remark!

"I don't wear a robe, either," he said. "At home or any-where."

"You don't?" That was just like him, trying to make her feel better.

"No, I don't own one."

"You just go around in your pajamas, then."

"I don't own any pajamas, either."

So much for trying to make her feel better. Her cheeks flamed and she grabbed up her bagel, taking a huge bite of it. Maybe if she kept her mouth full, she wouldn't talk so much. She was wandering into dangerous territory, territory a mother would tell her daughter not to venture into if she wanted to stay out of trouble. What had happened to that little talk she'd had with herself last night?

Well, Fiona certainly didn't want to find herself in trouble, but there was a knot in the pit of her stomach that didn't seem able to loosen. And it was as if that knot of nerves was somehow attached to her tongue. It wasn't a helpful attachment.

"It's a free country," he said. "You can wear whatever you want to breakfast. Especially since we're eating in."

A picture of Alex's apartment came to mind, the refrigerator and cabinets pretty much bare. This was a man who always ate out. She'd blown it again.

"You said you didn't mind."

"Didn't mind what?" He put his bagel back on his plate with a definite thud. "Don't mind you wearing a robe? Don't mind eating here in the apartment? None of these things matter. I really and truly do not mind any of these presumed inconveniences."

"Well, I didn't know," she said. It wasn't like she was used to having breakfast with strange men. "Would you rather have eaten out?"

His eyes flashed his exasperation. "I can take eating in, light margarine instead of cream cheese and even instant coffee instead of regular. But I cannot take sixty-seven questions before I've had a single bite to eat."

Her toes curled up under her just like she wanted to curl up and hide. She'd pushed and bugged and generally made a pest of herself until he was good and annoyed. All because she was just a touch nervous being here with him.

"I'm sorry," she said once again.

Alex just looked at her and then, with a deep sigh, sat back in his chair. "You don't have to apologize for everything," he said.

"I didn't mean to annoy you."

"Why don't you get annoyed back?" he asked. "Tell me to stuff it."

She just shook her head. "I couldn't do that. Not when you're being so nice."

"You worry far too much about other people being happy or comfortable or whatever. You should think more about what you want."

"I'm happy when other people are happy," she said.

"You should be happy when you're happy. Forget about everybody else."

"That's not me." For too many years, she'd worried about keeping people happy, thinking about them before herself. She couldn't just turn it off like a light that wasn't needed anymore.

Alex picked up his bagel, taking a healthy bite out of it. He didn't look like he was sighing in ecstasy and she couldn't help herself.

"Bagels are healthier," she told him. "Than eggs and bacon and sausage, I mean."

He grunted around his mouthful of food and she had to explain further.

"All that cholesterol isn't good for you."

"Fiona." His voice had a growly undertone to it as he quickly swallowed his food. "You don't have to justify everything."

"I'm not," she said. "I'm happy with bagels for breakfast and I'm telling you you should be, too."

He groaned and rolled his eyes. "If I promise to never eat a cholesterol blue-plate special ever again in my life, will you let me eat in peace?"

His tone made her frown. And made those nerves subside a bit. "You said before that I shouldn't worry about other people's feelings. Now are you saying I should?"

He looked as if he was in pain. "I'm saying that I'm not used to being badgered during breakfast."

"Well, excuse me, sir. I thought a little conversation at breakfast would help relax things. Encourage good digestion."

"I think the operative word is *little*."

"Fine."

She took another bite of her bagel, a big one this time, and chewed vigorously. She was acting like a silly schoolgirl, chatting on and on. She needed to relax. Ten days was a long time and she had to learn how to ignore his every move. Her gaze roamed and stopped on his hands as he paged through the newspaper. They were strong hands, capable and sure. A man's hands.

She swallowed hard and looked away. Annoying him with her chatter was better than letting her mind wander.

"I guess you must have had quiet breakfasts when you were a kid," she said. "I mean, being an only child like you were."

"Yes." His words came out slowly and carefully, as he lowered his newspaper. "My breakfasts were quiet. And very, very peaceful. When I finished, I was totally relaxed."

She pursed her lips. She should just take the hint and shut up.

"I usually ate alone. My mother didn't like to get up early." His words seemed tagged with bits of tiredness and he was concentrating on his food, macho pride radiating out like heat from a radiator.

Her heart heard the hurt behind the words and went out to him. "Do you still eat alone?"

"Most of the time I eat out," he said. "So, unless I'm with a client, I might as well be alone. Everyone else in the restaurant is into their own thing." He shrugged. "That's the way it is in the big city."

"That's sad," she said.

"Don't you live alone?" He was frowning at her again. "Your breakfasts have to be quiet also."

"Yes." She started peeling her orange. "But not entirely. I have two cats, remember?"

"Oh, yeah." He snapped the paper upright again. "Well, just pretend I'm a cat."

After a long moment, Fiona found herself glaring at the top of his head. Her warm feelings were cooling rapidly. She thought they'd been getting closer and he'd shot the walls back up again.

"You're ignoring me," she said.

"I thought that's what cats do best."

Suddenly Fiona noticed a suspicious quiver to Alex's shoulders. "You're laughing at me."

"No, I'm not." He looked up at her, his whole face filled with laughter. "I'm laughing with you."

"I'm not laughing."

"Maybe you ought to." His face was wearing a mask of male smugness. "Try it, you'll like it."

Not only was he pushing her away, he was laughing at her attempts to get close. Thirty years of being polite and following the rules evaporated as fast as the dew on a hot summer morning. She sprang up out of her chair and grabbed up a section of the newspaper. Rather than begin to read it, though, she started rolling it up.

"Hey," he said, as he watched her. "I thought you didn't believe in violence."

"It has its place."

"Come on, Fiona."

She whacked him on the shoulder. It was highly satisfying. He raised his arms and she feinted a blow toward his chest. When he lowered his arm, she whacked him on the head. It felt even better. She was tired of being nice and polite and unselfish.

"I like this," she said, and whacked him another couple of times. "I really do."

"Darn it." He grabbed her and pulled her down onto his lap. "Now, cut that out. The Andrewses don't want us doing anything dangerous."

Fiona stopped her assault as his eyes captured hers. The laughter in his gaze slowly faded as something else took its place—something hot and fiery and all too willing to consume her. She felt a wonderful warmth slip around her, promising something even more splendid.

His arms were lightly around her, but she couldn't move, couldn't breathe. Her mouth was dry and she licked her lips, trying to find a way to ease the fever in her blood. She was sitting in a man's lap, with nothing but a thin robe and even thinner nightgown to shield her. And her body told her that he was a hard man—well muscled and . . . and hard.

"And what would you call this?" she murmured hoarsely.

He stared deeper into her eyes. Fiona could smell the coffee on his breath and feel the throbbing of his heart, pumping blood to the farthest reaches of his body.

"Dangerous," he finally replied.

"Extremely dangerous," she agreed.

They slowly separated, pulling apart cell by cell. Fiona tried to straighten her robe, but her wayward eyes only wanted to devour him. His shirt was pulled half out of his pants and her hands itched to pull it all the way out. She needed—

"I need to do something physical."

He just blinked once. Like he wasn't sure she'd just said what she'd said.

"Like jogging along the lakefront," she said, quickly. "Or maybe a bicycle ride."

"Bicycling would be good," Alex said. "We can rent some bikes over by Lincoln Park."

"I'll go change."

"Okay." Alex stood. "I'll clean up while you do."

"That's okay," she replied. "I can—"

"Hey, you made breakfast, let me clean up."

She nodded and hurried across the room. Distance would ensure safety. But she stopped just at the hall. "You don't suppose bicycling counts as dangerous, do you?"

Alex didn't look at her; he was busily cleaning up the breakfast dishes. He just laughed, sounding as shaken as she felt. "Not as dangerous as staying here."

Chapter Six

"I thought you said it was just a little farther," Fiona said. "We've been biking for miles."

"You said you wanted some exercise," Alex reminded. Well, that wasn't exactly what she'd said, but it was close. And it was what he needed. Hours and hours of it. This morning had been a little too cozy for his peace of mind.

Unfortunately, they were nearing their destination. "Turn up here," he said. "I live in the next block."

"Oh, yeah?" Fiona slowed her bike as she looked around. "Cute neighborhood."

Cute? Alex looked down his street, at the old brownstones crowded up against each other, at the spindly city trees that hadn't yet leafed out. And at the parked cars lining both sides of the street. "If you think this is cute, wait until you see my apartment."

"I can hardly wait."

Suddenly he wasn't sure he wanted her to see it. Not that his apartment held all sorts of secrets. Except for his autograph collection, it was almost void of personality. But that in itself would mean something to her. And he didn't want to give her any further glimpses inside him. It was going to be hard enough to maintain their distance over the next week or so—as this morning's episode proved.

"This building on the right, here," he called to her. "I'm on the ground floor."

They stopped in front of the one he indicated and dismounted from their rented bikes. Fiona's face said nothing, but she probably was comparing it to the building she lived in. And hers was no doubt winning. They both were old houses converted into apartments, but hers had a yard around it and was in a quiet neighborhood. There was no such thing in the city.

But he liked it here. Showed how different they were.

"Better put the bikes down here," he said, nodding down the stairs to his little patio. "They'd probably be okay out here on the street for a few minutes."

"But best not to take the chance," she finished for him.

He started at her completing his thought, but then just grabbed up her bike and carried it down the short flight of steps. No big deal. What else would he have been going to say? She was not reading his mind.

He bounded back up the stairs to find Fiona lifting his bike. "What are you doing?" he asked, and took his bike from her.

"I can carry one," she insisted, following him down. "Bringing a bike down a few steps doesn't constitute danger."

No, just ungentlemanliness on his part. "I'm a full-service guy, remember?"

He leaned the bikes against the near wall, then emptied his mailbox. "My place is pretty ordinary," he told her, suddenly thinking of the worn rug in his living room and the scratches all over his kitchen table. And heaven knew when he dusted last. "I really don't spend a lot of time here."

"You want me to stay out here?"

He wished he had the guts to say yes but then, perversely, he wanted her inside, wanted her soft presence in his home. He opened his door and waved her inside.

"Sit down, look around, or whatever," he said. "I'm just going to check my mail and pick up some clean clothes."

"Okay." She'd followed him into the living room, somehow making the room seem lighter and warmer.

"I'd offer you something to drink but I don't have anything." That sounded strange even to him, like he was some anonymous ghost just passing through. "I knew I'd be in and out over the last couple of weeks so I didn't stock up on anything."

"No problem."

Of course not. When did she ever see a problem?

Strangely annoyed, he went into his office and flipped through the mail in his hand. Nothing of significance; a few bills and a whole lot of junk. He slipped back out into the living room on his way to his bedroom. Fiona was looking at his autograph collection.

Well, if there was one thing in the place that told who he was, that was it. It would be interesting to see what Fiona made of it. Not that it mattered to him one way or another.

He pulled a suitcase from under the bed and threw it on a chair, before rummaging in his dresser for some clean shirts, socks and underwear. He tossed them into the bag, added a few toiletries. Then, after snapping the case shut, he hurried out into the living room.

"You have a very interesting collection here," Fiona said, turning to face him. "But I'm not sure what the theme is. You have athletes, politicians, and other people that I don't recognize."

"Yeah." He could feel the left side of his face pull up in a crooked smile. "I have the world's best, and probably only, collection of people who put honesty ahead of everything else."

Fiona looked back at the collection, her face wrinkling up. He put his suitcase down and moved to her side.

"There's Walter Mondale," he said.

"Yeah?"

"He said taxes would go up even though it might've cost him the election."

"And why do you have this team?" She stepped closer to the picture of high school basketball players. "The Salem Sentinels? Why are they in your honest people's hall of fame? Did they tell the other team what plays they were going to run?"

"No." He shook his head. "But they made it to their state finals before learning that one of their players was ineligible. They reported it and it negated their whole season."

She moved down slightly and stopped. "Hey, this is Great-great-grandpa Horace."

"Yep. He believed honesty was more important than popularity," Alex said. "Refused to kiss up to anybody. He made a lot of people angry when he started a series on ethics in politics, but he didn't care."

She turned from the display. "You sure are into honesty, aren't you?"

He shrugged. "Guess it makes me pretty weird."

"No." She shook her head, her smile so gentle, so accepting. "It means I can always trust you," she said. "No matter what, I know you're going to tell me the truth."

Even as she said the words, he felt a cloud cover his sun. Would she always want the truth? Few people did.

She picked up the framed photo on a bookshelf. "This your mom?"

"Yeah."

"She looks nice." Fiona put the photo down, then looked around as if looking for others. "No other family photos?" she asked. "I thought you said your mother was married a number of times."

"She was." He made a small face, not really wanting to get into this discussion, but he couldn't not answer her. "She had too many husbands and I didn't want to waste wall space on them."

"Not even your father?"

He looked away, checking out the front window that their bikes were still there. "She never married him," he said. "I don't even know who he is."

He was surprised that the words came out like they had. It wasn't like him to tell people that; certainly not people he barely knew. Yet that didn't quite describe Fiona. True, it was less than a week since he'd driven up to her apartment, but they'd been through a lot in that time.

"I'm sorry," Fiona said.

He turned back to her. "What for?"

"You obviously still hurt."

"I don't obviously anything." He felt a frown growing on his face but he also felt pain from being too sharp with her. "We should get going."

She still had that knowing look on her face. Damn it. He should never have opened his big mouth. He didn't need her sympathy.

"I'm not upset that my biological mother and father never married," he said. "Those things happen."

She didn't look convinced and he found himself going on.

"Trouble was, I went along for years thinking that her first husband was my father." He looked away and took a deep breath. "They never said he was, but they never said he wasn't. So I guess it was my mistake."

"I'm sorry."

She put her hand on his arm, and for the life of him he wanted her to take him in her arms. He wanted to lay his head on her shoulder and let her arms surround him until he could hear nothing but the roaring of his heart.

Jeez, what was happening to him? That all happened ages ago. It didn't bother him anymore.

"It's not your fault." Thinking his words had come out too sharp, Alex paused and cleared his throat. "You're not the one who lied to me."

"I'm sure they had their reasons," Fiona said.

Alex couldn't help but laugh, although it had a bitter, hollow sound. Little Miss Fiona Sunshine. She'd find a good reason for anyone's meanness, from Judas Iscariot to Attila the Hun.

"Their reasons don't matter," Alex said. "They should have told the truth. That would have saved all of us a lot of embarrassment and pain."

"I'm sure they meant well."

He shook his head. "If they had, they would have been honest. Honesty isn't just the best policy, it's the only policy."

This time it was Fiona's turn to shake her head. Her eyes grew dark and troubled. "I don't like absolutes."

"What? You think lies are okay?"

Her look told Alex he'd again made a wrong choice of words.

"You think that lying is sometimes okay?"

Fiona shrugged. "My adoptive father says that secrets are like dirty socks. Sometimes bringing them out to the sunshine is fine. But other times, they should just be left buried."

"I don't agree. There may be some pain but, in the end, honesty leaves everything all clean and fresh."

For a while she didn't say anything, but the expression on her face said she stood with the fudgers of the world—people who didn't lie outright, but bent things to present a better view.

It didn't surprise him. It didn't even disappoint him. Strangely enough, he felt only a measure of relief. That stirring in his heart when his eyes met hers would pass.

"We'd been left with a neighbor, me and Cassie and Sam," she said, her voice quiet. "Our parents said they were going to Milwaukee about a new job for my dad."

Alex knew something bad was coming. There was a stillness about her, a fragility that said the pain she was holding in was great. "You said they were killed in an automobile accident."

"Yes." Fiona stood still for a moment. "In Minnesota."

On their way to Milwaukee and ending up in Minnesota? Alex waited.

"At the funeral, I overheard my mother's best friend talking. She said that my parents had never planned to come back. That they were abandoning us."

The pain he had sensed was in her voice and in her eyes. He had to somehow ease it, but this was where he always failed. Slaying the dragons was easy; reading the needs in a woman's soul was impossible.

"That had nothing to do with honesty," he said gently. "That woman you overheard was probably just mouthing off."

"Maybe."

The one word held all the fears she'd accumulated over half a lifetime. Damn. He wasn't good at this. He was blindfolded with both hands tied behind his back.

"So they were going someplace else," he said. "If they'd told you truthfully where they were going, you would never have given that woman's words a second thought."

"What if Mrs. Cochran's words were the truth?"

Time had made her fears a certainty, had cast them in stone. What dynamite could he use to reduce their size?

But no words would come, no vestiges of wisdom appeared. He didn't know what else to do, so he just opened his arms to her and drew her into his embrace. She came as if it were the only place in the world for her to go. And when his lips lowered toward hers, she rose up to meet them.

His kiss started out gentle, like a touch meant to soothe and ease, but it changed suddenly. Her lips seemed to ignite some spark within him, some buried need that only she could awaken. That only she could meet. The spark grew into a fire, trying to consume him, and he seemed powerless to fight it.

His arms pulled her tighter, closer, yet it wasn't near enough. His heart cried out for more. He wasn't satisfied with her lips melting beneath his, or her hands holding on to him. He needed more than just a kiss, or a tender caress. The flames of his hunger wanted to climb higher; they wanted to devour everything.

But then sanity returned. Alex let go and slowly pulled back. His breathing was ragged; Fiona's face was flushed. Neither of them seemed able to meet each other's eyes, yet kept darting glances at each other.

"We ought to get going," Alex said. His voice sounded as if he'd been running a marathon.

"Yeah." Hers didn't sound any stronger.

That kiss was a gigantic mistake. Not that it wasn't mind-numbingly, knee-rattlingly great, Fiona thought. But it still was a gigantic mistake. She was here to worry about Kate, not bat her eyelashes at Alex. She was going to have to be more careful.

And she kept her vow through lunch and even into the afternoon when they went to a bookstore close to the apartment. No romances with broad-shouldered heroes in passionate embraces with weak-kneed heroines. No, she chose books she'd always wanted to read. All right, ones she'd always thought she ought to read. *The Autobiography of Benjamin Franklin, Thirty Days to a Better Vocabulary,* and Thoreau's *Walden.* Plus an illustrated volume of Irish folk tales, leading off with the tale of Princess Fiona and her brothers.

"Boy, those look fascinating," Alex noted when she brought her pile up to the cashier.

"Yes, don't they?" She ignored his sarcasm. Her silly heart was going overboard in the fantasizing department. She didn't need to encourage it.

And why was it every good restaurant felt hungry patrons wanted dim lights and piped-in violin music? she wondered at dinner. And why did they assume every man and woman who dined together were a couple?

"We should eat in more often," Fiona said. They were in the middle of the restaurant's prescribed gaze-into-each-other's-eyes time. Except she was gazing anywhere but in Alex's eyes. The fake plant in the corner had seventeen leaves, spaced in a two-then-one pattern. The double swing doors into the kitchen weren't hung evenly.

"The Andrewses want you to be comfortable," he said.

Then they definitely should be eating in.

"I like to cook," she said.

"We don't need to be cooped up in the apartment all the time."

She thought back to that morning, to that little scene at the breakfast table. Maybe eating in wasn't all that safe, either.

"Fast food is fun," she said. No candlelit tables there.

"Fast food is dangerous," he said.

"What are you talking about? Maybe years of it increases your cholesterol, but—"

"I hate fast food," he said, with a gleam in his eye that somehow captured her gaze and held it fast. "I become enraged when I have to eat it. And that can be dangerous."

"I see." He was joking; she knew that. Yet that gleam in his eye was somehow unconnected to his words. It was talking to some deeply hidden part of her soul, and that traitorous part of her was listening. She grabbed at her water glass and sipped from it slowly. "Well, I appreciate your warning."

"Hey, you know. I'm—"

"A full-service guy." Her cheeks flamed with dancing images of just what that service might include. Thank goodness for dim lights.

"No, I was going to say I like to be honest."

Thankfully their dinner arrived and she was able to keep her mouth occupied. And to think this was only day one!

The evening didn't exactly speed by, but it finally got to be bedtime and, pleading exhaustion, she hurried off to bed. Only to toss and turn for the next four hours. If she wasn't thinking about Alex being just across the hall from her, she was hurting with loneliness and fear. On top of all that were her fears about Kate. She finally picked up a book. Ben Franklin put her to sleep in minutes.

Day two was slightly better, or maybe she was more prepared. She got up early and dressed, then went down to the lobby to get the newspaper. By the time Alex was eating breakfast, she had a whole list of suggestions for how to spend the day. They agreed on the Chicago Historical Society.

"This is a great place," Alex said as they entered the old brick building on the edge of Lincoln Park. "They have all this melted stuff from the fire."

"What fire?" He'd put his hand on her back to guide her through the turnstile and her brain had turned to oatmeal. Soggy oatmeal.

He frowned at her. "The Chicago Fire. You know, that little conflagration in 1871. Destroyed most of the city."

"Oh, that fire." Jeez, she felt like a jerk.

They walked through exhibits about the ancient history of the area and then dioramas of the settling of the Lake Michigan shoreline and the Chicago River. Obviously not everyone in the world had spring break at the same time, for all around them were school groups. It would be a great place to bring a class. It would be a great place to bring your own kids.

She sighed as she watched a group of kids that looked to be in about fourth grade—Kate's age. Would she ever have kids of her own? And how many would it take to erase that emptiness of not having Kate?

"You okay?" Alex asked. He took her arm, pulling her close.

She was grateful for the contact, for the reminder that for the moment she wasn't alone. "Yeah. It's just—" She shrugged, unable to finish.

"Hey, Kate'll be coming to all these places pretty soon. She's a strong kid. She's going to be fine."

But Fiona wouldn't be there to share it. "Yeah. You're right." That was the deal she'd made. And if it weren't for

Kate's illness, she would know nothing about her. At least now, she knew that Kate had a good family and was being well taken care of.

They moved into the room with the fire exhibit. Antique fire engines lined one wall while newspaper clippings and pictures lined the others. Maps, models of the city and half-burned toys and books and clothes completed the display. Everywhere she looked, though, were the kids, oohing and aahing over the display.

"Do you ever want kids?" she asked Alex.

The question seemed to catch him off guard. "I'm not sure," he said slowly, like he was thinking about it for the first time. "Since I firmly believe that kids should be raised by two parents, I wouldn't have them unless I was in a relationship that was going to last. And I can't see myself in that."

"Why not?"

He shrugged and stared at the map showing how much of the city had been destroyed by fire. "I'm like my mother," he said. "We don't wear well."

Fiona frowned at him. "Your mother doesn't think that way, does she? Or has she given up on finding love?"

"My mother is the ultimate eternal optimist."

"And so you have to balance it with pessimism."

"Realism," he corrected.

"Yeah, right." She didn't bother to hide her scorn. "Convenient excuse." She started into the next room, not certain why his dismissal of lasting relationships annoyed her, but certain that she was annoyed.

He hurried after her. "Well, I don't see you jumping at relationships," he said. "Judging from your family's reaction to my presence at your birthday party, I would guess you don't even date much."

"That doesn't mean I've closed myself off to love," she snapped.

"Maybe I don't see love as this so-great, all-wonderful thing that the movies make it out to be," he said. "It looks like a big waste of energy to me."

"Anything that you're scared of seems that way."

"Scared of?" he cried.

Fiona stopped, suddenly aware that people were staring at them. Alex seemed to notice at the same time. He took Fiona's arm and led her along the hallway, leaning in close to her.

"I am not afraid of love," he hissed. "I'm not afraid of anything."

"Oh, big macho man," she mocked.

She could feel him stiffen with annoyance. "You can't be afraid of something that doesn't exist," he whispered.

"One day you'll learn that it does," she said.

"Yeah. When some woman would rather get her feet wet than me catch a cold."

She just stared at him. "What are you talking about?"

"Your fairy-tale kind of love. It should be a fifty/fifty-type arrangement. Sometimes one person throws his coat over the puddle, another time the other one walks through and gets their shoes muddy. But it didn't work that way for my mother or for me. As long as we were willing to sacrifice our coats, everything was fine. But it was a different story when we needed something. It was goodbye, Charlie."

"It doesn't have to be that way."

He shook his head. "Right. If I don't ask for the impossible."

"Impossible's a relative term," she said. "Maybe you didn't ask the right person."

"Look, I never asked for miracles. I wasn't looking for the world, just a little compassion when I needed it. Face it. Love is a hoax generated by the greeting-card and candy companies."

What an attitude! Any sympathy that had been simmering in her soul vanished and she turned to concentrate on the

Native American exhibit they'd entered. It was a display of a typical forest-Indian clan—a wigwam, warriors, women, and children. And toward the back, partially hidden by the bushes, was an old woman.

"If love doesn't exist, why am I here to give Kate bone marrow?" Fiona muttered.

"That sappy romantic, last-forever kind of love is what doesn't exist," he hissed under his breath. "I don't doubt the existence of a mother's love for her child, even a child you've never met."

"That's big of you."

Fiona took a few steps down the exhibit, but her eyes were drawn back to the old woman in the display. There was something about her—

Fiona froze. From where she now stood, she could see more of the old woman. She looked just like the one who'd spoken to her and Cassie and Sam that day they'd saved Romeo and Juliet!

"What's the matter?" Alex asked.

She just shook her head for a moment before she could find her voice. "Who's that old woman there supposed to be?"

He looked at Fiona, then looked at the display, then walked down to the end of the scene where an explanation was posted. Fiona followed him, but her eyes stayed on the scene itself.

"She represents the Native American's belief in the interdependence of man and nature," he said, then frowned at her. "You okay? You look strange."

"Wow, what a line!" She forced herself to mock him even though her heart felt shaky. "With smooth talk like that, it's no wonder you're single."

He frowned at her, but she just hurried on to the next exhibit. Her unease stayed with her for the rest of the day, though. The old Indian woman did not look like that other one; Fiona had to be wrong. Her imagination was just working overtime, what with her attraction to Alex and her worry over Kate. If Cassie was here, she'd tell Fiona she was crazy.

Still, the old woman haunted Fiona's sleep, what little of it there was, and kept her uneasy over the next few days. They went one day to the Art Institute and then to the Museum of Science and Industry the next, but once they were back at the apartment each evening, Fiona could barely remember what she'd seen.

That old woman years ago had said that the spirits would return to help her fight for her love. But she didn't have a love, unless you counted Kate. So, were the spirits going to fight for Kate? Assuming any of that was true, which it probably wasn't.

"You've been quiet the last few days," Alex said one evening just before dinner.

She shrugged. "Guess I'm just tired." That was true enough. She was tired physically, tired of being worried, and tired of trying to second-guess fate.

"Want me to run out and get us Chinese takeout for dinner?" he suggested.

"Sure."

She saw the soft concern in his eyes and felt again that urge to let him shoulder some of her worries. Her heart wobbled for just a moment, wanting to give in and not daring to. One didn't lean on an ice sculpture, no matter how sturdy it looked. Come the sun and it would be gone. He'd admitted he wasn't around for the long haul—not that he'd needed to be. She knew this was just a job.

She picked up the newspaper from the table by the windows and sank onto the sofa. She was stronger when her gaze didn't meet his.

"I think I'll just get started on this crossword puzzle," she said.

"Okay."

He left a few minutes later. Fiona actually did attempt the crossword puzzle but tossed the paper aside when she couldn't answer any of the clues. She lay against the sofa back with closed eyes. When had things gotten so complex?

Weirdly enough, the phone chose that moment to ring, as if someone was calling with the answer. Fiona reached over the end of the sofa to pick it up.

"Fiona?" a childish voice asked. "It's Kate."

"Kate?" Fiona fell back onto the sofa. Her hand was suddenly shaking so that she could hardly hold the phone. "You're supposed to be in isolation."

The girl snickered. "They have phones in the rooms, you know."

Fiona felt a smile slide over her lips. "I forgot."

"Mom lets me call my friends," she said. "It's not like I can do much of anything else, and TV gets pretty boring after a while."

Fiona laughed at the fervor in Kate's voice. "I wish you could convince my kids of that. All they want to do is watch TV."

"You got kids?" the girl asked.

Something stabbed at Fiona's heart and she bit back a silent cry of pain. "I meant my class," she said, her voice almost calm. "I teach fourth grade."

"Wow, that's my grade," Kate said.

Fiona knew that. Or had known that was where Kate most likely was. Just as she had known last year, when she'd monitored the third-grade lunch period and had wondered if her daughter was like that group, giggling at the boys and fussing with their hair, or if she was more like those others, rushing through lunch to play kickball or tetherball or hopscotch on the playground. Or the year before, when Fiona had watched a little eight-year-old neighbor learn to ride a two-wheeler and had only been able to think that her own daughter might be learning to ride one, too.

"Maybe you could come over and do my lessons with me," Kate said, pulling Fiona back to the present.

Wouldn't that be wonderful? And impossible. "I think those kinds of tutors are supposed to be licensed teachers," she said. "And I'm licensed in Indiana, not Illinois."

"Too bad," Kate said. "That woulda been cool."

A dream come true. "Yeah."

"Hey, I got a question," the girl said, her tone suddenly different. "Everybody just laughs at me when I ask it and then, when Mommy brought me the butterfly phone book from home so I could call Candy and Steffie and I saw the apartment's number in it and knew you were there, I thought maybe you'd tell me."

"What, honey?" Fiona gripped the phone harder, somehow afraid of what Kate might ask. And more afraid of having to answer.

"Once I have your bone marrow in me, am I gonna start looking like you?"

"Looking like me?" Fiona was stunned by the question, and flooded with possible answers, all starting with the fact that Kate already did look like her.

"Not that I think that would be bad or anything," Kate assured her. "I'm just kinda afraid of not being me anymore."

The child's fear sent all Fiona's hesitations scattering like fallen leaves in the wind. "Oh, Kate, that'll never happen!" Fiona cried. "You'll always be you."

"Yeah, but..."

Obviously that was the answer everybody had given her, and it hadn't been enough any of the times she'd heard it. Fiona dug into her years of experience with ten-year-olds. How did you address a fear like this? In terms they can understand.

"Do you know where you get your looks from?" Fiona asked.

"From my mom and dad." But the hesitation in the girl's voice said beyond that her knowledge was vague.

"Right. Long before you were even born, a kind of recipe was made with parts from your mom and parts from your dad of what you were going to be like. Every one of your cells has a copy of that recipe, just like every one of my cells has a copy of my recipe."

"Yeah?"

"Now you're getting about two cups of my bone marrow in the transplant," Fiona said. "That seems like a lot, but it's really small compared to the number of other cells that you have. You'll have way more copies of your recipe than mine."

"I just didn't know," Kate said, her tone lighter, relieved. "I was afraid I wouldn't like our cat Caspar anymore, or wouldn't be good at soccer or would suddenly start acting like a nerd and my friends wouldn't like me."

Fiona laughed even as her eyes got watery. There was so much love in her heart, it had to overflow. "I think you're safe. Though I should warn you I was kind of nerdy as a kid and terrible at kickball."

"You probably kicked with your toe," Kate said. "That's what most people do wrong. They kick with their toe instead of their laces."

"That sounds too simple an explanation. I was a very complex nerd."

Kate burst out laughing. "I like you," she said when her laughter slowed. "And I didn't mean—"

"I know," Fiona said. "It's all right. Nobody wants to stop being themselves and start being someone else. Even if that someone is really cool."

"Yeah." There was talking in the background and Kate seemed to leave for a moment. "I gotta go," she said. "Dracula's here again."

It must mean more blood was being drawn. Fiona gripped the phone tighter at the resignation in Kate's voice. Fiona should be there, holding Kate's hand and watching over her. That was her child suffering and she didn't belong at the other end of the phone from her. She was always making a big deal about looking after people, but the one person she should have looked after, she'd given away.

"Well, take it easy," she said quietly. "It won't be too much longer till you're back playing soccer—at your level, not mine."

Kate hung up, but Fiona couldn't. Not for a long moment. She couldn't break that fragile connection between her and her daughter. A connection that wasn't even there anymore, she told herself. And with a sigh, she reached over and replaced the phone in the cradle.

"Food's here," Alex called out as the door shut behind him. "Anybody hungry?"

Fiona got to her feet. She felt like she'd just swum across the Atlantic and every step was an ordeal.

"Hey, I got—" Alex stopped and frowned. "What's the matter?"

Fiona tried to smile at him. "Kate called." The smile drooped, but she fought to keep some semblance of it on her lips. "She was afraid she was going to start being me once she had the transplant."

The food and a couple of videos got tossed onto the end table as Alex took Fiona in his arms. "You okay?" he asked.

She wanted to cry and weep and sob and kick and scream, but all she did was nod as she buried her face in his chest. His arms felt so good around her. They were walls that would hold her up, steel that would not let her fall into misery. He wouldn't let her down. She could lean on him now, just for the moment, just until she caught her breath.

"I should be there with her," she told him. "I should be the one taking care of her. I should never have given her up."

"Fiona," he said on a sigh, his breath ruffling her hair. "You *are* taking care of her."

She pulled away from him slightly, away from his strength that was so addictive. "Not like I took care of Cassie and Sam when we were little. Not like a mother takes care of her child." A sob shook her, echoing through her heart. "I was so selfish, just thinking how hard it would be to raise her.

But if I'd kept her, I'd be there at her side. I'd be there to—''

He gripped her shoulders, forcing her to look at him with the sheer determination of his gaze. ''No. If you'd kept her, neither of you would be there,'' he said. ''Giving her up years ago is probably the only thing that's giving her a chance now.''

''What?'' What was he talking about?

He loosened his hold on her, but his gaze wouldn't release her. ''Assuming that you could have finished college while raising her and would be teaching where you are now, would your insurance have covered the transplant?''

''Would it have...'' Her voice trailed off into uncertainty, into oblivion. ''I don't know,'' she whispered.

He just shook his head. ''Probably not. A lot of insurance plans don't. But the Andrewses don't have to worry about it. They have enough money to pay for the transplant themselves if they have to.''

She just stared at him. ''So giving her up saved her?''

''In a way,'' he said. ''Of course, you didn't know what would happen back then. But it looks like it turned out for the best for her.''

Fiona nodded slowly. ''And that's all that counts.''

''It's what counts most,'' he corrected, his voice gentle. ''Your feelings matter, but—''

''But better I hurt than Kate dies,'' she finished.

She lay back in his arms, feeling too weary to move, too weary to find the strength to stand alone. It was only for now, only for this moment of weakness; not a habit that would cripple her. She had to regroup. She had to settle her churning emotions and reaccept the fact that giving up Kate had been for the best.

She sighed, letting go of all the hurts and pains and fears that had been bottled up inside her. No more second-guessing. No more wanting to turn back the hands of time. It was right the way it was, with hope on Kate's side and the pain only here on her own side. She could handle it. She had in the past, and would again once her heart was strong again. Speaking of which, maybe it was time to test it.

She pulled away slightly, but foolishly looked up into Alex's eyes as she did and stopped. The tenderness in his gaze undid her. Her carefully constructed armor fell away and all she could do was watch him. Stare as his lips came down slowly to meet hers.

His touch was as gentle as the touch of the dew on the grass in the morning. As sweet as the scent of apple blossoms on a spring breeze. And as healing as time.

She gave herself up fully to the ministrations of his lips and let the healing warmth flow over her, wrapping her in a soothing cloak. For a moment, she was not alone in all this; there was another heart standing next to hers, another hand to cling to.

They pulled apart slowly. Fiona smiled up into Alex's eyes. They were cloudy and confused, as if he was just waking from a deep sleep.

"I guess I was taking care of Kate all along," she said. "I just didn't know it."

"Princess Fiona to the end."

How well he knew her. "I'd like to give her that book I bought of Irish folk tales. Do you think her parents would mind?"

His smile said he would, in turn, watch over her. "I'll take care of it."

She had never felt so sheltered, so secure. Even in the midst of all her fears, she felt whole.

And the feeling lasted over the next few days. She and Alex took the book over to the hospital, leaving it with Mrs. Andrews, who was pale with tension but polite and grateful, nonetheless. Then Alex took Fiona down to the Chicago River for a cruise along the lakefront.

"Thought we'd do something more relaxing today," he said. "Don't want to wear you out with all that hiking around museums."

"This is great." And it was. Since it was early in the sight-seeing season, the upper deck of the boat was almost deserted. They were alone with the spring breezes and the gentle sun, holding promises of the summer to come.

"Sure you're warm enough?"

They were standing at the rail, watching the dock recede. Under one bridge, then another. She felt as if she could toss her worries into the wake of the boat and they would be washed away for the time being. It was a good feeling.

"I'm fine," she assured him as she gazed up at the buildings towering over them. "It's beautiful out."

"It'll get colder once we're out on the lake."

"I'll worry about it then."

"Sure. And then when you're freezing, you'll want my coat," he grumbled in a mocking tone.

She turned away from the city, letting it grow distant on its own, as she smiled at Alex. "And would you give it?" she asked.

He just made a face, then turned back to watching the city. "That white building there is Tribune Tower and that one across from it is the IBM Building."

Fiona laughed and slipped her arm through his, leaning close to him. "You're not such a tough guy, are you?" she teased.

He frowned at her. "You keep trying to ruin my reputation."

She just laughed again and felt even more of her fears flow away. He was turning out to be a good friend, now that she had her silly emotions under control. It was just a matter of getting focused, and she was, now. She could enjoy Alex's company for what it was, without complicating it with her silly dreams.

Of course, there were a few shaky moments over the next several days, when her resolve weakened. One evening she was particularly tired and when he put his hand on the small of her back as they were led to a table in a restaurant, she felt a wave of desire wash over her. She wanted to feel his hands really on her, feel his lips take hers in hunger and need. She wanted to belong to someone totally, to have that lonely shadow gone from her heart forever. Luckily, the maître d' was reciting the evening's special to Alex and she was able to gulp down some water and take a few deep breaths.

The next morning at breakfast, she bumped the table and the carton of orange juice tottered near the edge. They both jumped for it, but somehow missed the juice and found each other. Their hands slowly slid around each other's, their eyes locked in an unbreakable bond.

Fiona's mouth went dry, as if his gaze was stealing all the fear from her. As if the flames flickering in her soul had turned her into a desert, with him as her rain. He leaned closer, bringing his lips down to meet hers in a slow dance of exquisite tenderness. Their lips touched and sang a sweet song of love and passion and "forever," then pulled apart as if scorched by the power in their hearts.

They touched again, harder and rougher this time, and the song became more strident. It was of winds and rain, of storms toppling barriers and washing away hiding places. Her fears were revealed and washed clean, melting down into a torrent of need. She was exposed and vulnerable; there was no escape from the barrage of emotions Alex's touch awakened. And no escape was wanted.

Then, suddenly, the storm seemed to fade and sanity peeked through the clouds. They pulled apart. Alex was breathing as heavily as she was, although she darted only a quick glance in his direction.

"I think we blew that," he said, his voice anything but steady.

Fiona forced a calm into her soul and looked at him. "We what?"

He nodded toward the floor. And to the puddle of orange juice there. "We didn't catch it."

"No." She just stared at it like it was a work of art, her sluggish brain trying to kickstart itself. Or maybe just kick itself. "I'll get some paper towels."

"I'll get a sponge."

Somehow they cleaned up the mess without touching, although it must have looked like they were magnetic fields, each repelling the other. But the worst slip came after Kate called again to thank Fiona for the book.

"Did you know there's a story in here about a Fiona?" Kate asked, her voice bouncing with excitement.

"Yep. My mother told it to me when I was little. I always thought I was named after her."

"Wow, that's cool. Do you have little brothers, too?"

"No, two younger sisters. They aren't too little anymore, though."

"No, I guess not." Kate paused. "The doc says things are going good. We should be able to do the BMT in a couple of days."

"Great."

"Yeah, I'm getting tired of everything here. Especially the food. You'd think they were trying to kill us all instead of get us better."

"Make your mom and dad take you out for a great pizza when you get out."

"I will." Another pause. "Well, I gotta go. Mom and Dad just got back from dinner and I'm going to beat them at Tripoly again. See ya."

"Right. See ya." Fiona's last words echoed back at her, though. Would she see Kate again? Not likely.

"How's she doing?" Alex asked.

Fiona shrugged. "Sounds real chipper. If energy counts for anything, she should be home free."

Alex was there to brush the fears from her heart as he brushed the curls from her cheek. "Hey, if love and genes mean anything, she's home free."

"Yeah." She found a smile from some forgotten corner of her heart and brought it out. "She's got a lot going for her."

Apparently she wasn't beaming as brightly as she'd thought. Alex's eyes studied her for a long moment. "But..." he said, waiting for her to finish.

She looked away. Why did she feel the need to open herself up to this man? Was she starting to care for him or was he a safe confidant who would be disappearing from her life in a few days?

"But after the transplant I won't get to see her again."

He said nothing, but just wrapped his arms around her. His embrace became a haven of safety, a refuge from the battering of the world. She wished she could just stay there forever. She wished she could just let reality become a distant memory.

She closed her eyes and buried her face into Alex's chest, realizing how her fears had grown in the last few days. No longer was she just worried about Kate and how to tell her family about her, but now suddenly she was afraid of losing Alex. Afraid of the time in the next few days when he would walk out of her life forever.

How had she let herself become so dependent on him? What had happened to that great strength that she used to boast about?

She pulled away from his embrace, away from the heaven his arms were to her. It was only a few more days. She just had to stay strong. She had to stay out of his arms.

Chapter Seven

Fiona was outside the apartment. Crowds of people were pushing past her but her feet weren't moving. She was waiting for someone and she had to stay here. If she left, they would never come. More and more people pushed past her. More and more time passed. A fear began to grow in her heart. Maybe she was in the wrong place. Maybe she'd missed her chance.

She began to race through the crowds, bumping and pushing as she fought her way, like swimming against the current. Then suddenly she was in a hospital nursery. All the babies were lined up in cribs, sleeping so peacefully. Fiona tiptoed among them, searching for soft brown curls, for a crooked little smile and a laughing voice. For eyes that would light up only when she came into the room.

But she was gone. Her child. Her baby. Her precious bundle of life.

"She can't be!" Fiona cried.

You're too late. Too late. Too late.

"No!" Fiona cried and sat up in bed, her hands over her ears. The words were echoing around her, taunting her. "No," she said on a breath. "No."

"Fiona?" Alex was at the door, with light spilling in from the hallway, silhouetting his broad shoulders, his strong arms that would hold her if she gave the slightest hint. "You all right?"

"Yeah." She took a deep breath and leaned back against the headboard. "Just a dream."

"Not a very pleasant one, I gather."

"No." If she made a move, he would come over. He would sit on the side of her bed and hold her. But it wouldn't stop with holding. Not now, not tonight. Everything was coming to a close. "I was looking for Kate, but I was too late."

"Too late for what?"

"To see her. She was gone. They'd taken her away from me."

She wanted the light on, wanted to fight back those demons that came in the night. Fear. Worry. Guilt. They sat off on the edges of her feelings, like hungry hyenas on the edges of the campfire's glow. But if the light was on, it would mean she wasn't going back to sleep. That she wanted—needed—company.

"You want a glass of wine or something?" he asked. "Might help you relax."

Fiona just laughed, trying for lightheartedness. "I think I was too relaxed," she said. "If I was tense, I'd never have fallen asleep."

"Maybe." He leaned against the doorframe, but his voice came in to surround her, to embrace with his caring.

She took a deep breath and wiggled her toes under the covers. "I'm like an alcoholic who hasn't had a drink for ten years. One slip, one sight of her, and I have this irresistible urge for more."

"Understandable."

"But not possible." She leaned her head back and stared at the spray of light across the ceiling. And how it made everything bright in the middle of the room, but the corners—where Fiona lived—were still dark and shadowed. "In a few days, I'll be out of her life again. It's going to be hard."

"I'm sure the Andrewses will let you know how things are with her."

"Maybe. I hope so."

"If not, I can keep an eye on things for you."

She laughed. "Mr. Honesty snooping around? Doesn't that sound wrong?"

"What's dishonest about it? Who am I misleading? There're certain rights we all have. Kate had the right to know if you could save her life. You have the right to know if that help was enough."

"You make it all sound so simple."

"It usually is," he said.

Was it? She gazed at him again, and suddenly saw him for the first time. "You have a robe on," she said. "I thought you didn't have one."

"Ever hear of a store?"

"Yeah, but you said—"

"One was needed and so one was acquired."

"But what a waste if you're never going to use it again."

He laughed then—a deep rich sound that pierced her armor and drew a slow, languid longing from her. "Who's to say I won't use it again? What about when you come to visit me?"

Early the next morning, Alex paused at Fiona's bedroom door for a long moment. No sound came from within. She must still be sleeping. That was good. She needed it. He'd heard her tossing and turning for hours last night after she'd awoken from her dream. It was probably just as well she chose that back bedroom. There was less sun in the morning.

After leaving a note on the kitchen table saying he'd be back soon, he slipped out of the apartment. The day was another gem—even though it was cloudy and threatening rain. There was such a promise of spring in the air, such a feeling of energy and possibilities. He couldn't remember another spring when they'd had a ten-day stretch of such great weather. It probably was going to be awful once Fiona left.

He frowned as he waited for the light to change. Fiona's presence had nothing to do with the weather. It wasn't like she could work magic or anything. And it wasn't like his perception of the weather changed when she was with him. That was all nonsense. Next thing he knew, he'd start thinking that the weariness that was starting to dog him was because she was going back home in a day or two.

The idea was so preposterous, so unbelievable, so insulting to his professional sense, that he couldn't stand still any longer. A lull in the traffic gave him the chance to dart across the street and that gave a few idiot drivers the chance to test their horns. Impatient jerks.

He hurried into the hospital and toward the bank of elevators at the back. It was still early, but that didn't mean the place wasn't already teeming with people. Not with visitors, but with hospital personnel—kitchen workers with carts of breakfast trays, cleaning crews finishing their rounds and aides wheeling patients off to who knew where. Hopefully it wasn't too early for the doctors to be arriving.

Luck was with him. Alex had barely gotten off the elevator when he saw Dr. Sears coming out of a patient's room, a small entourage of residents and medical students following him. Alex hurried over to catch him before he disappeared into another room.

"Dr. Sears," he called. "I need a minute of your time. We have a little problem."

With a flick of the doctor's head, the entourage drew back. "What's wrong?" he asked Alex. "Is Miss Scott ill? Has she changed her mind?"

Alex shook his head. "She needs to see the kid."

The doctor frowned and Alex could almost see him running to hide behind his rules and regulations. "That would be highly unusual, Mr. Rhinehart."

"What about this case isn't?" Alex snapped. "Look, she's already met Kate. The kid orchestrated that, and she's talked to her a couple of times on the phone. Fiona needs to see the kid for a few minutes before all this is over."

There was a mulish look in the doctor's eyes. "There's a lot more involved here," he said.

"It can be when Kate's asleep," Alex said. "It's not like Fiona wants to talk to her. She needs to see her. Just see her."

The entourage was getting restless and the doctor shot them a look that stopped them dead. He turned back to Alex. "All right. But late at night when Kate's asleep. And no physical contact."

"Fine." Though Dr. Sears wasn't exactly waiting around to hear Alex's agreement.

Alex restrained his desire to shout a "Yes!" of victory and just hurried back to the elevators. The day was even more gorgeous than he remembered, he discovered when he got back outside. True, it was drizzling now and there was a definite chill in the air, but it put a certain briskness in his step.

At the corner near the apartment, a florist was setting out a sidewalk display of flowers. The daffodils looked especially springy; their bright yellow faces looked like miniature suns. He bought a couple of bunches of them. Not for any special reason; just that it seemed like a good idea. When he opened the apartment door, he heard Fiona in the kitchen and found himself smiling.

"I'm back," he called out. "Anybody miss me?"

Fiona came to the kitchen door. "Hi."

She looked like spring itself in her pink blouse and green slacks. Even the slight shadows under her eyes couldn't hide the fact.

"You're back quick—" She stopped as she saw the flowers, her face breaking into a smile that put the daffodils' brightness to shame. "Oh, how pretty."

"I thought so." He handed them to her, suddenly feeling as self-conscious as a junior-high kid. "They made me buy them."

She just laughed, burying her face in the bright yellow and taking a deep breath of the sweet spring scent. "Is that right, Mr. Honesty? And just how did they do that? Pull a gun on you?"

He felt his cheeks get hot. "They called to me," he said.

"Uh-huh. In what language?"

"If you need to ask, you have no soul," he said. "There are times you don't need words to communicate."

Her face suddenly grew as red as his felt. She was thinking of the times they'd embraced. The times when they hadn't needed words to share their loneliness or fear, their excitement or their desire.

She turned away quickly. "I'll put these in water, shall I?" she said.

"Yeah, great."

He followed her into the kitchen. She looked to be almost done with her breakfast. "So, what do you want to do today?" A vision of the two of them locked in an embrace zipped into his mind, and he pushed it aside just as fast. Jeez, his mind was stuck on one track today. "The transplant is tomorrow. Want to do something special since it's your last day here?"

She'd put the flowers in a tall glass and placed them in the center of the table. They definitely took second place when compared to her.

"I'd really just like to do some shopping," she replied. "I want to get presents for everybody back home. You don't have to come."

He felt a moment's disappointment. Didn't she want him along? "I don't mind," he said. "Don't you need somebody to carry packages?"

"So you're offering your body up for service, is that it?"

"Any service you should desire, ma'am."

He enjoyed the further blazing of her cheeks, and wished that he had the right to swoop her up into his arms; that tonight wasn't going to be their last night here; that tomorrow she wasn't going off for the transplant and then back to her life without him.

He was going to miss her, he realized with a shock. He was going to miss letting her lean on him. He was going to miss fighting her battles and watching out that she wasn't taken advantage of. When had she gotten close to him? How had she slipped behind his defenses?

"I can't believe the ten days are up," he said.

"I know." She poured the remains of her coffee into the sink and rinsed out the cup. "T-day is just about here."

Jeez, how stupidly selfish he was! Here he was, thinking about how he was going to miss her, and she was worried about the transplant and whether or not it would work. It was a good thing this was just about over. He was no good in relationships.

"Bet you'll be glad to have it over."

She shrugged, her fears showing in every slight movement. "Yes and no."

"No more calls from Kate," he noted.

"No more being dragged by you through a million miles of museums, either."

He wasn't certain she was joking. "Just doing my job."

She came over, as quiet as a summer breeze, and touched his cheek. It was like a kitten's kiss—so soft that he could barely feel it on his skin although it sent rockets shooting through his heart.

"I was very lucky the Andrewses hired you," she said. "You are a good man, Alex Rhinehart."

Her words caressed his soul, setting it to trembling. His arms ached to hold her, his lips begged to kiss her. A fire smoldered in his loins that screamed to light an answering flame in her. Desire sent sparks into the air, seeking the kindling in her eyes. He just stared at her, not daring to breathe or move or even think.

One of two things was going to happen. Either he was going to sweep her into his arms and make mad, passionate love to her here on the kitchen floor. Or they were going to go shopping.

"I'll get my purse," she said, and turned away.

Slowly, he let the air out of his lungs. Shopping it was.

Fiona tried to pay attention. Alex had rented this movie because he had been sure she'd enjoy it, but she was having trouble keeping it all straight. And an even harder time pretending that she cared.

Everything was coming to an end. The waiting, the time here with Alex, the calls from Kate. She needed to let it all go and get used to being alone again.

"I think I'll go to bed," she said, although she knew that sleep was far away. "I've got a big day tomorrow."

"Already?" Alex looked at his watch. "It's only eleven."

"Hey, that's late for us small-town girls."

"I thought we'd take a walk. You know, to help you sleep better."

She wasn't sure anything would help her do that, but Alex was trying so hard to look out for her. She just nodded. "That would be nice."

So they went outside, bundled up against the suspected chill in the night air. Alex offered her his arm and she took it, leaning into his warmth as they started off into the night. It was dark, but only above them. The streetlamps threw circles of light over the sidewalks, and car lights chased away any lingering shadows.

"It's a lot darker at home at night," she said as they strolled down the sidewalk. Even at this hour, a reasonable number of people were out. "You can't even see the stars here."

"Too many lights competing for your attention," he said.

"Sort of like life, isn't it?" she said. "Little things are always claiming your attention so that you lose sight of what's really important."

They swerved around a couple walking a dog and reached the intersection just as the Walk sign flashed on. They started across the street.

"Pretty deep thoughts for eleven at night," he said.

She laughed. "Hey, I do my best thinking late at night."

"I thought you said you did your best thinking at the swan pond."

She looked at him. "Funny you should remember me saying that."

"Why?" he asked. "I remember a lot of what you've said."

"Part of the full service?" They were nearing the hospital. It loomed before them, the dark windows like eyes closed in sleep. But that was just pretense. Even though the front entrance was silent, sirens sang out from around back, warning that the place was still awake. "It's just not what I expected you to do for your clients."

"You aren't one of my clients."

Something touched her heart. Fear? Joy? Confusion? "Oh?"

"Technically, the Andrewses are my clients," he explained. "But I consider you a friend."

She liked the sound of that. "Thank you. I feel the same way."

He tightened his hold on her arm as he headed them up the front steps of the hospital. "I thought we could visit here."

It all came clear to her as if he'd written it out. He was taking her to see Kate. "Alex, we can't," she protested even as he pulled open the door for her. "Visiting hours are over."

"So?"

She went inside, but only so that they wouldn't be standing there with the door open, calling attention to themselves. "Alex," she said. "We're not. We can't."

"We can. We are."

She came closer to him, feeling the empty lobby was filled with watching eyes. "Kate's in isolation," she whispered.

He shrugged. "They'll bundle you up. Give you a mask and stuff."

"It's against the rules."

"I got it approved."

"How? By who?"

"By Dr. Sears," he said. "Kate'll be asleep, so it's not like you can talk to her. But you can see her."

It was the one thing she wanted to do, yet... "I don't know," she said with a sigh.

"You want to see your daughter, right?"

Fiona didn't answer. She couldn't answer.

"Fiona."

He laid a hand on each shoulder, looking her in the eye. She didn't remember seeing that piercing quality before.

"I'm not supposed to," she replied. "I agreed to that."

"You'll just go up there. You'll look in on her for a few minutes. Then we'll come back and put you to bed."

Oh, Lord. It sounded so easy.

She let him lead her across the lobby to the elevators where a security guard sat. She was sure he would turn them away. Or worse, hold them and notify the authorities.

But Alex just gave the young man some snappy patter that she couldn't comprehend. After signing a register, he hurried her to a waiting elevator, where he pressed the button for seven.

It was the same floor where she'd met the doctor and the Andrewses not even three weeks ago. The same floor where she'd met Kate for those few precious minutes.

A nurse looked up from the nurses' station when the door opened at the seventh floor. "Dr. Sears said you'd be here."

She came around the end of the counter, grabbing up a stack of plastic-wrapped packages. "This way."

The nurse, whose badge said her name was Stella, grabbed Fiona's arm and started leading her down the hall. Fiona looked back at Alex.

"Don't worry about him," the nurse said. "He'll be here when we get back."

She stopped at a door about halfway down the hall. A large yellow sign on the door proclaimed the patient therein to be in isolation. Fiona felt a quiver of concern run through her.

"Is this all right?" she whispered to the nurse.

"You got a cold?" she asked, handing Fiona the paper gown she'd pulled from a bag.

"No." Fiona slipped her arms into it and tied it shut.

"Any contagious diseases?" She gave Fiona an elastic-bound cap.

"Not that I know of." She slipped it over her hair.

"You're not going to hurt her any more than we do," Stella said. She handed Fiona some paper booties. "Put these on."

Fiona slipped them on over her sneakers, her hands shaking so that it took her two tries to get the second one on. "I don't want to hurt her," she said.

"Honey, you're fine. You're not hurting anybody." She waited until Fiona had the booties on, then handed her a mask. "The nurses here, we all think you're one special lady."

Fiona stared at her as she pulled the mask over her mouth. "Why?"

"To give up your kid, then come back and pretend to be a stranger? Now, that takes real love. It ain't everybody who could do that."

"Oh, I don't know about that."

"You ready?" the nurse asked.

Fiona nodded, her heart going at a thousand beats a second.

The nurse pulled the door to Kate's room open but Fiona stopped. "Won't we wake her up? I don't want to disturb her."

The nurse shook her head. "She's used to us coming in and out to check on her. She's a sound sleeper."

The nurse went in, gesturing for Fiona to follow her. The room was shadowy, but a soft light behind Kate's bed illuminated it enough to see Kate and any monitoring instruments they might need.

The nurse beckoned Fiona in farther. Fiona stopped when she reached the foot of the bed, her vision blurred.

Images of a dark-haired girl danced before her eyes. A baby being baptized. A little girl standing at the edge of a swimming pool, begging to go in. A preschooler on her first pony ride. A pigtailed little girl running to throw herself into the arms of her parents.

So many pieces. Pieces that Fiona had never seen and could never touch. She was an outsider who could only guess at her child's life.

Fiona felt a touch on her arm and saw the nurse there, gesturing that she would wait outside. Fiona nodded, her eyes filling with tears as she turned back to the bed. There on the nightstand was the book of Irish folk tales she'd given Kate.

"I'm so sorry about everything," Fiona breathed into the night in a voice so soft that the angels couldn't have heard it. "If this was all somehow my fault, I'm sorry. I never wanted to hurt you. I only wanted what was best for you. Alex says giving you up was, but I don't know. I want to think I did right, but I just don't know. It's so hard not being the one to look after you."

She took a deep breath and stepped back toward the door. "Take care, my darling," she breathed. Then before she was blinded by tears, hurried out the door.

The nurse handed Fiona a tissue as she led her back down the hall. Barely able to see for the tears, Fiona stumbled to take off her mask and the cap. Then Alex was there to help her with the booties and gown.

"She's so beautiful," Fiona said, her voice all watery. "How could I give her up?"

"Because you loved her," Alex replied. He pulled the gown off her arms, then took her into his embrace. "And you'll give her up again because you love her even more now."

Fiona just let his arms surround her, giving herself up to his strength. With slow, silent tears, she wept for Kate and her illness, for her own loneliness and pain, and for the goodbyes just ahead. Although the sorrow was there, somehow the fear and pain weren't. It was as if Alex's embrace could hold back some of the misery. Her tears slowed as she let peace claim her.

"You're doing everything you can for her," the nurse said, patting her back gently. "And you've given her a good, strong body. Those genes are what's going to help her pull through. You've done a good job, Mama."

"You've given a great piece of yourself to the world," Alex said.

She had, hadn't she?

Fiona fairly floated back to the apartment. "I can't tell you how much it meant to me to see her," she told Alex.

"I'm glad."

"I never expected it." The darkness seemed like a cloak of velvet, the streetlights like diamonds scattering their magic along the way. She wanted to dance and laugh and sing. "I just know it's all going to work out."

"Going to send all those positive vibes into your bone marrow?"

"It's going to be chock full of them."

She was almost sorry when they reached the apartment building. The rooms would seem too confining for her happiness. She was never going to be able to sleep now.

"Big day tomorrow," Alex said as they went into the lobby.

"Yep." The elevator came all too quickly and sped them upward. She needed a star to climb to, an ocean to swim.

Then they were in the silence of the apartment and there was nothing left to do but thank him again and go to bed. She stood in the apartment's foyer as Alex closed and bolted the door.

"No one's ever done something so wonderful for me," she said when he turned.

"No big deal," he said with a shrug.

"It was. It is," she insisted. "It was the one thing that made this all bearable."

She leaned over to brush his cheek with her lips. It was to be a quick thank-you, a chaste kiss that spoke of nothing but her gratitude. But then the faint scent of his after-shave closed around her and her chest brushed the strength of his arm and it felt like an earthquake rocked the world beneath her.

She pulled away slowly, trying to regain control of her wobbly senses, but her gaze met Alex's and she forgot all about control. There was a fire in his eyes that promised warmth and magic and belonging. It called to her, pulling her closer and closer like a magnet. She licked her lips, then tried to laugh away the spell.

"I guess I should go to bed," she said. Her voice was shaky, uncertain.

"Yeah."

But his eyes wouldn't release her. Or else it was her feet—they wouldn't move. As if they were bogged down in some invisible mire.

"I need to get some rest," she said, although why, she didn't know.

"True. And it's late."

"Way past my bedtime."

But even as her treacherous feet finally managed to free themselves from the mire, they forgot which way to take her.

She took a step forward and found herself in Alex's arms. Maybe her feet knew better where she belonged, after all.

Alex's lips came down on hers so softly that it might only have been in her dreams. She felt almost no pressure at first, then the fire that had been in his eyes started to smolder in her heart. It flickered and danced deep inside her, igniting all her secret fears and hesitations and worries. Suddenly her hopes and dreams and hungers were growing wildly, filling up every crevice of her heart.

The pressure of his lips increased, entreating her soul and calling for an answer from deep inside. She didn't know with her head what his lips were saying, but the hungers inside her grew, entwining around her natural caution until it was lulled to sleep.

Alex pulled back slightly, his breath coming fast and hard, his eyes dark with the ravages of their hungers. "I'm not sure this is wise," he said.

But she was lonesome away from his lips, and cold as if winter winds were whipping through her heart. "Why not?"

"Because it's almost all over," he said. "Tomorrow's the transplant. You'll be going home the day after."

"It seems a good way to say goodbye," she whispered and let her fingers brush his cheek.

He let her hand roam for a moment, then took hold of it, pressing his lips into her palm. "A cup of coffee and a game of rummy would be safer."

But she was tired of "safe," tired of watching life from the sidelines and then regretting her lack of daring. "I want to feel alive," she said. "Just for tonight. Just for this once."

"Oh, Fiona," he said on a sigh and pulled her back into his arms as if he no longer had the strength to keep her away.

His lips took hers again, all pretense gone. His hunger spoke to her. It raged and stormed and attacked her sensibilities. She loved it—loved the sense of power his desire gave her; loved the exploding need that he awoke in her.

Her hands roamed over his back, pulling him closer while hungering themselves to feel more of him, to touch his skin and feel his muscles tremble and quiver. He would be strong and his skin would taste slightly salty even as the heat of it would threaten to scorch her.

"Why do I feel like we're playing with fire?" Alex breathed into the night.

"Fire's only dangerous if you don't know how to handle it."

"And you do?"

"We do."

She led him down to his room. Through the wall of windows the city lay before them, its lights like a handful of gems scattered on the night. It lent magic to the air. She turned to him in the enchanted light, and began to unbutton his shirt. His hands stopped her, holding her hands still.

"Are you doing this because of your visit to Kate?" he asked.

She tried to see into his eyes. "What does that have to do with this?"

"I don't want you out of gratitude," he said.

"I don't think that's what this is," she said slowly. "I'm grateful, certainly, but this is something else. It's something that's been building since that first day."

"We don't have to give in to it."

She leaned forward, laying her head against his chest and willing his arms to come around her. They did.

"It's like I'm living in a whole different world here," she said softly. "Everything here is bigger and deeper and better than at home. The monsters that come out from under my bed at night are twice as big. The hopes I have for Kate are twice as huge as anything I've ever hoped for and the moments of happiness have been twice as sweet."

She closed her eyes and reveled in the nearness of him, in the riot of sensations dancing across her heart. "Right here, right now, this feels right. I don't want to think beyond that."

His hands were on her back, moving with infinite slowness. "I don't know how you can think," he said, his voice hoarse, but with a touch of teasing in it. "I think I gave it up about two seconds after I closed the door."

"Then why are we wasting time talking?"

His lips came back to hers and the world rocked and shook. It was as if they'd both taken the reins off their rigid control and it exploded out of the gate.

Under the pressure of his mouth, she let her lips open slightly. His tongue slid inside to explore, to dance, to tease her senses into a hunger that she'd never known before. She pressed closer to him, wanting their bodies as near as possible. But as near as possible wasn't near enough.

When his mouth left hers to blaze a trail down the side of her neck, she let her hands fumble with the buttons of his shirt. One undone. Another and another until her hands could creep inside and find his heated skin. Laying her hand flat, she could feel the racing of his heart and smiled, knowing hers was beating in unison.

"This is insane," he murmured into her hair. "This is crazy."

"I know." But for once insanity seemed to fit her, craziness seemed to match her soul. "Hell of a way to say goodbye."

But nothing about their relationship had been ordinary, so why should the ending of it be? And what if it wasn't to end?

That would be a story left for another day, she decided. She wasn't thinking of tomorrow or next week or next month. It was now that called her name and held her hostage.

His hands had slid under her blouse; his touch was electric, sending shivers through every inch of her. She gasped with pleasure, her heart seeming to falter as her breath did for just a moment. Then he was loosening her blouse and freeing her from the confines of her bra.

Somehow, in an embrace that spoke of bindings of the heart, they made their way to the bed and lay together. Soft light spilled in through the windows, bathing them with enchantment. Ever so gently, Alex reached over to caress her breasts, lightly touching the tips but somehow sending unspeakable waves of desire through her.

He leaned closer, taking first one tip in his mouth, then the other. His lips tugged at them. He teased them with his tongue. Just his very breath on them sent tremors into her world to demolish the last of her sanity.

She pushed his shirt off his shoulders, then unbuckled his belt. With his help, she slid his pants off and let her hands slip gently over the length of him. Her hands teased the trail of hair that ran down the center of his chest, then she let her lips follow their lead. As she slid ever lower, he moaned in pleasure. Then, with a boldness unknown to her, she took him in her hands, rubbing the rigidity of him with her fingertips.

"Oh, my precious little Fiona," he said on a sigh as he pushed her back against the pillows. "This isn't playing with fire. It's playing with dynamite."

He tugged at her slacks until she slid them off, then her stockings so that she was lying naked in the dim light. She could almost see the fire in his eyes as his gaze swept over her, his hands exploring as if he couldn't trust his sight.

"You are so beautiful," he murmured.

And for once she felt so. She felt she was just right; that her body was in sweet harmony with his. When his hands wandered over her, teasing and tormenting her ragged hungers into insatiability, she had no desire to hide under the covers or to close the drapes. Who could see them up this high but the stars? And she felt she was already halfway there, anyway.

Alex's hand moved lower, finding the core of her hungers, the key to her passion and desire. Under his caress, those hungers grew deeper and more voracious. Her body moved into him, needing a rhythm of love to ease the wild agony of her wanting.

"Now, Alex," she moaned and opened herself to him.

She took him inside her, burying his essence in the center of her heat, as they moved in an age-old rhythm. Outside the window the stars seemed to dance. Closer and closer they spun until their light was all around them.

She seemed to soar higher and higher, passing the stars as she found a light and a fire all her own. They were one and in some distant galaxy would always be so. The fire was close to exploding and she clung to him tightly, pulling him deeper into her heart. Then she was there; her world burst into flames and she knew only wild, unanswerable pleasure.

They held each other close, as if trying to hold on to the ecstasy, but it slipped from their grasp and let them glide slowly back to earth. But even that was magic as she lay in his arms and let sleep claim her.

How could this be a goodbye? she wondered, just before slumber claimed her. It felt so much like a beginning.

Chapter Eight

Fiona stepped out into the mild morning sunshine and took a deep breath. It was a beautiful day, just one in a line of beautiful days. But today was special. Today she was going to give her daughter health. A new life.

"You okay?" Alex asked.

She turned to smile at him. How dear he was. In just a few short weeks, she had found her very own champion, her very own guardian angel. She would never have gotten through this time without him.

"I am wonderful," she said and took his hand as she looked around at the people bustling along. She no longer feared she was lost. "Let's walk along the lakeshore. We have plenty of time."

He frowned, his eyes showing all sorts of concern. "Are you sure you'll be all right?"

"Walking along the lake won't be much longer than walking on the street."

"I wasn't thinking of walking at all," Alex replied. "I was going to get us a cab."

Darling, sweet Alex. Fiona felt like hugging him, but just squeezed his arm instead. "Don't worry," she said. "I'm fine. Not eating or drinking since midnight isn't that big a deal. Besides, you didn't have anything for breakfast, either."

"I don't need breakfast."

Oh, big macho man. He could skip breakfast but the fragile little woman couldn't. Fiona just gave him a look. She was feeling too happy and hopeful to give him a hard time for being overly protective.

"The exercise will help settle my nerves," she said and tugged him toward the corner. "And if I faint, I'll let you carry me to the hospital."

"I'll hold you to it," he said.

"And I might just let you."

Something in the air around them changed. Memories of last night's loving mingled with dreams for tomorrow. His hold on her arm tightened. His eyes seemed suddenly alight with desire, flashing something hot and fiery that made her soul come alive. She felt every inch of her sing with joy, and let a smile tell him just how special last night had been. It had been the perfect ending to the weeks of tension.

Hand in hand, they crossed Lake Shore Drive and stepped onto the walkway along the lake. It was so quiet, so peaceful here. It was the perfect place to put her thoughts back in order.

As perfect as last night had been, it really had been an ending. Their lives would go in opposite directions from this point on. She knew that this morning, even if her heart had wavered last night. But that would be a dream for a lovestruck little girl. Fiona was a woman and knew better than to waste her time wishing for something that wouldn't ever be.

The scent of the water mixed with the crunch of the sand underfoot and brought reality back to surround her. The only good thing that had to come out of this time was Kate's return to health. Fiona wasn't going to be greedy and ask for more.

They crossed the street and walked up the steps to the main door of the hospital. Fiona thought of last night when Alex had brought her here and the joy he had given her. Joy in so many ways.

"Well, here we are," he said. "Any second thoughts?"

"There's no reason to have any," she replied. "The procedure is pretty minor."

"You'll be put under."

Fiona shrugged. "It won't be the first time. I had a general anesthetic when they took my wisdom teeth out."

"Then let's do it."

They walked into the hospital and followed the now familiar path to the rear bank of elevators. This time they both signed in, then stepped into the elevator for the ride to the seventh floor. She'd already been preadmitted, so all she had to do was check in at the nurses' station before going to her room.

"I guess I'll be staying overnight," she said. Her voice echoed oddly in the elevator.

"That's what they'd like," he said. "Though you could leave tonight if you're feeling all right."

"Tomorrow'll be fine." She was handling all this well, she thought. "I can catch an early train out to South Bend and be home before lunch."

"I can drive you home."

"There's no need. You'd have to get a car and everything." The elevator doors opened and she hurried out. There was no reason to tie him up anymore. Although she did hope that he would visit her once or twice before she checked out tomorrow morning.

"We're all set for you, Fiona," the head nurse told Fiona even as she started down the hall. "Your room's down here."

Fiona glanced at Alex, not wanting their goodbyes to be said here in the hall by the elevator, but he appeared ready to follow the nurse with her. He took her hand and gave her an encouraging smile as they walked to her room, passing a cart of breakfast trays that was in the hall.

She wiggled her nose. "Don't think I'm going to miss not eating that."

"I'll put in an order for a great lunch for you," he said.

"With my luck, I'll miss lunch by a few minutes and starve all afternoon."

"I'll smuggle you in a subway sandwich," he offered.

"What if I want one of those six-foot-long ones?"

"I'll find a way."

Fiona stepped into the room the nurse had entered, then stopped in astonishment. Her sisters stood by the window.

"Surprise!" they called out.

"When did you get here?" Fiona asked as she hugged first Cassie, then Sam. "Why didn't you call?"

"About thirty minutes ago."

"We were going to call."

"Yeah, I bet."

"But we didn't have time."

"We had to get your cats settled and taken care of."

"Are they all right?"

"Then there was Mr. Kaminsky."

"And Mrs. Torcini."

Suddenly, Fiona remembered Alex. She pulled him over to her side. "You may not remember but you met Cassie and Sam at my birthday party."

"You still taking care of Fiona?" Sam asked.

"Poor guy," Cassie added.

"It wasn't so bad," Alex said.

"Wasn't so bad?" Fiona repeated.

"She didn't make you eat healthy foods?" Sam asked.

"Well—"

"Or bring your jacket even if it wasn't cold?" asked Cassie.

"Actually—"

"I hate when she does that," Sam agreed.

"It's even worse when she's right and you need it."

Alex's gaze was going from one to the other, like he was watching a tennis match. Fiona didn't much like the amused smile that was growing on his lips. It was time to take a stand. "So how long are you staying?" she asked her sisters.

"However long you are," Samantha replied.

"We're going to take you home," Cassie said.

A little bubble of disappointment zipped through Fiona. Yeah, she'd already told Alex that she was taking the train home, but now there was no reason for him to insist on taking her.

"That's great," was all she said, though. "That saves me a ride on the old bump, rattle, and roll line."

"Where you guys staying?" Alex asked.

"We haven't looked for a place yet," Cassie said.

"You can stay at our apartment," he said. "Fiona'll stay in the hospital for the night and I have to get back to my own place."

Our apartment? The sound of it sent a warming sense of belonging through her. For a time, she guessed it had been.

"You guys stayed together?" Cassie asked.

"In the same apartment?" Sam added.

Not having had a drink since late last night, Fiona's mouth was already dry and sticky. Now it felt like someone had poured in a bucket of sand. "Well, you know..."

"Everyone wanted to make sure that Fiona was comfortable," Alex said.

"And your job was to..." Cassie said, letting her voice trail off into the silence.

"Well, he—"

"Miss Scott?" A bearded man in a long hospital coat stepped into the room. "I'm Dr. Wenger, your anesthesiologist. I need to ask you a few questions, if I might."

Saved by the needle sticker. "Hey." Fiona turned toward the others. "I bet you guys haven't had breakfast yet. Why don't you go grab something? I'm going to be pretty busy for a while now."

"You sure you don't need us?" Samantha asked.

"We can stay," Cassie said. "There'll be plenty of time to eat later."

"No, just go, already. I don't want you guys keeling over and fainting."

Her sisters started walking out, but Alex just stayed where he was. "I could stay and keep you company."

She shook her head. "I'm fine, really. I'm fine."

Slowly, very slowly, he walked out the door and left. Fiona strained until she couldn't hear his footsteps out in the hall anymore. He was gone. Suddenly the doctor picked up her hand, causing her to pull back and wince.

"You're not going to start crying now, are you?"

"Of course not," she snapped, blinking back the wetness. She was used to being on her own. It was the way she liked it best.

Alex got off the elevator. It wasn't even nine in the morning and he felt like he'd lived about two lifetimes today. This was one hell of a job. One of the easiest he'd had in ages, and for some reason, one of the hardest.

"Fiona's already down in surgery."

Alex looked up at the young nurse. "I was actually looking for her sisters."

"In the visitors' lounge around the corner."

He thanked the nurse and hurried to the lounge. Cassie and Sam were seated in a far corner, murmuring to each other.

There was a strong physical resemblance among the three sisters. But according to Fiona, they had completely different personalities. He doubted that they were all that different, but he wouldn't be around to find out. This business with Fiona was done. It was time to move on, even if his heart was having doubts.

"Hi, Alex."

"It's all set," he told them. "You two can stay in the apartment tonight."

"Great," Cassie said.

"It's only a couple of blocks from here. A steel-and-glass tower right on the drive. The address is 880 Lake Shore Drive."

"Is it high up?"

"Can we see the lake?"

"Yes and yes," he answered.

"Cool," they chorused.

"Do you need me to show you where it is?" he asked.

"No, we can find it," the athletic one said.

"Here's the key." Sam took it. "It's 21B."

"Thanks," Samantha said.

"You're welcome." Alex turned toward the door. "Nice meeting both of you."

They all stood there nodding. The silence hung heavy in the air around them. It was time for him to fly. "Well..."

"We're going out for some breakfast," Sam said. "Why don't you join us?"

"I'm not much of a breakfast eater," he replied. "If I don't eat soon after I get up, I lose my appetite until lunch-time."

"You mean you didn't eat because Fiona couldn't?" Cassie asked.

"You're a sweet guy, Alex," Sam said.

Her sincerity made him uneasy. "Actually I'm Nutra-Sweet," he joked. "That's why I'm so slender."

They just stared at him. It was time to go. He gave them a quick wave, then hurried down the hall to the elevators.

Once he was outside he considered hailing a cab; that would get him to his apartment the fastest. But then what? He didn't have anything he was all that anxious to do. The bus or the elevated would do just as well. But neither interested him. He let his feet take him to the lakefront.

Alex crossed at the same crosswalk he and Fiona had taken to get to the hospital a few hours ago. Once he was across, he stepped to the edge of the breakwall and looked out over the lake. He took a deep breath and shook his head, trying to clear his mind.

Fiona was as good as gone. She was going to make her marrow donation, rest overnight, then head back home. Keeping her memory alive wasn't going to make anyone happy.

Besides, he wasn't that kind of guy. He wasn't the type to look back. And Chicago was a big town. If too many memories of her lingered here on the city's gold coast, then he'd have to stay away. Wait until all traces of her were gone. Blown away across the lake. Back to that Indiana-Michigan area where she belonged. And he belonged here.

He took another deep breath. It was a beautiful April day with a gentle breeze coming from the west. A good day for a walk, a long walk. Like north along the lakefront, up to Lincoln Park, and then across to his place.

He started off at a good pace, fast enough to work up a sweat. That's what he needed—something physical to clear his body and mind of the past two weeks. Put him in the mood to jump back into his own life.

It was a good walk. He moved his feet and swung his arms. He checked out the action on the beaches while he dodged the bicyclers and skaters. His heart was pumping and he had a good sweat going. He flirted with the notion of going up to Foster Avenue. Hell, it was only another four miles.

But his feet slowed at Fullerton Avenue, just about where he'd planned to cut across the park—a path that he knew would take him along the north edge of the zoo, right by the lagoon where the swans lived.

Since he'd already slowed, Alex decided that he might as well slow down all the way and sit down. A little rest would do him good. Park here awhile and look out over the wide expanse of beach that stretched before him. And the water beyond that. He'd heard it was restful to watch waves like those that danced on Lake Michigan today. He leaned back and stared.

There were a zillion different ways to get to his apartment, any number of which would avoid the zoo entirely. But he couldn't spend the rest of his life running. What was he to do? Leave? Move up to the Yukon or something?

It certainly wasn't a surprise that Fiona's memory clung to him so tenaciously. After all, they'd lived together, twenty-four hours a day, for the past two weeks. Hell, that was more togetherness than married couples had, what with jobs, different friends and hobbies. So she'd gotten engraved in his psyche. But that would pass. It had to.

Time was like the wind, eroding even the hardest rock. Things would get back to normal once he plunged back into his own life.

Of course, he shouldn't just ignore her. It wasn't like they'd had a spat. They were friends. And like any friend who was having an operation, she deserved a little something.

Like flowers?

Yeah, flowers were good. He could have some sent.

No, you didn't just send flowers to a friend, not if she was a good friend. You delivered them yourself. And a sandwich in case she missed lunch.

"Hey, you got a visitor already," the orderly said as he pushed Fiona back into her room.

She turned on her bed, trying to focus her bleary eyes on the figure in the chair. She felt all disconnected from the anesthetic, like the various parts of her weren't plugged into the right sockets.

"You look beat."

It was Alex's voice. He stood and came over to the side of the bed.

"Nice talk," she managed to say, although her words seemed slurred. Her eyes slipped closed again. "You gotta be honest all the time?"

"I should let you get some rest," he said.

She got her eyes open somehow. "I'm okay. Just dopey. Give me a few minutes." Those stupid eyes closed again.

He mumbled something that sounded like wanting to give her forever, then she thought she felt his lips on her forehead. But by the time she got her eyes to open again, he was gone. Cassie was sitting where Alex had been and Sam was looking out the window. Absurdly, she felt abandoned and close to tears.

"Hey, Sleeping Beauty's awake," Cassie said.

"'Bout time," Sam said, coming over to the side of the bed. "How are you feeling?"

Lonesome. But Fiona just moved slightly in bed, testing out her limbs. "A little sore," she said. "Not bad." Had Alex even been there or had she just been dreaming?

"Where'd the flowers come from?" Sam asked.

"And the submarine sandwich?" Cassie added.

Fiona craned her neck to see the table next to the bed, discovering she was a little more sore than she'd thought. And discovering that the thought of Alex bringing her her sandwich and a gorgeous pot of tulips made the discomfort a lot less uncomfortable.

"Alex must have brought them," Fiona said.

Sam's eyebrows rose. "This sounds serious. Not just flowers, but food."

"Good food," Cassie said, unwrapping the sandwich and showing it to Fiona. "Want a bite?"

Fiona shook her head. "It was just a joke. Just part of his job."

"Uh-huh."

Cassie and Sam exchanged knowing glances; they didn't believe her.

"It's true," she insisted. "He's just a nice guy doing his job. There's no big romance." She pushed aside memories of last night.

"Sure."

Fiona was getting annoyed. It was just like always. They never listened to her, never believed her. "I'm about as likely to see him once I leave here as I am—"

"To kick a home run in kickball," Cassie finished for her. "We know."

"We always know," Sam added.

Fiona just made a face at them, but a nurse coming in to check her blood pressure saved them from a scathing retort. They just didn't understand the real world, she thought. They thought love was just out there waiting to be picked like a flower. They didn't know just how rare it was; how you could look for it your whole life and never find it.

"Lookin' good," the nurse said. "Need anything for the discomfort?"

Fiona shook her head. "No, I'm fine."

"Well, just call if you need anything."

Once the nurse was gone, Fiona turned back to her sisters. "You guys don't have to hang around here all day, you know."

"That's okay," Samantha said. "We don't have anything else to do."

"You could go shopping," Fiona replied.

Cassie made a face.

"The art museum isn't too far," Fiona said.

Her sister made another face, but not as bad as the one she made at the mention of shopping. Cassie hated shopping.

"I don't think we're in a museum mood," Samantha said. "We'll just stay here and bug you."

They fell back into silence. Cassie turned on the TV, but even with that to stimulate conversation, it was a hospital room. And there was something about hospitals that seemed to suck the conversational juices out of people.

Of course, people in hospitals were usually sick and Fiona wasn't at all. She was a little sore, but the residual of the anesthetic was wearing off, leaving her feeling restless and impatient. Like an animal in a too-small cage. Even the arrival of a fruit basket from the Andrewses didn't seem to provide them with much to talk about.

"You know, you could go to dinner with us," Cassie said as evening loomed over them.

"Yeah, I know," Fiona replied. "But I'm not really hungry. And I've got my sandwich and all that fruit."

"Your sandwich has to be all soggy by now," Sam said.

Her sisters waited while Fiona hesitated. It wasn't like she didn't want to go out with them. She just didn't want to go out with anyone. Well, that wasn't exactly true.

"I don't feel bad," Fiona said. "But I don't feel top-notch, either. You don't want me along. I'd just be a drag."

"We've never let that bother us before," Cassie said.

"Thanks." Fiona waved them away with a laugh. "Now I know that, I don't want to go out with you."

"Fiona," Sam whined.

Jeez, now Sam was afraid they'd hurt her feelings. "Cassie," Fiona said with a sigh. "Take your sister and go feed her."

"Come on, Samantha," Cassie said, pulling on Sam's arm. "You know how she is when she gets stubborn."

Samantha whined a little bit more, but it was more out of habit than conviction. Her sisters were gone within minutes, promising to bring back a treat.

Fiona waited until she couldn't hear them anymore, then she dropped her head back on the pillow. It was time for her to go home. To return to her life. So why wasn't she happy?

Chapter Nine

"Thank you," Mrs. Andrews said the following morning. Her voice was quiet and tight as she pressed a small something into Fiona's hand. "We can't ever thank you enough."

"Let's just hope it works," Fiona replied. She glanced down to see the other woman had given her a wallet-size photograph album. Pictures of Kate! Fiona clutched it to her.

"It will, I'm sure of it."

Mrs. Andrews pulled her into a hug as Fiona blinked back tears. This wasn't the place for them—not here with Alex and Cassie and Samantha all watching her. Later, at home, there would be time for tears. Fiona pulled away slowly.

Keep in touch, please. The words lay flat in her mind. She wanted to ask the Andrewses to let her know how Kate was getting along, but the fear of being refused was too high a hurdle.

Mr. Andrews reached over to shake her hand. "We'll let you know how she's getting along," he promised. "And our number's in there." He nodded at the small photograph album. "Call anytime."

"Thank you," Fiona whispered, her voice overwhelmed by her gratitude. She tightened her hold on the album, wanting to look at it now, wanting to study the pictures of Kate and embed every speck of her into her memory. But she didn't dare. Not with everybody here.

"Well," Mr. Andrews said. "We need to get going and I'm sure Fiona wants to get home."

"Yes," Fiona replied. "My cats miss me."

"I'm not sure they do."

"Thanks, Cassie." Fiona grimaced and looked at the Andrewses. "The joys of having sisters."

"We've kept you long enough," Mrs. Andrews said. "Have a safe trip home."

They were quickly gone, leaving Fiona standing alone near the door. She turned and found Alex's eyes on her. The look was gentle and understanding. He knew what those pictures meant to her and how her hands itched to open the book.

"Well, is that it?" Cassie asked. "You free to go now?"

"Yeah, I guess." Now that it was time, she wasn't all that anxious to leave. It felt like part of her was about to be torn away.

"Let me take your bag."

Alex picked it up from the bed while Cassie grabbed the fruit basket and Sam took Alex's tulips. Fiona felt like a tagalong. She got her purse and just followed along after them with her precious little photo album.

Once out in the hall, Cassie and Sam hung back so that Fiona could walk next to Alex. She knew it was silly, just as Alex must know it, but they were both mature. They let her sisters play their little game and walked side by side.

"Bye, Fiona," a nurse called out.

"Take care of yourself," said another.

She kept a smile on her face and returned their best wishes, holding on tight to her lower lip until the elevator came. She hadn't thought leaving was going to be so hard. She had to focus on Kate's chances to be well, and on saying goodbye to Alex.

There were two orderlies with patients in wheelchairs on the elevator so the four of them had to squeeze in alongside the wall, with Fiona standing tight up against Alex. It brought up a whole wild array of memories that she should ignore. The hard feel of his body pressed against hers. The gentle touch of his hands when she was feeling blue. The fire in his eyes when they'd kissed.

But what good did it do to remember? She didn't need to remind herself of all that she was leaving. Yet neither could she stop. It was as if she had to reopen all the wounds to see if they were healing. The elevator reached the ground floor and Fiona was flooded with relief.

Cassie exited first when the door opened. "I'll run and bring the car around," she said. "You guys wait by the front door."

"That's all—"

"I'll come with you," Samantha said, stepping in on Fiona's words.

Fiona sighed as she watched her sisters hurry off. "You wouldn't know I was the oldest, would you?"

Alex just laughed and took her arm. "You probably were unbearably bossy when you were growing up and they need their chance for revenge."

"I was never bossy," she protested. "And somebody had to look out for us. Cassie would have led us all to reform school."

"Sure." His tone was mocking, but his voice was so gentle.

Regrets washed over her again and she took the time to flip through the photo album. Kate as a baby, as a toddler, as a grinning little schoolgirl. Getting her first haircut, wearing Halloween costumes, clutching a huge white cat.

Fiona slammed the book shut, her control about as steady as a cobweb.

"Good stuff?" Alex asked.

She nodded and took a deep breath. "It was really nice of them to give me these."

"They owe you a lot."

"They don't owe me anything. I did it for Kate, not them."

They'd reached the front doors, and Alex stopped. "I have something for you, too," he said and took a small box from his pocket. "I saw it when you were buying presents for your family the other day."

She untied the ribbon and lifted the lid. Lying on a soft bed of cotton was a pin of a silver swan with a baby swan behind it. "Oh, Alex, it's beautiful," she said. More tears welled up in her eyes and she didn't seem able to blink them into oblivion.

"Jeez, I'm like a sprinkler system today," she said.

"It's been a stressful time for you."

"I'm usually better than this." She took a deep breath and let it out slowly, willing her backbone to stiffen and the weepy faucet to turn off. The world stopped being blurry in a moment and then she took the brooch out of the box, pinning it to her blouse. It would remind her of both Alex and Kate, and this special time when they both belonged to her in a way. "It's perfect. I'll keep it forever."

He just took her arm and led her out the door. Cassie wasn't in sight yet. She was either thinking she was being considerate in giving them more time to say goodbye or seeing this as another chance to exact revenge for childhood grievances. Fiona felt the weepiness creeping back like vultures waiting to feed. Where was Cassie?

"You don't have to wait," Fiona said.

"No problem."

No problem. Hear that, heart? Fiona asked herself. This was no problem for him. It should be no problem for her. She didn't come into this expecting anything but goodbyes at the end. And he'd given her a whole lot. He'd made the whole thing bearable with his kindness and support.

"It was fun," he said.

She nodded. "I enjoyed myself. Thanks for all your work."

He took her hand and smiled. "It wasn't really all that hard."

She should pull her hand away; slip back into her shell and run for Indiana. But her treacherous hand didn't move, no matter how loud her brain screamed.

Suddenly a car horn sounded right next to her and Fiona jumped so high that she scraped some clouds coming back down. Her sisters just sat there grinning.

"Come on, Alex," Samantha said. "Are you going to kiss her or aren't you?"

Fiona contemplated murder. Why had she worried so about keeping the three of them together when they were kids? She should have ditched them and billed herself as an only child.

"That's a good question." Alex took a step closer to her, his voice a silky caress. His eyes were looking into the depths of her soul. "Are we or aren't we?"

"They're asking you," Fiona said, even as her heart wobbled and stammered. She wished he wouldn't look at her like that.

His eyes kept piercing through all her barriers and slaying all her fears, even as her mind knew that this was the last time. Then, ever so slowly, he moved closer and put his arms around her. His lips sang an easy song of memories to her soul. Of fears faced and conquered. Of boat rides and swan cookies. Of secret midnight visits and of finding peace in another's arms.

She wished it could go on forever—the sweetness, the peace, the longings that wanted to explode across the sky like fireworks. It couldn't. She knew that. But for the moment, she clung to him, treasuring the safety and magic his arms had offered. Then, suddenly, her surroundings came crashing back around her—a horn sounding and her sisters' raucous cheering. She pushed away from Alex. Time to get back to her real world.

Cassie was out of the car and opening the trunk, while Fiona climbed into the back seat. Once Alex had put her suitcase in the back, he came around to her window to smile at her. She gave him a quick little wave in return. Much more dignified than the silly nonsense her sisters were indulging in.

"Don't be a stranger," Cassie called to him.

"Come to South Bend anytime," Sam said.

"It's not that far."

"You know where she lives."

Finally, Cassie slid into the driver's seat and turned on the ignition. After the three of them gave Alex one last wave, she pulled away from the curb.

The traffic was heavy so they moved slowly down the street, but Fiona didn't look back, not even once. She was leaving Alex behind as well as Kate. It seemed that she was always losing the people she cared about.

"Hello, honey." Alex's mother was waiting at the foot of his stairs.

He paused for a moment before continuing on down to his door. His mother met him partway and he bent down so that she could kiss him on the cheek.

"I was expecting you an hour ago," Alex said.

She'd told him she would be at his place by nine so they could go to breakfast together. He figured that meant ten and they'd go out for coffee. It was now eleven-fifteen. He guessed they were doing lunch.

"I've been waiting fifteen minutes or more," his mother said. "Where were you?"

"I was upstairs with Mr. Fourier." He unlocked the door and stood aside to let his mother go in.

"Mr. Fourier? Who is this Mr. Fourier?" she asked, walking straight into the living room where she dropped down on the sofa. "A new client?"

"No." He heard the sharpness in his voice and paused a moment to settle himself. Just because he was having one of his moods again, he didn't need to take it out on everyone else. It was three days now since Fiona had left. Time to get some new assignments started. "He's my upstairs neighbor."

"Were you interrogating him?"

"I'm not a cop anymore, Mom."

She jumped back at his words, although he hadn't thought his tone was as impatient and irritable as he felt. He forced his voice to be extra calm.

"I was just seeing how he was, okay?"

"Sure," she replied, trying to find her reflection in the dusty glass in the coffee table in front of her so she could make minor adjustments to her hair. "It's okay."

"I was just being neighborly."

"Alex, dear, I said it was okay."

"Then why are you asking me so many questions?"

His mother let loose one of those big sighs of hers, the ones that filled a room to near bursting. "Okay, I'll never ask you another question in my life."

"Mother, you know you'll never do that. So why do you say it?"

"So why are you so grumpy?" she asked.

"Me, grumpy?" He shook his head. "I'm not the one who came late and then started complaining that I wasn't there to meet you."

His mother rolled her eyes to the ceiling and sighed again. Alex clenched his teeth tight.

"I have a new fella." A broad smile lit up her face and she suddenly looked like a different person. That was his mother—the eternal junior-high sweetheart hoping the boy across the aisle would notice her. And sinking into ecstasy if he did. "He's real nice, you'll like him."

Alex sat down in his chair by the window. "I've liked all your husbands, Mother."

She snorted. "You didn't like any of them."

"Hell, I never had a chance to get to know them. You didn't keep them around long enough for me to even remember their names."

"You don't have to be cruel, Alex." Her voice had that all-too-familiar quiver to it.

"I didn't mean to hurt your feelings," he said and turned to look out his window. It was overcast outside, looking like rain any minute. Good. The weather was just right for his mood.

"It's hard to find somebody that's really right for you."

"Sure, Mom."

"Not everyone is lucky like you, you know."

His mother's words brought him up short, like a dog hitting the end of his leash. "Lucky like me?" he asked, finding himself turning back to look at her.

His mother was smiling softly at him. "How is that young lady of yours?"

He had this feeling that he was interrupting something. It was as if he were walking into the middle of a conversation.

"Mother, what are you talking about?"

"Alex, don't act silly. You know exactly who and what I'm talking about." She was wearing one of her smug little grins. "The young lady you've been squiring around town these past couple of weeks."

"She was a client, Mom."

"You sounded so happy when you were with her."

His mother had called when he first was hired to take care of Fiona. She'd wanted him to drop by and he'd had to explain that he was working. Of course, part of that explanation included telling her what he was doing.

"I was getting paid," he replied. "It was just a job."

"It's nice when a person finds that special someone."

Alex clenched his jaw tight. "Like I said, she was just a client."

"She made you happy."

He winced as if in pain. Once his mother was on a track there was no derailing her.

"You even put on some weight," she said. "Has she cooked anything for you?"

"She was my client so I took care of her. That's how it works with clients."

His mother stared at him a long time and suddenly he could feel the back of his neck grow warm. He remembered those hours just before dawn, after Fiona had visited Kate. God, he hoped that his mother wouldn't start prying. Trying to find out just what he did to take care of a client. Especially a young, beautiful, female client.

"So," Alex said, forcing a load of heartiness into his voice. "How about some lunch?"

"And where is your client now?"

"Today's Monday." He could play that game, too. He could ignore a question as well as his mother. "You know what that means?"

"Is she still at the hospital?"

"Anne Sather's has their chicken-and-dumplings special for lunch. I know that's your favorite."

His mother just shook her head. "Why are you trying to deny something like that? It's a fact and it's there just like the nose on your face."

They'd been through this kind of conversation before. Only this time his mother was persisting a lot longer than she ever had. She was holding on to Fiona like a bulldog to a bone.

"Fiona's back in South Bend."

"Why?"

"It's her home," he replied. "It's where she came from."

"We all come from someplace, Alex. It doesn't mean we have to stay there."

"I'm going to wash my hands." He pushed himself up from his chair. "Then we can go to lunch."

"She sounds so perfect for you, Alex."

"I'll be right out," he said, hurrying toward the bathroom.

"Alex."

He stopped. He knew that he should hurry on and do his business, but it was his mother talking. Not a person he always agreed with, but a person who had always done the best she could for him. "Yeah, Mom."

"You remember how you used to play you were one of King Arthur's knights?"

He squeezed his fists up tight. "Five-year-old kids do a lot of weird things," he replied. "That doesn't mean they're going to be warped the rest of their lives."

"Find her dragon and slay it. That's how you'll win her heart."

"I'm not trying to win her heart, Mom. I'm lousy at relationships. You know that."

"What do you mean you're lousy at relationships? You've never had one."

"I've had a few."

She snorted rudely. "A couple of dates with someone isn't a relationship. When did you ever forget who you were because of someone else? When did you ever let yourself be miserable just so somebody else could be happy?"

"I know myself. I've saved all those somebody elses from misery by ducking out early."

"Saved yourself is what you mean," she snapped. "Sometimes I can't believe that you're my son, the way you run from love."

"I don't run from anything." But this was not a conversation he wanted to pursue. There was no winning it, he knew. His mother didn't recognize the truth when he told it to her. He cleared his throat. "We have to get going. I have a three o'clock appointment in Hammond."

"Hammond?"

His mother was a Chicagoan, born and bred, but she didn't recognize anything beyond the city limits. "It's in Indiana, Mom. Just over the Indiana-Illinois border."

"Indiana?" The smug little smile slipped back on her lips. "Isn't that where your lady friend lives?"

"Yeah, South Bend's in Indiana."

"Isn't that nice?" his mother said. "As long as you're there already, you can drop in and see her."

Yeah, right. After his meeting in Hammond, he'd drive another hour and a half, pull up to Fiona's apartment and say, Hi, I was just in the neighborhood.... That was the stupidest thing he'd ever heard.

Although it wasn't a bad drive. And it would be polite to find out if she feeling okay after the transplant. More important, seeing her again would no doubt get her out of his system.

Fiona put her car in the garage and then walked around the front of the house to check for the mail. Sometimes Mr. Kaminsky brought it in and sometimes he forgot. She sighed and shook her hair free of the barrette she'd had it clipped back with. But even the mild spring afternoon failed to perk up her weary heart.

It was harder to get back into the swing of things than she'd expected. School was fine; her kids had been well taken care of in her absence. Plus, she got a chance to teach them a bit about human biology when she talked to them about the transplant. And she wasn't all that sore anymore.

Life just seemed so empty. Besides the constant worry about the success of the transplant, there was no chance that when the phone rang it would be Kate; or when she was feeling blue, that Alex would be there to hold her.

As she came around the corner, she noticed a man sitting on the front stoop. Fiona frowned. "May I help—" She stopped as the man started to stand and she could see who it was. "Alex!"

Her heart suddenly darkened with fear. "Did something happen—?"

"No, Kate's doing fine," he said quickly. "I just dropped by to say hello."

The day came alive with joy and laughter and magic in the air. She wasn't sure how she moved, but the next thing she knew she was in his arms and he was holding her like he'd never let her go. She clung back, like she'd been afraid for years and was suddenly safe. It was a crazy notion, but she refused to let sanity into her world just now.

"What's going on out there?" Mr. Kaminsky called from up above.

Fiona fell back from Alex like she'd been stung and looked up at her neighbor leaning out his upstairs window. "Nothing, Mr. Kaminsky."

"Fiona? What's wrong?"

"Nothing," she yelled a little louder. Mr. Kaminsky could hear fairly well but sometimes he got confused. And she certainly didn't want him alerting the whole neighborhood "Everything is fine."

"What's going on?"

"I have a visitor. I was just excited to see him."

"Oh, were you?" Alex muttered, his voice teasing and sending little shock waves down her spine.

"A visitor?"

"Yes." She pushed Alex back up the steps and unlocked her door even as she continued calling out, "Everything's just fine. There's no problem."

Then she jumped into the building and hurried to open the door to her own apartment, hoping to get in before Mr. Kaminsky came out and started yelling down the stairs.

Once she shut the door behind her, she and Alex fell to laughing like little children who'd pulled a trick on their baby-sitter, but then the laughter faded and they were in each other's arms again. It had seemed like a lifetime since she'd seen him. More than a lifetime since she'd held him.

She let her lips whisper all the things to his soul that her heart could never say aloud. How she'd missed him. How in just a few short weeks her life had learned to revolve around him. How she couldn't keep her silly smile under control now that he was here. Finally she pulled away slightly, just enough to rest her head on his heaving chest.

"What are you doing here?" she asked.

"I was just in the neighborhood," he replied.

"You have a client in South Bend?"

"Close."

"I'm glad you came."

He looked into her eyes like he was trying to look into her soul, like he was trying to find answers to questions he didn't even know he was asking. "I am, too," he said slowly.

Then there was no more need for words. He bent his head and took her lips again. There was a hunger in them, a savagery that her own needs met in kind. She opened her mouth to his longing just as she wanted to open her heart and herself to him. She had never felt this way before—so much like she belonged to someone. It was confusing. It was scary. It was wonderful.

He pulled back, struggling visibly for breath as he leaned against the living-room wall. "So how's your class?" he asked. "They do okay without you?"

"Just fine." Her voice was no stronger than his. "I told them about the transplant. They were really interested."

He nodded. "How're you feeling?"

"Good." A smile crept over her lips even as her hand crept out to run lightly over his cheek. "I miss her terribly, but it's getting better."

He captured her hand and held it against his face for the longest of minutes before bringing it down to his mouth. He kissed her palm and lightning seemed to crash through the air around them. Heat raced up her arm and exploded into flames in her heart. She couldn't breathe. She couldn't think. She could only want, and that she did very well.

She wiggled her hand from his and slid her arms back around him—wanting him, needing him close so that her heart would know a rhythm to beat to. It had been hell without him. She hadn't known how to breathe or feel or laugh or play. She hadn't known how alone she'd been until he'd come.

He pulled away slightly. "I thought of you."

"Me, too." She touched his chin gently, then his cheek and then his lips, drawing her fingers over them with a soft touch. "Elvis isn't nearly as much fun to aggravate at breakfast."

"Glad I served a purpose." His voice was ragged.

"We all need to feel useful."

"Speaking of feeling..."

His lips came down on hers again and the fire took over. There was no time to think or analyze. Sensation after sensation washed over her. It was wonder and splendor and magical rides on a roller coaster. Her heart was flying and knew no boundaries.

Her hands slid over his chest and slipped the buttons free so that they could touch his chest, run through the hair and feel the cool smoothness of his skin. He was hers in so many ways.

His touch said he felt the same, as his hands roamed over her back, then found their way under her blouse. She came alive at his caress, found life in a way that she'd never known before. She closed her eyes, giving herself up to the wonders of his embrace.

"Do we have a thing for foyers?" he whispered in her ear.

She opened her eyes and looked around. They were still standing just inside the door. "Maybe we just can't wait," she said, smiling up into his hungry eyes.

She took his hand and led him down the hall. In the quiet stillness of her room, she helped him undress, then undress her. The sunlight streamed in, lighting her bed with warmth and rapture. She lay there, her eyes feasting on his lean body, and letting his gaze devour her. Then his hands took the place of his eyes, touching and feeling and bringing every inch of her to hot expectation. There was nothing but fire and passion in the room, nothing but delight in the touch of their hands.

When she could no longer wait, she took him inside her, welcoming him into her warmth and heat as her lips sang a song of awe into his heart. They danced and flew and moved to the rhythm of their souls until all marvels exploded and they were bound together by the power of their needs.

Then they lay softly, barely moving, as peace came to claim them. His lips touched her forehead, not in passion but almost in reverence. She just closed her eyes and prayed for the moment never to end.

"You're sure this isn't a problem," Alex said.

Fiona smiled across her kitchen table at him. For all the world he looked like a little boy hoping Santa wasn't joking when he'd promised him a new bike. "No, it's no problem. I'd love to have you stay here."

"All this wasn't what I had in mind when I dropped by," he said, waving his hand toward the bedroom. "I just wanted to see how you were feeling."

An impishness took hold of her. "And how did I feel?"

He reached across the salad and the plate of bread to take her hand. "Oh, lady, better be careful." His voice was low, pulled tight with tension.

Some rare burst of courage had invaded her soul, though, and she just looked back at him, not afraid of taking a chance. "It's good to see you again. I missed you."

He let go of her hand and looked away as if about to say something painful. Her heart skipped a beat.

"I missed you, too," he said.

"Was that so hard to say?"

He turned back to her, his eyes troubled. "This isn't like me," he said. "I don't do relationships."

"What's there to do?"

"It's just the whole idea of it. Of somebody leaning on me. What if I'm no good at it?"

She brought his hand back to her and held it tightly. "I'm not looking for anything," she said. "I'm not expecting anything but a houseguest for a few days. Somebody that I can talk to and be totally honest with. Can't we just relax and see where we go?"

"You're too easy to get along with," he grumbled. "Why can't you be demanding?"

"Because I wouldn't know what to demand. One minute, this thing scares the hell out of me. The next, I can't believe how happy I am."

"So what do we do now?"

She gave his hand a last squeeze, then let go. "Eat dinner."

Chapter Ten

"I don't know how you can be so cheerful in the morning," Alex said as he poured a cup of coffee and stumbled toward the table. "It doesn't feel natural."

Fiona frowned at him as she poured herself more coffee. "You don't look all that grumpy this morning, sir."

He didn't feel grumpy at all, if the truth be known. He felt like singing and laughing and generally acting like an idiot. But his natural caution kept it hidden. "Don't you know that if you're not careful, your system'll jam in the mood you wake up in?"

"I'm cheerful when I wake up."

"I know. That's my point. If you aren't careful, you could stay that way all day."

She just laughed and brushed a light kiss on his forehead. "You should be used to my mornings. This isn't your first exposure, you know."

"I thought maybe those others were an aberration." He

sipped at his coffee, then discovered Fiona was looking worried. "Hey, it was a joke. I was just trying to be funny."

She looked only slightly relieved and he sighed. "See, I told you I wasn't good at relationships."

"No, you're lousy at jokes," she said. "Want a bagel?"

"Sure." He saw that she was taking it out of the freezer and he got up. He didn't want her waiting on him. "I can fix it. Don't you have to get ready for work?"

"That's okay," she said. "I just have to throw a few clothes on. My school isn't all that far from here."

He took the bagel from her hand and sliced it himself. "Yeah, but you might miss. Then one thing would lead to another and before you know it, you'll be late."

He looked up and found she was staring at him, not even blinking.

"You said you just had to throw a few clothes on. And I said that you might miss."

Fiona still didn't say anything.

Alex shook his head. "These kinds of things don't work if you have to explain them."

"Do you talk to your clients this way?" she asked. "How do you get any business?"

"I'll have you know I'm in great demand." He popped the bagel into the toaster.

She slid her arms around him from behind. "I'd better be more respectful, then."

"You betcha." He clasped his hands over hers, liking the feel of her near him. He could get used to this, used to the sense of belonging.

"Elvis," Fiona said, pulling away. "Get down."

Alex turned. The calico cat had jumped up on the table to sniff at his coffee. Fiona's firm words bought her a glare while her second cat, Prissy, joined the first on the table.

"Looks like there's going to be a power struggle here," Alex said.

"Not for long." Fiona pushed away from him and put both cats on the floor. "Now, shoo. Scram. Beat it."

Grumbling, the feline duo stomped off toward the living room.

"Is that how you're going to send me on my way in a few days?"

Fiona just laughed. "Only if you jump on the table one too many times."

"I'll try to behave." He didn't want to have her mad at him, didn't want her to send him on his way. From being scared to try a relationship, he was finding it easier and easier to take.

The phone rang and Fiona hurried over to answer it. It was Mrs. Andrews. "That's wonderful," Fiona said to her, giving Alex a thumbs-up sign even as she spoke into the phone. "That's great."

He slowly let his breath out. It appeared that Kate was progressing nicely. Super.

A few more words were exchanged before Fiona bid Mrs. Andrews goodbye, then she flew into Alex's arms.

"I take it Kate's doing well," Alex said.

Fiona looked up at him, her eyes glistening. "It's too early to know for sure, but there haven't been any signs of rejection yet."

"That's such good news."

"The best."

He felt a weight slide from his back, as if he, too, had been holding his breath for good news of Kate. His hold on Fiona tightened and his lips touched hers. He meant it to be just a soft touch, a quick little kiss to share her joy, but the pressure she returned was anything but. That fire in his groin wanted to take hold again; that blinding need to bury himself in her softness fought for control of his sanity.

Fiona just pulled away with a laugh. "Enough of that," she said, and dashed off toward her bedroom.

Alex took a deep breath and went to the toaster. Would a cold bagel be the same as a cold shower? He somehow didn't think so, but he spread it with the low-fat cottage cheese Fiona used—a strange combination but surprisingly tasty—

and ate it. Then he cleaned up their breakfast dishes. This trip wasn't exactly going as planned. Unless he was trying to cure his dreams of Fiona with an overdose.

"I'll be home soon around four."

Fiona had come out of the bedroom, dressed in peach-colored slacks and a flowery print blouse with splotches of peach in it. Alex hurried out of the kitchen to take her into his arms. She fit so perfectly there. She could stay there the rest of his life.

"Are you going to be back by then?" she asked.

"I should be," he said. Considering he basically had nothing to do with his day, it shouldn't be a problem.

But then the thought of being here waiting for her so ignited his heart, filled him with such a sense of belonging, that he wanted to give her something in return.

"Got any dragons you need slaying?" he asked. "In case I have some free time."

"I don't have any dragons."

"Worried about Kate?"

"Not too much. Not that you could slay my worries even if I was."

She was so damn self-sufficient. Did she need him for anything? "How about your parents?"

She stiffened, her muscles drawing out tight and taut. But this wasn't what he wanted. He hadn't wanted to awaken hurts. He'd wanted to pay her back for making him feel alive.

"I have to get going," she said, pushing herself out of his arms and hurrying over to the kitchen counter where her purse and briefcase were.

Something that still caused pain had to be a dragon. "You told me you were born in South Bend," he said. "Did you live here all the time or did you move around a lot?"

"When Mom and Dad were alive, we lived out on the west side," she said. "The only times we lived somewhere else was when we were in foster care. Then we lived for a time in Mishawaka and in Wakarusa. That was all before the Scotts took us in.''

Her body language said she didn't want to talk about it, but how could he slay something if he couldn't find it?

"If I remember right, your parents were going to Milwaukee to look for work?''

She nodded, locking up her briefcase.

"Did your father tend to bounce around different jobs?''

"No.'' She put her purse strap over her shoulder and picked up her briefcase with her left hand. "That was one of the things that was so strange. He had worked at Bendix for years and years. It seemed like a good job that paid well with loads of benefits. And he must have had seniority.''

Alex's wheels started spinning as he processed this new bit of data. He'd gotten the idea that Fiona's father had been a blue-collar worker. In the mid-seventies such work was getting scarcer. He would have had to have a strong reason to leave a good job when a replacement would be hard to find.

Unless he had been let go. There were a lot of questions to be answered. And Alex didn't think Fiona was going to answer any more.

"I left my spare key on the counter here in case you get back before me,'' she said. "I thought we'd eat dinner out.''

"We don't have to do that,'' he said. "I'm a good cook.''

"I don't do things because I have to. I do them because I want to.'' She carried her bags to the door. "And I want to celebrate Kate's progress.''

He didn't let her get away that easily. Before she could open the door, he was there to kiss her goodbye. And then to kiss her good-morning. And have a good day. And have a nice lunch and a great afternoon. And finally, that he'd miss her.

Then she left and he was alone. Four o'clock was almost nine hours away. Or fifty-seven centuries, depending on how you looked at it.

He walked over to the window and watched as her car pulled out of the garage. He continued staring long after she disappeared around the corner. Fiona's father's name was Joe—Joseph Fogarty—and he'd worked for years at the Bendix plant here in South Bend. Probably in a union if he was a blue-collar worker. A place to start.

After a morning of searching through old newspapers, Alex found an article placing the accident in Witoka, Minnesota, and telling a few facts about each of her parents. Fiona's mother had been born in South Bend, had graduated from Washington High School and had volunteered at the local hospital. Fiona's father worked at Bendix and was a member of the machinists' union. There was no mention of his relation to Horace Fogarty.

The afternoon was less productive. A fax of the accident report would be sent, but not today. Bendix—which was now a division of Allied Signal—wanted a written request for information that it would pass along to the union steward. The house where Fiona had lived with her parents no longer existed—that end of the block had been wrecked to enlarge a nearby church parking lot.

Alex knew that everything took time, but still he was discouraged when he drove back to Fiona's apartment. He'd wanted to lay the slain carcass of her dragon at her feet. He'd wanted to mount its head on her wall and prove to her that he could take care of her. And what did he have? Nothing.

"Hi," Fiona called as he came into the apartment. "Have a good day?"

She was right there, walking into his open arms and feeling so good and right and necessary in his embrace, that everything else fled.

"Sure," he said as his lips came down to meet hers. "It was a great day."

And getting better.

"So, Fiona, when are we going to meet this fella of yours?" Amy O'Brien asked.

Fiona dropped the pencil she'd been holding. It fell, clattering onto the desk and bouncing down to the floor with more noise than a ton of bricks. The fifth-grade teacher stood in the doorway, grinning at her.

"What?" The word came out as a squawk, like a chicken that had been grabbed from behind. Fiona cleared her throat once, then again. "What are you talking about?"

Her fellow teacher just shook her head and laughed. "When a woman's floating up in the clouds the way you have for the past couple of days, it only means one thing."

The blood rushed up across Fiona's cheeks, spreading through her body like a fever and making her feel hot enough to broil steaks on her skin. She bent down to pick up her pencil, taking it slow and hoping that she would cool down before she had to answer. She had lots of things on her mind—missing Kate, worrying that the transplant would continue to work, wondering how and when to tell her family the truth. If she'd been distracted lately, Alex didn't have to be the reason.

"Fiona," Amy said, a rising sharpness entering her voice. "Have you fainted down there?"

"I was just getting my pencil." Fiona straightened, holding her pencil up for her fellow teacher to see. "I didn't want to lose it."

"Oh, yeah," Amy said with a snort. "Those number-two lead pencils are hard to come by."

"So when do you want to get together to plan the class picnic?" Fiona tried changing the subject.

But the woman's grin just wouldn't go away. "So we're not going to meet him."

Fiona's frown dissipated into wrinkles of annoyance as she began gathering up her papers. She would have liked to say, Meet whom? But Amy had been a teacher for too long. If the kids couldn't fool her, Fiona would have no chance.

"Come on," Amy pleaded. "We just want to eyeball him. We're not going to bruise the merchandise in any way."

"I'll make up the notices to send home with the kids. Last year a couple of them got the date mixed up and wore picnic clothes on the wrong day."

"He's not married, is he?"

"No." Fiona's mouth quickly closed, but it was too late. The denial had been made. And in denying she'd confirmed Amy's question that there was indeed a man in her life. "No, he's not married," she added.

"So why the secrecy?" Amy asked.

"There's no secrecy," Fiona denied. "We just haven't been seeing each other all that long. And he's not even from around here. So it could be over tomorrow, for all I know." Although the mere thought of that made her heart pause.

She had to be honest, though. Alex had already been here three days. That was how long he'd said he was staying. It literally could be over tomorrow.

"I guess we'll just have to come peek in your windows," Amy said.

That damn pencil hit the floor again. Fiona stared in bewilderment at her friend and co-worker.

"Luther Benjamin lives just a block up from you," Amy noted. "He's got to be tall enough to look in your windows without a ladder." Amy flashed a triumphant smile before going on her way.

"Boy." Fiona bent down and retrieved her pencil again, throwing it into her drawer. The joys of living in a small town where everyone knew your business. "Anybody who comes peeking in my window is going to get their head knocked off."

She stuffed a stack of math exams into her briefcase, then let her feet dance her out to the parking lot. Although Kate was constantly in her thoughts, Fiona knew Alex was the reason she found herself smiling so often, that she couldn't wait each day to get home. It wasn't like she loved Kate any less; it was just that it was time to let go again.

She told herself she had to be careful, though. Not to hold on to Alex all the more tightly because of loosening her hold on Kate. She told herself not to count on anything; she and Alex were just seeing where things would take them. Nobody was making any promises. But it was impossible not to fly from the car to the apartment.

"Hello," she called as she opened her door. "I'm home."

Elvis gave his usual "So what?" yowl while Prissy bounded over to greet her. Otherwise the apartment felt empty. Her words echoed through the rooms as if it was an abandoned mine shaft. Fiona could feel her stomach tighten up as she put her bags down on the kitchen counter.

There was a note on the bulletin board by the phone. Alex would return by five at the latest.

"Shoot, guys." She bent down and picked up the demanding little female. "Now what are we going to do?"

Prissy's purr said "Scratch me," which Fiona did. She walked to the window, carrying the cat and scratching as she went.

It would be at least another hour before Alex was home. What should she do in the meantime? Correct those papers she'd brought with her? Naw, it was too nice a day to stay inside. Maybe it was time to pay a visit.

"I'm going out for a while, Prissy." Fiona put the cat on the floor. "Take care of your sister, Elvis."

Both cats grumbled their protests at being left again, but Fiona skipped into her bedroom for a pair of sneakers, grabbed some bread crusts from the freezer, and then bounded out the door.

Within minutes she was at Clements Woods. She followed the familiar roads to the parking lot near the lake, then hurried down the path. It had been a few weeks since she'd been here. The last time had been when Alex had come to find her about Kate. How her life had changed since then!

Soon after she got to the lake, the birds glided gracefully toward her. She threw pieces of bread out into the water. "Remember when I came here a few weeks ago? Well, I went to Chicago to help my daughter. She was really sick, but it looks like she'll be okay now."

Fiona took a deep breath, then tossed a few more pieces of bread onto the water. "You know that guy that was here with me last time? Well, he's back again. Came all the way from Chicago to see me." She frowned. "Well, actually, I guess he's got some client out here, so it's not just to see me."

Juliet gave her a look that she probably gave all her little daughter swans when they were mooning about some new boy swan that had come around.

"It's not like that," Fiona protested. "He cares about me. I can tell. And I care about him."

She stopped as many images came rushing around her. Her joy at seeing him. Her emptiness when he was gone. The sense of being whole when he was close.

"I love him," she said simply. Although she hadn't realized it before, the words sounded right. They were true. "I love him," she repeated and smiled. "I really do."

She tossed the last of the bread onto the water with a laugh. "I never thought I had a Prince Charming out there somewhere. I thought it was just a silly story. But I was wrong."

Once the bread was gone, Fiona sat down on a stump and watched the birds swim about. "I don't want him to leave," she told them. "Ever."

Alex stopped at the red light; the cross street was Olive. A gas station on one corner and a Polish National Alliance lodge hall—PNA No. 1183—on another. That meant the bar should be coming up soon.

The light turned green and he crossed the intersection, moving along the tired, old commercial strip that had probably been at its peak about fifty years ago. Back when huge factories provided full employment and the neighborhood was filled with corner grocery stores, bars, and bakeries. Now the buildings that weren't boarded up were thrift shops and package liquor stores. But the bars still remained. The last bastion of the independent small businessman.

The marquee advertising Rosie's Kazbar came up on his left and Alex slowed down. The sign in the window said the joint's specialties were *pirogi* and tacos—Slavic ravioli and a Mexican staple.

After parking the car, Alex turned and walked in through the back door. The first thing that hit him was a dense, stagnant cloud of tobacco smoke that almost brought tears to his eyes. If the smog outside was this awful, the government would have recommended the elderly and respiratory patients stay inside.

Alex stepped into the main room and saw four men at the bar and a female bartender. She was the only one smoking. Apparently, the smoke in the air had built up over the years, embedding itself in the walls and fixtures.

Alex walked up to the old-fashioned bar, which was dark and deeply polished, and put his foot up on the shoe railing. "I'm looking for a couple of guys," he said. "Crawford and Gus."

"I only sell booze," the barkeep replied.

"You Alex?" a stocky gray-haired man sitting around the corner of the bar asked. "I'm Gus." He tilted his head toward a slender black man sitting next to him. "And this is Crawford."

"You want a beer?" the barkeep asked Alex.

"Sure, a draft would be fine." He looked at the two men's near-empty glasses. "You guys use a refill?"

Both men agreed they could and, once they'd been served, Alex suggested they sit at a table. He led them, with Gus limping very noticeably, to a table farthest from the bar and the smoking barkeep, hoping for cleaner air. He sniffed the air as he sat down. His wish was not to be fulfilled.

The man called Crawford smirked at him. "The EPA's declared this a toxic area," he said. "There's no place you can breathe fresh air in this joint. Not even down on the floor."

Alex sipped his beer and waited as the two men sampled theirs. "So," he said. "You remember anything about Joe Fogarty?"

"Why you nosing around in old Joe's life?" Gus asked. "Man's been dead over twenty years now."

"Family's got some questions," Alex said. "His kids were real young and nobody told them much of anything."

Both men nodded.

"I suppose you know I was the crew chief back then," Gus said.

"Yep," Alex replied. He'd spent yesterday and most of today tracking down somebody who would have worked with Joe. It had been pure luck that he'd stumbled across Gus Svoboda's name. And even better luck that the man had been home when Alex had called about an hour ago. Gus had told him about Crawford Marling and, after some chitchat, agreed they would meet Alex at Rosie's.

"I understand that Joe was taking a medical leave," Alex said, revealing about the only piece of information he'd uncovered in his digging. "Do you know why?"

Gus shook his head. "Didn't even know he was sick. Joe was big as an ox and strong, too. Sure didn't look sick."

"I don't know," Crawford said. "He talked to me a lot his last few days. Main thing I remember him saying was that he had to get his heart healed."

"Had to get his heart healed?" Alex repeated. "He had heart trouble?"

"Might've," Gus said.

Suddenly it all fit. Minnesota and all. Fiona's dad had had a heart problem. He didn't want to tell his kids about it, but was going to the Mayo Clinic up in southeastern Minnesota.

Hot damn. Three days of work, and one slain dragon.

"How about another beer, guys?" Alex asked.

"Hell, yes," Gus replied. Crawford just nodded.

Alex went over to get the two refills, but excused himself from joining them. He could hardly wait to get home.

Home. He smiled at the thought. Funny how brave a man got after slaying a dragon.

Chapter Eleven

"I'm sorry, Prissy." Fiona glanced away from her cats to the clock on the microwave. Her visit to the swans had taken about forty-five minutes, then she'd fed the cats. It was now past five-thirty and Alex had said he would be home by five. Prissy rubbed against Fiona's arm, calling her attention back. "But you don't have to be so fussy. Look how nicely Elvis ate."

The little gray female looked disdainfully at her chunky male partner, who was now cleaning up her dish.

Fiona looked at the clock again. Darn. Where was that man?

He couldn't have gotten lost. South Bend and the surrounding area weren't all that difficult to find your way around. There were a few rough places, but nothing that should cause Alex any problems.

"He's probably working late, guys," Fiona told her cats. "I bet something came up and he had to follow through on it. P.I.s don't have regular hours, you know. Not like teachers or accountants. There's nothing to worry about.''

Although he could have called. But that was something she was going to have to get accustomed to, she thought, as she dried the cats' dishes. P.I.s didn't spend much time in their offices, either. And Alex didn't have a car phone.

There were a lot of things she was going to have to get accustomed to if she wanted to keep this relationship going. And she did. But what were Alex's feelings? He'd said he was going to stay a few days and they'd pretty much reached that point. She had no idea how to ask him where they were headed. Maybe she was just afraid of the answer.

Suddenly Elvis jumped off the counter and ran to the front door. Fiona's heart made a sudden jump for joy. Alex must be home. Elvis always ran to the door to welcome him.

On the other hand, it could be one of her neighbors or sisters. Elvis liked company.

The door swung open just as Fiona got there, framing a grinning Alex. Something must have gone well with his work.

She was in his arms before either said a word. She'd missed him and had let silly worries creep into her garden. They were foolish; the realization of her love for Alex didn't change anything. Just because she no longer had Kate, it didn't mean that she would lose Alex, too. She kissed him hungrily, then kissed him again. Not caring or needing to breathe, for his touch was nourishment enough.

She wasn't used to the power of her love—the needs it awoke in her or the fears it left her prey to. She was going to have to be stronger. Or else be in Alex's arms more often. It was only there that she truly felt alive, truly felt able to love. All her rule-abiding common sense seemed to have fled over the last few days.

''I was getting a little worried,'' she said, as they paused for breath. ''You're late.''

''I'm sorry.''

He pulled her to him and kissed her again as if he could not get enough of her touch. His lips seemed to embrace her with sunshine, seemed to melt her silly reservations and fill all the dark corners of her heart with flowers. It was riotous spring all around her, with warmth and laughter and the promise of something wonderful and magic just ahead.

His arms tightened around her for a long moment, then he let her go. "I have a surprise for you."

"Should I close my eyes?"

His hands took hold of her shoulders, sliding down her arms as if he couldn't bear not to have some contact. "I found your dragon, Fiona. And I slayed it."

"You what?"

"The damn thing is stone-cold dead."

His voice was overflowing with excitement, but she just shook her head. She didn't have a clue what he was talking about.

"What's your biggest dragon?" He looked at her intently for a moment. "Besides Kate's health."

As hard as she tried, she couldn't get her brain to work. She felt like she was walking through a pond filled with molasses. Maybe it was because he was so close, because she could still feel the taste of his lips on hers.

What was he talking about? What dragons? She'd talked about some problems at work but those were normal things. Certainly not major. Kate was a major concern. And the other—

She looked into his eyes, a tight little bud of fear poking its head up. "My parents?"

"Bingo." His smile stretched to the far corners of his face.

Her hands went cold and clammy as the fear opened up, trying to claim her as it usually did. "What did you find out?" She was almost afraid to ask, but surely Alex's smile said it was safe to know. He wouldn't be bringing her more pain.

"Your father wasn't going to Milwaukee," Alex said. "He was probably going to the Mayo Clinic."

The bud started to shrivel in the brightness of Alex's certainty. "He was what?" she asked.

"Apparently your father had a heart problem. He was on medical leave when he died."

"I didn't know that," she gasped.

"Most parents probably wouldn't have told little kids about that. Not unless they had to know for some reason."

"He didn't seem sick."

"The auto accident occurred in southern Minnesota, not that far from Rochester. And that's the home of the Mayo Clinic—one of the premier medical centers in the country."

"I had no idea he wasn't well. He always seemed so strong. So able to take care of us."

She was stunned, numb almost. She had lived with her fears for so long—they'd been such a part of her—that she felt her whole world was capsizing. Alex must have sensed it for he took her gently in his arms, letting her lie against his chest as she fought to reach shore.

"All these years I thought maybe there was something wrong with me," she said, only realizing she was crying from the quiver in her voice. "I was afraid I had done something wrong, or didn't do something I was supposed to. Or just wasn't lovable."

"That's crazy," he said, his voice a caress in itself.

She felt his lips brush her hair and she just closed her eyes. "I used to tell myself I was wrong," she whispered. "But I never really believed I was."

"So you should be jumping around, not crying," he said. "This was supposed to make you happy."

"It does," she assured him and tried to make her eyes stop watering. "I'm really happy."

He just laughed softly and pulled her closer to him. "That's what I thought."

"It's just that I had this sword hanging over my head," she said. "And now I find out it's made of chocolate, not steel. My whole life was spent being afraid, my whole self was built around fear. But I never had anything to be afraid of. What did I miss out on because of being afraid? Who could I have been if I hadn't worried so?''

''You can't go back and undo anything,'' Alex said. ''You have to look at it as freeing you up in the future.''

''I know, and it will.'' She pulled back slightly to show him that her tears had stopped. She smiled up at him, loving him even more for what he'd given her. ''And I know who I am—Horace Waldo's great-great-granddaughter and Kate's bone-marrow donor.''

He bent down to kiss the tip of her nose. ''And one very nice lady besides.''

''I think your sisters are here,'' Alex called out. ''That looks like Cassie's truck.''

He'd barely left the window when Elvis was at the door yowling his welcome. Fiona wiped her hands on a dish towel and came into the living room.

''Nervous?'' he asked, taking her into his arms.

''Yeah,'' she admitted. ''Kind of.''

''Nothing to worry about,'' he said. ''You're just setting the record straight. I'm sure your sisters will take it as you did. They'll feel a lot better knowing what really happened.''

''I hope so,'' Fiona murmured. She didn't need him to remind her that there were other things she had yet to tell them. Maybe telling them about their parents would open the door for her to tell them about Kate.

''Hey, the truth shall set them free,'' Alex was saying. ''As descendants of Horace Waldo Fogarty, they wouldn't want anything less.''

''Good old Horace,'' Fiona replied. ''Our whole-truth-and-nothing-but-the-truth ancestor. May he be with us always.''

''There you go,'' he said, hugging her hard.

Fiona snuggled into the safety of Alex's arms. He was such a wonderful man. She couldn't even begin to count the ways that he had brought sunshine into her life. He was caring, considerate and had such a fantastic sense of humor. And he knew what was important to her. She wasn't an expert on love, but she sure thought she'd found a treasure.

"I don't know if I ever thanked you for finding out the truth for us," she said. "I was so stunned and then all I could think about was telling Cassie and Sam."

"You didn't need to say anything," he told her. "I knew."

He brushed her forehead with his lips. It was a gentle kiss, like a butterfly landing for a brief moment before skipping off again. Then he just held her. Firmly enough to let her feel safe, yet gently enough to let her know she was loved.

She turned her head to look at him, to will his mouth down to hers. And, as if their hearts could speak to the other without words, he leaned down and pressed his lips to hers. Each kiss seemed to contain new pleasures, new wonders to behold. Yet each kiss also woke that slumbering fire in the core of her soul; that sweet tension that pulled her heart tighter and tighter until only his touch could release her. She wanted this moment to go on forever.

The banging on her door told them that the kiss had come close.

"Alex," Fiona said, pushing against him.

"Tell them to go away," he said. "Tell them they misunderstood. That they were supposed to come over tomorrow."

"You're awful," she scolded, squirming out of his grasp and lunging for the door.

"Hi, guys," she said, flinging her door open wide. "Come on in."

But instead of coming in, her sisters stood out in the hallway staring at her. "Are we interrupting something?" Sam asked.

"They were probably exercising," Cassie said. "Look how rosy Fiona's cheeks are."

Fiona could feel her face grow even warmer. "You two want me to sic Elvis on you?" she asked.

"Oh, now there's a threat."

"What's he going to do—purr us to death?" Her sisters came into the apartment.

"What's up, Fiona?" Cassie asked.

"Yeah, that was quite a summons," Sam said.

Fiona waved them over to the sofa and waited until they were seated. Then she sat in one of the easy chairs with Alex perched on the arm. "I don't exactly know where to begin," she said. "It's about our parents."

"Mommy and Daddy Scott?" Cassie asked.

"No," Fiona replied, shaking her head. This was all so complicated. "Our biological parents."

"I hardly remember them," Sam admitted.

"We never really talked about stuff when they died," Fiona said. "But Mom told me they were going to Milwaukee to look for a job for Daddy." She paused to take a deep breath. "But, as we all know, they never made it. They were killed in an automobile accident."

Fiona paused to take another deep breath, then let it out slowly. Alex took her hand and she realized how lucky she was to have him to lean on.

"I don't know about anyone else," she said, looking at her sisters, "but that accident always bothered me. If they were going to Milwaukee, how did they wind up in Minnesota?"

"I wondered that," Cassie said slowly. "I just thought I had it wrong. Where they were going, I mean."

"I remember the funeral," Sam said, leaning forward slightly as if it would help her see into the past more clearly. "There was some really bossy woman there who acted like she knew everything."

"Mrs. Cochran," Cassie said.

"She kept talking about what pests we all were." Sam shrugged. "I don't know. She made me feel like it was somehow all my fault."

"I didn't think you guys had heard all that," Fiona said.

"How could we not?" Cassie demanded. "The woman was broadcasting her views at the top of her lungs."

Fiona nodded. "Well, the stuff she said bothered me for a long time. And Alex decided to do something about it and—" She paused to look at him. He squeezed her hand and she swallowed the lump in her throat. "And he found some answers for us."

Nobody's expression changed. The room had grown totally quiet as if everyone was holding their breath.

Fiona faced her sisters squarely. "It appears that Daddy had a heart problem. He and Mom weren't going to Milwaukee at all, but were probably on their way to the Mayo Clinic."

There was absolute silence until Cassie spoke. "Jeez." She must have been holding her breath, for she let it out all in a rush. "How did you ever find that out?"

Alex shrugged. "Asked the right questions."

"But who'd you ask them of?" Sam wanted to know.

Alex looked at Fiona as if for permission to tell it all. When she nodded he turned to the others. "I found a couple of guys that your dad worked with. One remembered your dad talking about going to get his heart healed just before they left."

"Wow," Fiona muttered. "Imagine him remembering that."

"It was the way your dad phrased it," Alex explained. "'Getting his heart healed.' It stuck in this guy's mind, especially then with the accident and all."

"It sure answers a lot of questions," Cassie said.

Alex glanced at Fiona, his eyes dark with a hint of worry. "Now, I haven't talked to any doctors yet," he told them. "Or to the Mayo Clinic. I can pursue this further if you want. You know, get proof of my suppositions."

Fiona just looked at her sisters; the two of them stared blankly back at her. They were letting her take the lead.

Finally Fiona just shook head. "I don't think we need written proof. This makes so much more sense than Mrs. Cochran's ramblings. I don't know why none of us ever considered the possibility."

"Because you trusted the source of your information," Alex said. "Hey, I'm the investigator and the truth took me by surprise at first, too."

Sam leaned against the sofa back, her eyes distant. "I wish I remembered them more. If it wasn't for the pictures we have, I don't think I'd remember what they looked like."

"I'd like to know all sorts of little things," Fiona said. "You know, stories about when they were growing up. Or how they met. But if I had to choose one thing to know, it was this."

She smiled over at Alex, clutching his hand tightly. "We all owe you," she said. "Big time."

"Hey, glad to be able to help."

Help? That made it seem so minor, so simple. He really *had* slain a dragon that had been attacking her for twenty years. There was no way she could pay him back.

"Well," Alex said, although his two feline companions were pretty much ignoring him. "The breakfast dishes were all washed and put away. The bed is made. Now what?"

Prissy yawned.

"Naw, I don't really want a nap."

Elvis scratched his ear. Then he began washing the top of Prissy's head. It was obvious that they didn't care what Alex did or did not want. They had their own lives.

"Well, the heck with you little bums," he muttered.

Fiona had been so pleased with his discovery about her father. But it hadn't seemed quite enough. There was more that he could give her. There had to be. Hell, he was a good P.I. If she wanted to know more about her parents, he was going to find out more. She wanted to know about them as kids. All he had to do was dig up some relatives. How hard would that be?

He went back to the newspaper clippings he had, frowning when he realized that the three girls were the only living relatives listed. No brothers or sisters. No aunts and uncles.

He got out the phone book. There were three Fogartys listed and by some miracle all were home. But the miracles ended there. None was a relation. None even knew of Fiona's branch of the family. He went back to the death notices and got Fiona's mother's maiden name—Mentzer. There was one in the phone book and it was no relation.

"Katherine Mentzer?" the woman repeated. "I kinda remember another bunch of Mentzers when I was growing up, but they weren't related. Don't think they had any other family in town. At least not Mentzers."

He even tried Cochran, Cochrane, and Cocharan. The mother's friend could help find other relatives or even with some info herself, but nothing. So much for his great skills at detective work. He needed some place to start. His gaze drifted and he stared into space as if an idea might be found there, when suddenly he stopped at the pictures on the wall. Horace Waldo Fogarty looked back at him. He was a relation, but since he was long dead, he wasn't someone Alex could talk to. Still, he could provide a trail.

Alex scanned Fiona's bookshelves to no avail, then called the reference desk at the library.

"Horace Waldo Fogarty?" the librarian repeated. "Why, he was born just down the road in Mentone."

"Where's that?" Alex asked.

"Oh, thirty miles from South Bend, I'd say. Take you about forty-five minutes to get there."

Hot dog. He pulled out Fiona's road atlas and found Mentone. Just as the librarian had said, it was about thirty miles away. He grabbed a scrap of paper and jotted down the route—Route 31 south to Route 30 east. Through Etna Green and bingo! He'd be there.

"You guys are in charge," he told the cats as he shrugged into his jacket. Both cats were already asleep on the windowsill and didn't even flick an ear or a tip of the tail at him. "What a life," he muttered as he made his way to the door and outside to his car.

After several minutes he was on U.S. 31 going south, where he kicked back and put his driving on automatic pilot. He and Fiona had been having a wonderful time these past few days. And although he really needed to check in at his apartment, he had no desire to leave. What did that mean? Was he luckier than his mother in love? Or was he just as foolish as she was, believing each little pang of the heart was a signal that this was the real thing?

A sign warned that the turnoff for Etna Green was coming up, so Alex slowed and turned onto the county road. At thirty miles per hour, he sailed through Etna Green in the blink of an eye. Within moments, he was outside of town again. Out where the land—green and flat as a pool table—stretched out for miles on either side of him. There was a sense of peace in the air, as if it grew there and was free for the taking. He let himself breathe deeply and actually felt his whole body relax. This was right. Mentone came up a few miles later.

It was a quiet little burg with an undertaker at one end of Main Street and a bank at the other. The undertaker had a giant chicken guarding his parking lot, while the bank was next to a big stone that looked like an egg. The town's economy must depend on eggs and chickens.

There were no signs directing visitors to Horace Fogarty's birthplace or grade school or fishing hole, but Alex wasn't surprised. He just headed toward the public library. That would be the best place to find out about the local writer. For all he knew, Fogarty's house might still be standing. He got out of his car and went into the building.

There were no obvious displays about Fogarty's life so he wandered over to the reference desk. An older woman was behind the desk, talking to a younger redhead who was carrying a baby in a pouch that hung in front of her. The older woman wore a name tag proclaiming she was Mrs. Mac-Allister.

"Well, I'll let you go, Mom," the young woman was saying. "Sean will come straight home from school. Make sure he finishes his homework before he goes to baseball practice."

"Fine, Merry. I'll take care of things." The older woman bent down and kissed the sleeping baby on the head. "Bye, Holly, honey. Have a nice visit with your doctor."

The young woman gave him a nod before hurrying away. The older woman turned to face him. "May I help you, Mr.—?"

"Rhinehart," he said. "Alex Rhinehart. And I'm looking for information on Horace Waldo Fogarty. I understand he was born and raised here."

"My goodness," Mrs. MacAllister said. "We don't get many people looking into Mr. Fogarty's early life. Not many people connect us with him, even though he was born here." She came around the counter and led Alex toward a file cabinet in the corner where she pulled out a number of notebooks. "I'm actually working on a display about him. Next fall it'll be the 125th anniversary of his birth."

"Oh?" Alex flipped through some of the copies of newspaper clippings she'd pulled out. They were clippings of editorials he'd written. "How long did he live here?"

"Until he was sixteen. Then he went to college—Princeton University—and never came back."

"Not even to visit his family?" Alex found that a bit bothersome. Fogarty was a hero to him and he didn't like learning that the man had no interest in his family.

"His family home burned a few months after he'd left for college and his parents perished in that fire. I'm sure he came back for the funeral, but there was no reason to come back after that. He had no other family here."

No reason? That didn't sound positive.

"Are you a reporter?" the woman asked.

Alex looked up from an article Fogarty had written for his college newspaper and shook his head. "No, I'm trying to gather some information for one of his descendants."

"One of his descendants?" the woman repeated, frowning. "But he had no descendants."

Alex frowned back. "He had to have."

Mrs. MacAllister was shaking her head. "He married twice but never had children with either woman. Records were kind of sparse from his early life but there was an epidemic of mumps around the time he was a teen. It's assumed that he must have had it and was unable to father children."

"But—" Alex closed his mouth abruptly. The woman had to be wrong.

"In fact," she was saying as she paged through a notebook of plastic-enclosed papers. She stopped near the back of the notebook at a copy of a handwritten paper. "We have a letter here that he wrote one of his friends late in his life where he expressed regret at not leaving any progeny."

Alex cleared his throat. "Maybe—"

Mrs. MacAllister was skimming the letter, her finger running down the page. "Here it is," she said. "'How it saddens me to leave this life with nothing but my words to live on. What a weak legacy, for who has listened even now? Would that I had sown some wild oats in my youth, for I would embrace gladly any child of my loins.'"

The woman looked up at him, shrugging slightly. "No descendants. And apparently not even the possibility of illegitimate ones."

"Sounds like that." Alex was thoroughly confused. "Maybe I misunderstood." Although he knew he hadn't.

"Perhaps it was a different Fogarty family," she said. "It's not that uncommon a name."

"That could be it." Alex closed the notebook. "Well, thanks so much for your help."

"I wish it had been more helpful."

Alex just nodded and wandered back out to the car. What now? His search to find Fiona some relatives had turned up information that would devastate her.

He thought back to all the times she'd mentioned Fogarty—he hadn't just been some famous relation to brag about. He had been her anchor when she had needed it most. Hell, she was still clinging to him. He was still just as much a part of her life as he had been years ago.

So did he tell her the truth? Or did he pretend that he'd never learned it? Did he destroy her self-image or did he live a lie?

Well, he sure as hell wasn't going to take away her pride in old Fogarty. What purpose would that serve? He'd just pretend like he never found any of this out. It wouldn't matter to him.

Chapter Twelve

Fiona put the jug of orange juice in Mrs. Torcini's refrigerator and closed the door. Two more bags to empty and she'd be able to rush back to her apartment. Mrs. Andrews had called with another report this afternoon and Fiona could hardly wait to tell Alex that things were looking even better.

"Fiona!" Mrs. Torcini shouted. The old woman was standing by the sink, holding out a large head of cauliflower. "Why did I buy this?"

Fiona took the vegetable and put it in her neighbor's crisper. "You're making a cauliflower casserole to take to your Sunday-evening church supper. Remember?"

"Oh, yeah."

Mrs. Torcini paused, as if contemplating some eternal truth, while Fiona stacked the canned cat food in the pantry. It didn't look like Mrs. Torcini's Oscar would go hungry. At least not in this century.

"Are you going to remind me to make it?" Mrs. Torcini asked.

"Sure." Fiona gathered up the empty grocery bags and put them under the sink. "That's what neighbors are for."

After straightening up, she checked that everything was in order. She always took her elderly neighbor grocery shopping after school on Friday. It was when she did her own, so it was no problem. And she enjoyed the company.

"I saw that young man of yours the other day," Mrs. Torcini said. "He was going out to his car."

That young man of yours. Her neighbor's words sent a warm glow washing over Fiona, which immediately caused her to force some common sense into her euphoria. She didn't own Alex or even want to. Well, maybe a little, but not too much. No more than any two people who cared about each other as they did.

"He looked happy." Mrs. Torcini paused to rub her nose. "Too happy, if you ask me."

Fiona's smile got hung up on some question marks. Too happy? "How can anybody be too happy?"

"He had that spring in his step."

"Spring?" Fiona felt especially dense.

"The kind men have when they're getting it regular," Mrs. Torcini said. "You know. He ain't gonna buy milk at the grocery store if he can get it wholesale at the dairy."

Fiona's face grew hot as she stuttered and stammered. Sounds fell from her lips, but no words. Certainly nothing intelligible.

"You got him talking marriage yet?"

Her treacherous cheeks were glowing like a Yule log. Mrs. Torcini had grown up in another time; she didn't understand how things were done these days. Fiona settled for a noncommittal shrug.

"You young people." Mrs. Torcini shook her head sadly. "All you think of is fun. Me and the mister, now. We didn't start having fun until after the boys were born."

Fiona didn't know what to say. She wished goodbye was possible, but she couldn't run out in the middle of a conversation. Sometimes her damn rules were a pain.

"It wasn't like we didn't know how everything worked."

"Uh-huh." Fiona looked around the kitchen, searching for diversion. Some of Mrs. Torcini's conversations were like sitting in a wagon pulled by a team of runaway horses.

"We just didn't have the touch. You know what I mean?"

"Yes, yes." Lord, she could feel her cheeks getting hot again, and she shoved the last of the canned goods onto the shelf. She was going to assert herself for once. "I have to get going, Mrs. Torcini. I have my own groceries to put away."

"You and your young man going out tonight?" Mrs. Torcini suddenly asked.

"Ah..." Fiona's hands fluttered for a moment. "Probably. I don't know. He wasn't home when I got back from school."

"He's gone?"

"Oh, no." A teeny ripple of concern shot through her heart, but Fiona immediately squelched the emotion. He wouldn't leave without telling her. Not after all they'd shared. "He was just out. He has work to do."

Mrs. Torcini nodded and reached down to pick up her cat. Oscar was of indeterminate age with one good eye and tattered ears, souvenirs of numerous back-alley battles. He was a foul-tempered old reprobate but Mrs. Torcini loved him unconditionally. She started scratching Oscar behind his ears while he shone his one hate-filled eye on Fiona. He wasn't too fond of Fiona and was obviously telling her that she was dismissed.

"Men wander, you know," Mrs. Torcini said.

Oscar was right; Fiona could leave now. "I'd better get going," she said. "I still have my own groceries to put away."

"Just like Oscar here." Mrs. Torcini paused to smooth his fur, eliciting an almost-obscene groaning and purring. "He used to wander all the time."

"Male cats are like that," Fiona replied.

"Yep, he went all over town. Maybe even to Lydick, for all I know."

This was not a conversation she needed to hear. "I bought some ice cream. I hope it's not melted by now."

"But then I got him fixed."

Fiona stepped toward the door. "I'm going to the mall first thing in the morning. I'll call and see if you need anything."

"You know." The old woman moved two fingers like they were a scissors. "Snip, snip."

"I'll call you by nine."

"Mr. Torcini, he sometimes used to wander. I thought about—" she made the scissors motion again "—snip, snip. But then what would I have?" The old woman laughed heartily for a moment. "It'd be like living with my sister."

Fiona pulled the door open. It was time to go. "See you tomorrow."

"Of course, I mighta been better off with my sister," she said. "At least I wouldn't have had someone leaving the toilet seat up all the time."

Fiona slipped out the door and closed it firmly behind her, fighting the urge to laugh until she had grabbed two bags from her car and was carrying them up to her apartment. And then, laugh she did. That woman was a real pistol.

"Hey, about time you're home." Alex was at the door and took the bags from her arms. He leaned forward to brush her lips with his. "I missed you."

"That's what you get for working," she teased and slipped down to the car for her last bag.

When she got back to the porch Alex was there waiting. He took the bag from her, leaving one arm to slip around her shoulders. He was so good to come home to.

"Mrs. Andrews called," she told him. "It really looks like the transplant's working."

"That's the best news," he said and punctuated the words with a kiss. "You must have given her some great bone marrow." He let go of her as they went inside. "Why don't we go out to dinner tonight to celebrate? My treat."

"We don't have to," she said. "I got some steaks and a bottle of wine."

"Then let me cook them," he said. He put the bag on the counter and took her in his arms completely.

"Why don't we do it together?" she suggested.

"Because I want to take care of you tonight."

She smiled up at him, her heart melting at the fervor in his eyes. She reached up to meet his lips and drank of the wonder there. Life was so perfect; so magical. She'd never dreamed that love could be like this. She'd thought it was full of anguish and fear, not of sharing joy and happiness.

"So, what do you want to do after dinner?" Alex asked as he pulled away and went back to unpacking the groceries. "Want to go down to the Comedy Club?"

She shrugged, feeling just a little uneasy away from his touch. It was almost like there was a storm coming. Not close enough to see, but close enough for the barometric pressure to drop.

"I don't care," she said and started unpacking a bag. "Do we have to do anything? We could just rent some movies."

"That'd be great." He put her ice cream into the freezer, then took the lettuce out of her hands.

"What are you doing?" she asked.

"Putting away the groceries," he said as he opened the refrigerator. "You just relax and put your feet up."

"I'm not tired."

"Maybe I'll run out and get the movies before I start dinner," he said and folded up the last bag. "You know, get there before all the good ones are rented."

"If you want," she said, although her unease seemed to be growing. There was no reason for it. He was being extra-attentive. He was everything a woman could ask for, so why was it her heart was seeing shadows? Maybe he liked a more action-packed life than they'd had the first few days. That was no reason to get scared.

"Why don't we go together?" she suggested. Maybe there was something in the air here that was making her crazy. She'd get out and find that the only shadows were in her imagination.

"We can make it a date," he said and brushed her lips in passing as he went to put the grocery bags away. "You know, I was thinking I should zip back to my apartment tomorrow."

Her heart almost froze. He was leaving. She had sensed it, had felt it in the air.

"If I leave before lunch, I should be back by dinnertime," he said.

She let her breath out in a rush. "You're coming back?"

He turned to frown at her, then came over to take her in his arms. "Hey, you aren't getting rid of me that easily."

His lips took hers again. This time the touch was stronger, more determined, more filled with his passion and desire. She felt a hunger rush up inside her, answering the love that she felt in his touch, that she heard in his words. There was warmth and safety and honesty in his embrace. And nothing at all to fear.

He pulled back, but still held her loosely in his arms. "You plan us a special evening for tomorrow," he said, coming back for a quick taste of her lips. "Whatever you want to do is fine with me."

"All right, already," Alex said. "Here's some for you little guys."

He stood on the bank and threw the scraps of bread onto the lake as far as he could to his right where some ducks were waiting. Then he did the same to his left. And finally he deposited a couple of handfuls immediately in front of him.

"You two are just big bullies," he told the swans. "You want everything your way."

But wasn't he just like that himself? Saying he wanted Fiona's happiness, then letting the truth about Fogarty eat away at him until he felt like Atlas carrying the weight of the world.

The white pair swam in graceful circles before him, quickly grabbing the crusts, while on either side of them various breeds of ducks scrambled and squabbled, snatching up any stray morsel that came close. Alex threw another handful to the swans and then dumped the remainder of his goodies where the ducks could get them.

This wasn't the first time he'd run across something unexpected, something with the potential to hurt, but it was the first time the hurt would go to someone he cared about. And the first time he had the option to remain silent. Fiona hadn't hired him to find out about Fogarty; he'd done it on his own. So the results were his own to keep or share as he saw fit.

Just how did he see fit?

He sat down on the bank and stared out at the swans. They just stared back, sharing no insights into the longevity of relationships, why they liked soggy bread crusts or what he should do. They were not much help.

Alex looked away, glancing at the woods around him. It was nice here, and quiet. Nicer now than it had been when he and Fiona were here almost a month ago. Now the trees were all leafing out and the air was warmer. And he and Fiona were much closer. So why did it feel like winter was about to descend?

He looked back at the birds. "It wasn't as easy as I thought it'd be," he told them. "It was like I was living a lie last night."

The swans paused in their gliding to look at him.

"But what difference should it make? So what, if she believes something that's not true? Who's it going to hurt?"

A brown duck came over to stare at him.

"It's not like it's a life-and-death situation," he told them. "It's not even something that affects her and me."

The duck dove for something under the water, then swam away—probably only willing to listen to whining if he was being fed.

"And it's nothing like what happened to me," Alex went on. "There's nobody around acting the part of her great-great-grandfather so that she thinks that's who he is. And she's not going around capitalizing on this supposed relationship, so she's not going to find out when some nosy jerk shoots her down. There's no reason why she shouldn't go right on hanging on to Fogarty's coattails if that makes her happy. No reason at all. Not one teeny-tiny one."

The swans moved away, as if sensing the conflict in his voice. Once they were gone, the ducks came careening in, circling in their space and muttering at him. But they wanted food, not philosophy.

"I'm all out." He spread his empty hands as if to show them. "That's it. No more."

The swans seemed to believe him, as their circles took them farther and farther away from him; while the ducks, skeptics that they were, stayed around quacking and otherwise making nuisances of themselves.

"Hey, so I didn't bring enough. So sue me."

Everybody wanted something from him. The ducks just wanted food. Fiona wanted someone that she could rely on. She wanted someone who put her happiness and well-being ahead of his own.

Maybe he didn't bring enough, ever. Maybe he didn't bring enough bread for the ducks and maybe he didn't bring enough to his relationship with Fiona. Maybe he just didn't have enough to give anyone.

"That's stupid," he said, rising to his feet. "I just need to try harder. Get out of my rut."

He just had to believe that he could make a relationship work. That was all it would take.

And he had the next several hours to figure it out. He needed to pick up his mail and check his apartment. Four hours, max. Long enough to come up with some faith.

"How do you like it?" Fiona heard the worry in her voice and wished she could have bought a little more gumption as easily as she'd bought Alex this shirt. "It looks like it fits okay."

"Fits great," he said, his voice enthusiastic.

She looked at his face in the mirror as she ran her fingers across his broad shoulders. He looked like he liked it. And he sounded like he did, but he was such a nice guy, he could just be saying that. She should never have bought the shirt, no matter how much she liked it. They weren't at that point in their relationship.

"Cassie said you'd hate it."

"Well, Cassie's wrong. It's great." He turned to kiss her with sweet tenderness. "I've never had a cowboy shirt before."

"I was afraid it was too early in our relationship."

Confusion danced across his brown eyes. "Is there some schedule we're supposed to be following?" he asked. "No cowboy shirts before a certain date? You'd better get me a copy. I don't want to make a mistake."

She knew she was being silly, even without his good-natured teasing, and just shrugged. "I don't know. I've never gotten this far in a relationship before. I just didn't want to get too presumptuous."

"You worry far too much," he said, touching her cheek with a gentle hand. For a moment, his eyes took on a shadow as if some cloud had passed in front of his sun, but then he smiled. And the hint of shadows disappeared like a bad dream. Or like something she'd imagined. "Now where's my cowboy hat and horsey?"

She was such a worrier, she scolded herself. She needed to just relax and do what felt right. She forced herself to laugh. "If you really want a cowboy hat, we can swing by Dudes and Darlin's on the way to the restaurant,'' Fiona replied. "But you'll have to handle the horsey part yourself."

He looked sad. "If I can't have a horsey, then what's the use of a cowboy hat?"

"Oh, stop whining." Fiona threw her arms around his neck and pulled herself to him. "Now, do you really like your shirt?"

"I love it."

His arms wrapped themselves around her, powerful well-muscled arms. A hungry smile filled his face and eyes as his lips came down to hers. There was such need in his touch, such desperation, that her heart seemed to swell in response. She wanted to give him everything. She wanted to ease his hurts and calm his fears. She wanted to give him all the love her heart held and more. She just had to stop getting caught up in her own silly worries.

Ever so slowly she was letting Kate go. It was hard, having memories of the girl to tug at her heart, but she knew it was for the best. Kate was getting better and slipping back further each day into her own life. And that was the way it should be.

But it was different with Alex. He was becoming more and more important to her. She knew there would come a day when he'd go back to his life, too; but she wouldn't let herself look at that. There was time enough for loneliness later.

The heat of his passion started to melt her coherency and she only knew her own needs and her own hungers. His touch ignited her desires, sending shivers of want all through her. That delectable knot tightened up in her soul, wanting him to find her release. She moved closer into his embrace, her mouth on his with silent words of love passing between them.

When they finally separated, Fiona could barely catch her breath. "Hey, cowboy," she said. "That was some thank-you."

All he did was laugh, a tight little croak that he seemed to have difficulty pushing out. Fiona's stomach told her that she was ready for dinner, but the rest of her had other hungers.

"Our table's reserved for six-thirty." Fiona snuggled into his arms. "Wanna be late?"

He gave her a quick kiss, then eased her away. "Let's go eat," he said, regret in his voice. "I'm hungry and we have the rest of our lives for everything else."

The rest of our lives? Fiona rushed off to finish dressing, her heart on high.

He loved her. He must. He wouldn't be talking about the rest of their lives if he didn't. The certainty of that fact melted her heart just like the hot July sun of an Indiana summer softened the blacktop country roads.

Prophesies by mysterious old women weren't all they were cracked up to be, Fiona thought as she pulled on a new pair of jeans. Her and Alex's souls were fueled with love, each wrapped so tightly around the other that nothing could pull them apart. Fighting for Alex's love would be like fighting for the heart that beat within her breast. It was already there. There was no need to fight, just accept.

She went back into the living room, grabbing her purse from the counter as she waved to the cats.

"Bye, guys." They were sleeping on the sofa, one on each end, and chose to ignore her. "Well, don't get so upset. Don't even bother to wake up. We can see our way out."

Alex took her by the arm and pulled her to go out. "Cats are a gift from the gods," he said.

"Oh, yeah? What are they good for?"

"They make sure we stay humble."

"Well, they've made me very good at that."

"You're very good at lots of things, actually," he said.

"You're so sweet," she replied, giving him another kiss.

Once they'd parted, he closed the door behind them. "How come we're dressed like cowboys?" he asked. "We taking a spin down to Texas for a barbecue?"

"There's a country-and-western nightclub downtown," she explained.

"And they have a dress code?"

"No, they have dance lessons every Saturday night."

"Dance lessons?" A quizzical look came over his face as he stopped halfway down the steps. "You're kidding?"

"I thought it would be fun," she said softly.

All her worries came flooding back. Why hadn't she dated more? Just because she hadn't ever met that certain someone who felt like the other half of her soul was no reason. She should have been dating just for practice, so that she wouldn't be so scared she was going to break some unwritten relationship rule.

"Dance lessons sound good to me," he said, as they continued down the stairs.

"Really? Remember you're Mr. Honesty."

That darkness came back to his eyes. Was it pain? It clutched at her heart like a steel claw, sending icy shivers all through her.

She tried to smile. "Hey, we can do something else, if you're not into line dancing."

He grinned and the darkness left his eyes. He reached over for her hand. "I was just worrying about stomping on your pretty feet," he said. "Just as long as you realize that you're going to have to move fast to stay safe."

She wanted to believe him. "No problem," she said. "I'm known as fast-footed Fiona."

As they reached the sidewalk, she stopped, waiting for him to lead her to his car du jour. She didn't see the blue Ford he'd been driving so he must have traded it in for something else.

"Here we are." He led her to a new-looking Jeep Cherokee right in front of her building.

"This doesn't look very used," she said.

"Less than a couple hundred miles."

"Goodness," she said. "How did it get on your friend's used-car lot?"

"It didn't." He shrugged at her silent question. "I kind of bought it."

"You bought a new car?" She turned to stare at him. This meant something. She wasn't sure what, but she knew it represented a change. And one that should send her worries packing.

"It's a beautiful car."

"Want to drive?" Alex asked, holding out the keys.

"You trust me?"

"With my life."

She reached out and grasped the keys, feeling like she'd grabbed the key hanging off the end of Ben Franklin's kite. Her arm trembled as the electrical energy of the universe poured through her. He trusted her! Wasn't that another way of saying he loved her?

"Come on," Alex said. "Or we'll be late and for no good reason."

Laughing, she grabbed the keys and ran around to the driver's door. The wonderful new-car smell welcomed her. She put the key in, starting the motor. It wasn't until she was shifting the car into gear that she noticed Alex pounding on the window.

"Sorry," she said, after unlocking the door.

"What were you going to do?" he asked, his voice filled with a growl. "Take the car to dinner and leave me out in the parking lot?"

"If you're not nice," she replied. "Yes."

The car was great, purring beneath her like a lion held in check. How could he let her drive it? If it was hers, she'd want to be behind the wheel all the time. No, she'd be willing to share with him. She drove downtown—all too short a drive, suddenly—and pulled into a parking spot down the street from the club.

They got out of the car and walked hand in hand down the street. It was still light out, and other couples were strolling by, but somehow they seemed all alone; wrapped in a warmth that surrounded just the two of them. It was a nice feeling, a feeling of belonging and oneness. But then she saw their reflection in a passing window and some warp in the glass made Alex seem more distant, as if he was somehow pulling away from her.

She had to push her worries aside, bury them once and for all. "So how come you went and bought a car?" she asked. "Aren't you afraid you're going to need something different before you're done paying for this?"

He just shrugged. "Seemed like the thing to do."

Spending twenty-thousand dollars on a car seemed like the thing to do? They were so different; sometimes it scared her. "You make it sound like a whim," she said. "I don't even buy a dress impulsively, but think through when I'll wear it and how many times and would I get my money's worth."

"You're not a risk taker," he said.

"And you are?"

He didn't answer and just opened the door to the club. A wave of laughter and music and noise washed over them.

"Come on," she teased. "Great-great-grandpa Horace says you've got to tell me the truth."

"What's with this Horace Fogarty stuff all the time?" he snapped. "You'd think you didn't exist if it wasn't for him."

She was taken aback by the vehemence of his response, but just grinned at him. "Well, actually, most of us wouldn't exist if it weren't for our ancestors."

He sighed as the maître d' came over toward them. Fiona gave her name and the man led them to a table up near the dance floor where you could hardly hear, let alone think.

"You know what I mean," he said above the music. "Sometimes I think you believe your only value lies in your relation to someone famous."

"It's not that at all," she said. "You make it sound like I'm conceited."

He shook his head as they sat down. "No, you have about the lowest self-esteem I've ever seen. You should like yourself and feel you're worth something even if you don't know any of your ancestors. Or if they were just all bums.''

He looked so serious, so worried about her that she just squeezed his hand with a laugh. "How did we get on such a serious subject?" she asked. "This is a night for dancing and partying, not gloom."

He held her hand tightly and smiled at her. It looked forced for only a minute, then his eyes were filled with sunshine. "You're right," he said. "So when are we going to learn line dancing?"

Chapter Thirteen

Alex crept out of the bedroom and sank onto the window seat in the living room. Two little furry buddies jumped up next to him, ready to watch the dawn arrive. They'd been doing this for almost a week now—ever since he'd found out about Fogarty leaving no descendants. But no great knowledge arrived with the light; no insight on how to live with the lie.

"Still pretty dark out," he told the cats, but neither paid him the slightest attention. They were concentrating on the scene outside. Some of the early birds were already singing out their announcements for the coming day.

Soon other birds, louder and more numerous, joined in the wakeup chorus. He felt—rather than saw—the agitation growing in the cats as they glared outside, but he doubted they would want the birds to disappear. Cats always hated birds. They were products of their genetic history.

Just as he was?

"Can't sleep again?" Fiona was in the doorway.

"I'm sorry," Alex said. "Did I wake you?"

He could hear Fiona padding across the rug and closed his eyes, clenching his fists as he waited for her to flop down into his lap. His natural inclination was to fold her into his arms and it would take all his willpower to keep from holding her. But thankfully she just sat in the recliner.

"I didn't hear you get up," she said. "I just sort of felt you were gone."

He suddenly felt nauseous, wishing the earth would open up and swallow him. Oh, Lord, what had he done? He'd made himself a part of her life, taken someone nice and good and kind and made her care about him. Why couldn't he have stayed out of Fiona's life? There was a good reason for his being a loner. He'd never brought anything good to anyone yet.

"Alex?"

The tension in his own body seemed to have been absorbed by Fiona. She was sitting up straight, her back stiff as a rod. The increasing light from outside was chasing the dimness of the night to the far corners of the room. He could see dark clouds of concern filling her eyes and wished the darkness had stayed.

"Is something wrong?" she asked.

"Why do you ask that?"

Damn, but he was a coward. Not only wouldn't he tell her the truth but he wouldn't tell her anything. He ought to get out of her life before he really hurt her.

"You haven't been your usual self," she said.

He'd been moody, slogging about in a deep, dark depression and not wanting to talk to anyone. Just wanting to run away and be alone. Hell, that was his normal old self. It was the other Alex who had been the fake. The happy, always smiling, wisecracking character had no relationship to the real Alex Rhinehart. There was a slight physical resemblance, but beyond that—nothing.

"You're usually joking around and making everyone laugh." Fiona leaned forward so she could reach him, her fingers playing gently with the hair by his left ear. "And now I have to fight to get the teeniest smile out of you."

The good humor was a facade; a shield he used to keep the rest of the world at bay, a mask he hid behind. But he couldn't do that to Fiona. He wanted to be honest with her. He'd asked her to bare her soul and he wanted to do the same. That was the only way to have a relationship. That was one thing his life's experiences had taught him.

They'd also taught him that he wasn't suited to relationships. Why hadn't he listened?

"I just have some stuff on my mind."

He was a damn coward. A dirty, rotten, low-down, side-winding chickenly coward.

"Got a problem at work?"

Shame washed over his heart and soul, filling every crevice in his being. Damn it all to hell. Why couldn't he just face up to things and tell Fiona the truth about Fogarty?

Because he was a coward. Because, although he knew that she had every right to the truth, he was afraid that once he told her she would be devastated. The very foundation of herself as a person would be destroyed. And then she would hate him for the rest of her natural life. It wouldn't be the first time that the recipient of an unpleasant message killed the messenger.

"I know that you don't like to talk about your work," she said. "And I know how devoted you are to client privilege and all that kind of stuff, but sometimes you have to let things out."

The only thing he'd like to let out right now were tears. Big, huge, crocodile tears, because he was about to lose the only beautiful thing that had ever walked into his life.

"You try and keep things bottled up inside and you'll just explode," she said.

"Bloods and guts all over the walls and ceiling." He made a face and shook his head. "Ugh. That would be a mess."

She laughed softly, deep in her throat, and kissed him on the side of his neck. "That's my guy," she whispered in his ear as she slid into his lap, letting her arms slide around him.

He couldn't fight it. He let his arms wrap themselves loosely around Fiona. It wasn't right for him to take advantage of her warm, loving nature, but he was only a man.

"Want to go back to bed?"

Her teeth were nibbling gently on his earlobe now, making his body silently scream out the pain of his desire. Alex wanted to scream along with it, a primeval sound that the first man must have made when the first woman smiled at him.

"And I don't mean to sleep," she murmured, the huskiness in her voice only hinting at the passion in her heart.

Yet, as much as he wanted to, he couldn't. His body grew tense again, his agony overflowing his loins and filling his soul. If he couldn't be open and honest with Fiona, there was no reason for him to enjoy the fruits of her love. To do that would be to cheapen something more precious than life itself.

"I need to get back to Chicago." His throat was filled with pain and it was hard to get the words out. Kind of like pushing a banana through a window screen. "Things are sort of piling up."

He forced himself to look into her trusting eyes. The only thing that was piling up was the crap he was putting out. He needed to either tell her the truth or get out of her life. And he knew which would hurt Fiona the least.

"This just isn't working," he said.

"What isn't?" she asked. "Us? Or trying to work so far from your office?"

"Both."

A shadow filled Fiona's eyes and, although she hadn't moved out of his arms, he could feel her drawing away from him.

"I guess I was stupid to think it would," he said, as he slowly let his arms slip down and off her body.

Getting him out of her life would be the best thing in the world for Fiona. The longer he stayed around, the bigger the chance that he would hurt her.

"I see." She slid off his lap. "So this is it?"

"I wanted it to work," he said, although it sounded as lame as could be. "I thought maybe I could beat the odds."

"And just what's convinced you you can't?" she asked. Her voice was quiet, as was everything about her.

He shrugged. He didn't want to get into any of this, but he owed her some sort of explanation. "I know myself. Let's leave it at that, okay?"

"Maybe I don't want to leave it at that," she said, her voice rising. "I have a right to know if I did something."

"For God's sake, Fiona, everything isn't your fault," he snapped. "It's me, okay? Just me."

"It can't be just you." Her voice was quivering and he could see her fighting to regain control. "If it's not something I did, then it must just be who I am."

"There's nothing the matter with who you are," he said. Damn it, anyway. She ought to slug him, not be so civilized. "I know that if I stay, I'll only bring you pain. And I don't want to do that."

She got to her feet, not looking at him. "It's all right. You don't have to make excuses. I never thought it would last anyway."

He got to his feet also, wanting to take her hand for one last time, but he couldn't. "You're a very special woman," he said softly. "One of these days you'll find that right man. I wish it could have been me."

"Better be careful, Mr. Honesty," she said, her back to him. "Now's not the time to start lying."

It wasn't a lie. He truly did wish he had been the one for her, but to protest would only mean more explanations. Best to let her think him a cad, than the alternative.

"I'll be out of here in a few minutes," he said.

"Fine."

* * *

"So, Fiona!" Mrs. Torcini shouted from her front window. "Ain't it a beautiful day?"

Fiona would have preferred to hurry down the sidewalk and be on her way, but she couldn't ignore her neighbor. "It's just great," she agreed. "After being cooped up in the classroom all week, I couldn't stand another minute inside."

That was certainly true. Although the beautiful spring weather wasn't the real reason she was out taking a walk. What she really couldn't stand was another minute inside, alone in her apartment.

Of course, she wasn't really alone. Elvis and Prissy were there. But, unfortunately, so were all sorts of memories. Of Alex. Of Kate. Of a time when she hadn't been alone.

Why had Alex left? She'd thought they were on the verge of something really good. She'd thought everything had been going along wonderfully. Showed how stupid she was about relationships. If she only knew what had happened . . .

"Where's that young man of yours?" her neighbor asked.

Fiona's stomach took a little twist but she fought to keep her smile in place. "He went back to Chicago a couple of days ago."

"Ah."

"He has a lot of work to catch up on." The old stomach twisted around even more. "That's the joys of being self-employed," Fiona replied. "You have to work when there are things that need doing."

Mrs. Torcini just nodded.

"He's a private detective," Fiona said.

Her neighbor nodded again.

"Sometimes he has to travel." Fiona shrugged helplessly, wishing she could walk away from her neighbor's knowing stare. Wishing she'd never got so involved with everyone here so that they all knew her business. "And he doesn't always know from one minute to the next where he might be.''

This time Mrs. Torcini only blinked. Fiona had steeled herself for some more probing questions, but an odd look came into the old woman's eyes. And suddenly Fiona had to look away. She was prepared to handle anything—the old woman's ''I told you so'' or another lecture on the wanderings of men—but not this. Not the pity she saw filling her neighbor's eyes.

''So,'' Fiona said. ''Is Robbie coming to take you out for Mother's Day?'' Mrs. Torcini's favorite nephew was always a good source of distraction.

''Oh, yes!'' Mrs. Torcini shouted. ''He said he'd take me anyplace I want to go. I was kind of thinking of the Wagon Wheel in Warsaw, but I don't remember how to get there.''

''You can take my atlas,'' Fiona said, starting back up the stairs to her apartment. ''It's got a good state map in it.''

''You're such a good girl,'' Mrs. Torcini said and disappeared from the window. A moment later she was at Fiona's front door. ''Your young man was a fool to leave, but he'll be back.''

''Sure.'' Fiona just unlocked the door and let the woman inside. Alex was about as likely to be part of her life as she was to be twenty again. As she was to swim the Atlantic. As she was to kick that home run in kickball. ''It's just over here.''

She got the atlas from the shelf, but as she pulled it out a paper fell from it, fluttering to the ground.

''Losing your laundry list?'' Mrs. Torcini called out.

Fiona stooped to pick it up. ''Nope, it's directions to someplace.'' In Alex's handwriting. ''I wonder where to.''

''Well, you got the map in your hand,'' the old woman said loudly.

True enough. Fiona opened the book to the Indiana map and traced the route. Route 31 south to Route 30 east. Through Etna Green.

''Mentone?'' Fiona said. ''What's in Mentone?''

"Maybe your young man," Mrs. Torcini replied. "You said he travels."

"I kind of doubt it," Fiona said. "Here's the atlas. Keep it as long as you need it."

"He left 'cause men ain't got the sense of melted ice cream!" the old woman shouted. "That's why God made women. Somebody's got to take care of things."

After Mrs. Torcini left, Fiona just sank into the nearest chair, too weary to resume her walk. Why had Alex left? She suspected he had more intelligence than melted ice cream, but he really hadn't told her anything.

If he'd just said that he hated the shirt she'd bought him. Or thought her cats were pesty. Or that she was too clingy. She could deal with that. Maybe not change it, but she could at least deal with it. Now, she was left with nothing. Nothing but doubts.

And the directions to Mentone. Why in the world would he have gone there?

Rather than her thoughts eat away at her, Fiona grabbed up the newspaper. A church on the south side was having a garage sale. She made a face and went on. Samantha liked that kind of thing. Maybe she ought to get out of the house before Sam came and dragged her down there.

A nature preserve, just over the line in Michigan, was conducting a signs-of-spring hike on its grounds. Plants and nature were Cassie's thing. Double reason to get out of the house. If Samantha didn't get her, Cassie would.

Fiona tossed the paper aside and picked up the directions to Mentone. Why not? She'd never been there—had barely heard of the place—and it was a beautiful day for a drive. If she stayed home, she'd just spend her time brooding about it being Mother's Day tomorrow. Better to get out than to ponder on all she had lost in the past few weeks.

Fiona grabbed her purse. "Bye, guys," she called to the cats, who ignored her.

The day was perfect for a drive. It was sunny, spring was bursting out all over the place, and the roads were empty.

She sped south past farm fields being awoken from their long winter's sleep and pastures of frisky horses. She couldn't stop her hope from building until a smile was on her face. Maybe she would find out the truth. And maybe it would be something she could fix.

Etna Green was a tiny little place that she zipped through in half a blink. After a few miles of flatter-than-flat fields, she was in Mentone. Now what?

She drove slowly along Main Street, finding a giant stone egg at one end and a concrete chicken at the other, with a handful of stores in between. What would Alex have been doing here? There were hardware and feed stores in Mentone, not to mention family-run restaurants. There were no billboards proclaiming Alex's mission. Gloom settled back over her shoulders as surely as if the sun had hidden behind storm clouds. It had been stupid to come here. Stupid to think she was going to find an answer.

He probably had a client here, or was sent here by a client. It probably had nothing to do with her.

Up ahead was a gas station. As good a place as any to grab a soda and stretch her legs before heading back. She pulled into the lot and sauntered inside. They had a lunchroom counter on one side, tires and batteries on the other. Behind the counter were hundreds of pictures taped to the wall in a collage effect. Athletic teams and people with trophies. Multigenerational photos and posed pictures of beauty queens. A guy with a helicopter and—

Great-great-grandpa Horace.

"Is that a picture of Horace Fogarty?" she asked the cashier, pointing to the one she meant.

The man turned around. "Ain't too many that recognize him," he said slowly, staring at the picture himself. "Been kinda forgotten about. But the man was born here."

"He was? I thought he—" What had she thought?

"He lived out east nearly all his life, but was born here, all right," the man went on.

"Of course, that makes sense," she said. Why else would his descendants have settled around here?

The man gave her an odd look as he moved over to take care of a customer. She waited as he rang up a young man's purchase of corn chips and soda. She was on to something; she just knew it.

"Is his house still standing?" she asked, once he was through with the transaction. "Does he have any relatives around?"

The man just shook his head. "Best check at the library. Alma MacAllister knows about that kind of stuff."

Alma MacAllister not only knew about that stuff, but she was willing to share her knowledge. The older woman pulled out large notebooks with newspaper clippings and copies of family photos. Fiona glanced through them, eagerly looking for a sign of his family. She found none.

"His family's been kind of ignored," Fiona said as she closed the last book. "I was hoping to see pictures or mention of his children or grandchildren."

"He had no children or grandchildren," the woman replied.

Fiona felt her mouth go dry. "But . . ."

The woman shook her head. "I'm sorry, but I have to tell you the same thing I told that young man last week. Horace Waldo Fogarty never sired any children."

So she wasn't a descendant. Fiona tried hard to remember just how she'd come to believe she was and, though she had vague memories of her father talking about Great-grandpa Horace, she didn't think her father'd ever said his great-grandfather had been *that* Horace Fogarty. No, she'd jumped to that conclusion somewhere along the line when she'd felt particularly alone.

So all her pride and belief that she was somebody, that she had inherited his writing talent, was all a lie. But her mind barely registered the fact as the woman's words sank in. "What young man?"

"I don't remember if he gave me his name," the woman answered. "But he discussed the very same thing with me. It was as if he'd already had Mr. Fogarty the father to a horde of children and couldn't accept the fact that he left no heirs. On either side of the blanket."

"I see." Somehow Fiona must have thanked the woman for her help and managed to walk outside to her car, but she had no recollection of any of it.

She wasn't Horace Fogarty's great-great-granddaughter and Alex knew it. The pain of having her anchor ripped away was nothing compared with losing her heart.

Had Alex left because she wasn't related to Fogarty? Was her only attraction for him her supposed relative?

It seemed like such a shallow reason. Such a nothing excuse for ending a relationship.

But it was the only reason she'd been given. And maybe even Mr. Honesty couldn't bring himself to tell her that truth.

"Oh, hell," Alex exclaimed, as he glared at the broken glass now scattered across the countertop and kitchen floor. "Damn it."

"Here," his mother said. "Let me get my own glass."

"I'm not a cripple, Mom." He reached up for another glass and this time he didn't drop it. "It was just an accident."

"You better clean that mess up before you do anything else." She had on her no-nonsense mothering look, but the best he could do was look away.

"Don't worry about it." He threw some ice cubes in the unbroken glass and filled it with diet cola. "I'll get it later."

His mother frowned at him. "It's not a good idea to leave broken glass laying around like that."

"What's the problem?" Alex asked. "I don't have any kids or pets." He didn't have anybody or anything to call his own. Life was like it had always been.

"The kind of shape you're in, you're liable to cut yourself."

"Mom." He walked over to her, kicking aside some of the bigger pieces of glass, and handed her the drink. "I'm all right. There's nothing wrong with me."

"Yeah." She took a long drink. "Sure."

There was no arguing with his mother. So, making a face, he turned to retrieve another glass and poured some diet cola for himself. He wasn't particularly thirsty but it was something to do.

"Honey," she said. "If there's anything I'm expert on, it's being in the dumps."

There was no arguing with her there. When she was right, she was right. He sipped his own drink.

"But what I'm mostly expert in is screwed-up relationships."

Alex clenched his teeth for a moment, before forcing himself to relax and take another sip of his drink. His mother had been on this relationship nonsense ever since she'd walked through his door. She had a million questions about Fiona and he didn't want to answer a single one. So he didn't. He sipped his drink again.

"You can pout all you want, Mr. I-Don't-Need-Nobody, but truth is truth."

He squeezed his hand tight. So tight that for a moment there, he was afraid he was going to crunch the glass in his hand. Then he'd have a real mess.

"I'm not pouting, Mom."

"Don't tell me," she said. "I may not have been the best mother in the world, but I do know when you're pouting."

Jeez, mothers could be a pain. Especially his. And when did she suddenly become such an expert on relationships? Hers weren't any great shakes. Of course, that's what she's telling you, a little voice whispered. She's telling you that she knows pain.

"I made reservations for dinner tomorrow at Bowers," he said. "That okay?"

Instead of replying, his mother just took another sip of her drink. Then, after setting it down on the table, she went to the small pantry where his cleaning supplies were and took out a whisk and dustpan.

"Mom," he said. "I said I'd clean it."

"Where's your little Indiana honey?" She cleaned the glass off the counter and then bent down to sweep up the shards on the floor. "I thought you two were getting on real well."

"I don't have any kind of a honey, Mom."

He didn't have anyone and wouldn't. Not now, not ever. He stared out his kitchen window at the high rise across the alley from him. The image was a bit blurred—what one would expect on an overcast day like today.

Alex wished the damn rain would just come instead of hanging around in the clouds. Get it over with; wash out the air, clean the streets, and bring back the sunshine.

"She had a very pretty name," his mother said, dumping the broken glass into the trash. "What was it?"

"Fiona."

"That's right." His mother put the dustpan and broom back in the closet before turning to smile at him. "Fiona. A pretty name for a pretty woman."

"Mom, it's no big deal remembering her name. I worked with her for two or three weeks."

"Is that what you call it?"

His mother was just looking at him. Usually she was very flighty, easy to stare down. But then there were times, like today, when an inner strength seemed to bubble up from within. Today Alex broke first. He looked away.

"I have a lot of work to do," he said, talking to the window. "Want me to drop you off at home?"

The sigh that split the silence told him that he'd won. Actually, there were no winners. Although if anybody was winning, it had to be Fiona. She did not need him in her life. And she did not need one more foundation of her life destroyed. It was best for everyone if things went back to what they were before. He had his life here and she had hers back in Indiana. Everybody would be happier if it stayed that way.

Chapter Fourteen

Fiona was in a foul mood by the time she left church on Sunday morning, clutching the white carnation that every woman had been presented with. What a way to spend Mother's Day—with a flower but no kid. Her mood only got worse when she stopped at the grocery store for a carton of milk. They were giving out red carnations. It was enough to make a person a hermit. Maybe it was time not to be a solitary hermit.

She never had Kate—her brief time with her had been a gift. She no longer had Great-great-grandpa Horace. And was trying hard to forget she'd briefly had Alex. Although actually, she ought to be grateful to him; her irritation at him dulled the pain of everything else.

She parked in front of her apartment, meaning to run in and grab the cake she'd made before heading off to her father's, but Mr. Kaminsky met her in the hallway. He was holding a bouquet of yellow roses stuck in an old coffee can.

"Missed you yesterday," he said.

"Oh?" She was staring at the flowers, her heart a mass of confusing emotions.

"These came for you, but you were out," he said, thrusting them at her. "I put them in water 'cause I was afraid they'd die."

She took the flowers, immediately swallowed up in their sweet scent. They wanted to chip away at her hurt and anger and she had to work hard to keep her walls in place. "Thank you," she said. "I'm glad you took such good care of them."

He nodded, then hurried off to his own apartment, leaving Fiona in the tiny foyer with roses so bright it was like the sun had come inside. She couldn't help but smile at them slightly, even as her heart wanted to break. She hurried inside.

Prissy and Elvis rushed over to sniff at the roses as Fiona pulled the little card out of its envelope. It read, "Happy Mother's Day." That was all. No name. No hidden messages. No expressions of regret.

He was being considerate, but he was still a Horace Waldo Fogarty groupie. She tossed the card onto the table, wishing she had the guts to throw the flowers also, and went into the bedroom to change. Luckily, they all went over to her dad's on Mother's Day, even after her mother died. If she was on her own here today, she'd be a basket case in about an hour.

She refused to even glance at the flowers as she left and hurried on over to her dad's. A swarm of nieces and nephews ran out to her car to meet her.

"Is that your marble cake?" someone asked.

"Of course."

"All right." High fives were exchanged.

"We're gonna play kickball when Aunt Cassie gets here," someone else told her.

"You're on her team."

Again? "Aren't we getting tired of this?" Fiona cried. They played kickball at every family gathering in the warm weather, and she was always on Cassie's team. It was like a life sentence.

"You gotta play."

"Yeah, 'cause we got Missy's mom on our team."

She knew all that. She was her team's prerequisite klutz, placed there to balance out the other family klutz—Missy's mom, Rosemary. "Cassie'll be thrilled."

"She's used to it."

"Maybe I'll break a leg before she gets here and breaks it for me." They all stared at her, uncertain if they were supposed to laugh. She climbed the stairs to the house. "Call me when it's game time."

"We will," someone called as the horde ran off.

Fiona went into the house, and tossed her jacket with the other coats in the den. After greeting her brothers and sisters-in-law, she found her father in the kitchen, putting a ham in the oven. The counter was covered with the salads and cakes and vegetable casseroles that the rest of the family had brought.

"Hi, sugar," he said, coming over to kiss her cheek. "You hear from your young man?"

"No."

"What a fool he is." He squeezed her hand. "How you feeling?"

"Good," she said.

"Not sore anymore?"

"Nope." At least, no place except for her heart. "And it looks like the transplant is working."

"Oh, yeah? That's really good news."

"It is," she agreed, and stood staring at her father. The silence grew around them for a long moment, then she sighed. It was time to open some of the doors she'd kept shut. "Can I tell you something?"

Her brother Bobby stuck his head in the kitchen door. "Hey, you two want to see the video of Kyle's school play?"

"In a minute," her father called.

He took Fiona's arm and led her into the little room off the kitchen that had always been his retreat. Books filled the shelves and family photos were all over the walls. Once inside, he closed the door and she felt like a kid again, safe in Daddy's special place. Why had she waited so long to tell him?

"What's on your mind, honey?" His voice was so gentle, so understanding, as if he knew how hard it would be for her to get the words out.

She took a deep breath as she sank onto the small sofa. She let her purse slide off her shoulder and onto the floor. "You know that little girl I gave my bone marrow to—Kate?"

He nodded.

"Well, she's my daughter." She couldn't meet his eyes and let her gaze drop to her hands, then rushed on as if hurtling down an icy hill. "When I was in college, I was really stupid and got pregnant and didn't know what to do. I had the baby but I knew I could never take care of her—not the way I'd want to—so I gave her up for adoption."

"Oh, Fiona." He reached over and took her hands tightly in his. "Why didn't you come to us, honey? Why didn't you tell us?" There was no anger in his voice, no recriminations; just sorrow. Just love.

The silence seemed so silly now. "I didn't know how."

He came to sit next to her, pulling her into his arms. "I am so sorry, honey. So sorry that you felt so alone. That there was no one you felt close enough to to trust with it."

She pulled back. His acceptance made her all weepy and weak-feeling and she still had things to say. "It wasn't your fault. I wasn't afraid you'd get angry or anything. I was just..." She didn't know why anymore.

He took back her hands. "You were always the hardest," he said with a sad smile. "I think that's maybe why you've been a little more special than the rest."

More special? Someone thought she was more special? She stared across the room, at the framed pictures that covered every bare inch of wall space. It wasn't just photographs that hung there, but pictures drawn in second-grade art class and stories written in fifth grade and awards for science fairs and perfect attendance. Everyone in this family had been made to feel special and important.

"You were so afraid when you came to live with us," he went on. "It was like you thought you had to be perfect. You don't know how your mom and I tried to get you to loosen up, to relax and feel secure. We thought we'd done pretty good, but I guess there's only so much a person can change."

"I knew you loved me," she said, her voice small. "It wasn't that."

"I'm glad." He loosened his hold on her hands. "I'd hate to think you doubted that."

"I just never have been able to admit certain things. I don't know why."

"You don't want to be vulnerable," he said. "You've lost a lot in your life and if you hold yourself apart, you won't be hurt when you lose someone again."

"I guess."

"No guess about it," he said softly. "Dads know these things."

He won a small smile from her.

"Did you meet her?" he asked.

She nodded. "I wasn't supposed to. They didn't tell her who I was, just that I was her donor, but one day she was in the lounge when I came in." She clutched at his hands, as she tried to make him see. "She looks so much like me. And sounds just like Cassie, telling me how silly I am when I worry."

She pulled the little photo album from her purse and opened it for him. He paged through the book slowly, a small smile on his lips as he saw Kate growing from a chubby little baby to an energy-charged little girl to the gangly young lady she was now.

"She's beautiful," he said simply, as he closed the book. "Will we ever get to meet her?"

"Well, right now, you and Alex and her parents are the only ones who know the truth. I will tell Sam and Cassie and the boys, but not just yet."

Fiona took the book back and stared down at it, thinking what a pitiful little piece of her daughter she owned. But also thinking how lucky she was to have it. If the Andrewses felt it would be better for Kate that they slip back totally into their former life, she would be able to bear it. She was learning a lot about the difference between giving someone up because you love them, and losing them in spite of loving them.

They heard the kitchen door slamming.

"Aunt Fiona?" someone cried from the kitchen. "Come on, Aunt Fiona. It's time for kickball."

Fiona got to her feet and pulled open the door. "Coming, Missy." She turned back to her father. "You know, this is one tradition I could live without."

"Fiona." Her father had gotten to his feet also. "Don't be so alone. Let people into your life."

Let people in? Wasn't that what she'd done with Alex? "I think the problem is with them running out of it, not my letting them in."

"But do you really let them in?" he asked. "Or do you only let them in so far and no more?"

She just shook her head, not liking the feeling that a lot of the blame might lie on her shoulders. "Kickball calleth."

"Come on, Missy."

"Go, Aunt Cassie!"

This had to be the first time in her life that Fiona had been quite glad to cross the street to the little neighborhood park and line up on Cassie's side for a kickball game. She felt better after telling her father about Kate, but he was wrong about her life. She wasn't pushing people away or keeping them at a distance. She hadn't done that with Alex, and yet he'd left.

Fiona watched her niece—a short, chubby little girl—race toward third base while the other team ran into the outfield after Cassie's kick. Someone caught up with it and threw the ball toward second base.

"Go, Missy!" Fiona shouted. "Keep running."

Suddenly there was a moment of silence; Cassie's team all held their breath. Fiona's nephew Timmy had tagged his brother Kyle out at second. Cassie was safe at first, but Missy had slowed down to a discouraged shuffle as she neared third.

"Don't quit, Missy!" Fiona shouted. "You're not out yet."

Timmy picked up the ball and threw it toward the third baseman—his dad, Bobby—but the throw was wild. Fiona and her teammates all gasped, then broke out in wild cheers.

"Come on, Missy!" Missy's brother Jerry called. "Come on. Go for home."

"Yea, Missy!"

The cries of encouragement continued and Missy was racing toward home plate, her chubby little legs going like pistons. She crossed home and was mobbed by her cousins and aunts and uncles.

"I scored a run!" she shouted happily.

"Yeah!"

"We're only down by one."

"The tying run's on base and the winning run's at the plate."

Fiona was suddenly gripped by the excitement herself. They were in the bottom of the last inning with two outs and Cassie on base. Two more runs and they would have achieved what Cassie's kickball team hadn't done since they started this tradition eight years ago—beat Samantha's team.

"We need a home run," Cassie called from first base. "Who's up next?"

"I don't know," Fiona replied. "I think everybody's been—"

A deathly silence fell over her group and they stared at her, a sickly look of horror etched on their faces.

Everybody had had their third turn at bat. Everybody but her.

"Sub, sub, sub," the kids all started shouting in unison. "Sub!"

"No, no!" Samantha yelled. "No subs."

"She can't play."

"She's sick."

"Lie down on the ground, Aunt Fiona," Missy hissed at her. "Pretend you're sick. Roll around in the dirt and cry and whine."

Fiona was tempted, but shook her head. "No," she said. "That wouldn't be right."

"I can kick you," Cassie called out her offer. "Then you'll be lying on the ground and whining."

"You kick me and you get no marble cake."

Cassie looked as if she was weighing the issue, although Fiona knew she was only teasing.

"It's my turn," Fiona said. "And it wouldn't be right to pretend I couldn't do it."

There was no reply from her team.

"That would be cheating."

The expression on her nieces' and nephews' faces said they didn't think this was the time and the place to have an ethics discussion. Well, too bad. Fists clenched, head down, Fiona strode briskly up to take her place at bat.

She was tired of feeling inadequate. She couldn't hold on to Alex; she couldn't keep Kate. She didn't even come first with her cats. But she could try to kick the hell out of this kickball.

When she got in position and looked up, her heart had misgivings. Sam's team had moved Timmy in as pitcher. He grinned at her; his smug smile said he was certain of victory. Her "prowess" at kickball was well known. No one had ever wanted her on their team. Not now and not ever.

As she stared at Timmy and his smug smile, Kate's advice came back to her: Never, ever kick with your toe.

Fiona took a deep breath and forced herself to stare at Timmy. With a wickedness added to his grin, he flung the ball toward her. Faster and faster and faster it seemed to come. But she could do it. Kate was a good athlete. Somewhere deep in Fiona's bones, she had to have some athletic ability. All she had to do was call it front and center.

The ball was there and Fiona drew her foot back, forced her toe to point down, and kicked.

She connected with the ball, feeling the jarring all the way up to her hip. Then the ball was gone and she just stood and watched it soar into the air, flying over Timmy's head, over Betsy's head and into the outfield, where it bounced toward the fence.

"Run!" someone screamed.

"Run!"

"Go, Aunt Fiona! Run!"

"You hit a home run, Aunt Fiona. Run!"

She hit a home run? Oh, my gosh. Suddenly Fiona was racing down the baselines. She was vaguely aware that Cassie was ahead of her, but all she could do was laugh. "I hit a home run!" she screamed to Betsy as she passed second. "I hit a home run."

"Faster, Aunt Fiona. Faster."

She sped past Bobby at third who patted her back in congratulations and then she was coming home.

"Faster!" her team was screaming.

"Slide!" Cassie yelled. "Slide!"

How did you slide? Fiona thought briefly. No one had ever taught her that. No one had ever expected it of her. But she threw her feet out in front of her and slid across the mud and grass to touch home plate just an instant before the ball came in. They'd won the game on her home run! Fiona got to her feet, collapsing into Cassie's arms.

"We won!" the kids were shouting.

"Way to go, Fi!" Cassie was hugging her hard. "I knew you could do it."

"'Bout time you figured out how to play," Fiona's sister-in-law Nancy teased.

"Talk about letting me down," Samantha grumped, but her eyes were laughing as she hugged Fiona in turn. "I was sure I could count on you to stay a klutz."

After more congratulations and good-natured grumping, the group began to move toward the house. Fiona was left with her sisters.

"You know what this means, don't you?" Cassie wanted to know.

Fiona stared at her. "We won."

"Oh, that." Sam shrugged it off. "It's just a game. We'll win next time."

"Then—" Her sisters were both grinning at her, but she just shook her head.

"I'm as likely to find Prince Charming as I am to kick a home run," Sam mimicked.

"I'm as likely to see Alex once I leave here as I am to kick a home run," Cassie said.

"I'm as likely to find a good parking place as I am to kick a home run," Sam finished.

They both just stopped and stared at Fiona, their faces expectant, but of what she didn't know. Their grins were definitely ones caused by little sisters seeing their big sister getting her due, though.

"What?" she finally said.

"Don't you see?" Sam asked, her voice ripe with exasperation. "You were wrong! You thought you'd never kick a home run but you were wrong about that."

"So how much else have you been wrong about?" Cassie demanded.

Fiona just looked from one to the other, a strange awareness growing in her. They were right. She had scored her home run. She had been wrong about that. Might she have been wrong about other things—like why Alex left?

But why else would he have left? He'd gone home so soon after learning about Fogarty, it had to be related. Although she would have thought Mr. Honesty would have told her the truth—

She stopped, feeling as if all the breath had been knocked out of her. Could that be it? Could he have left because he couldn't tell her the truth?

She shoved her hands into her pockets, and felt something in her right one. She pulled it out—it was a swan feather. The one she'd found on her birthday.

Everything came back all of a sudden. That anger she'd felt years ago that had enabled her to break all sorts of rules and help rescue Juliet. That need she had to find a way for happiness to bloom. That certainty that love was more precious than anything else.

Suddenly things looked possible. A slow anger started percolating in her. Alex had left because he couldn't tell her about Fogarty. He'd tossed aside their love for that? Didn't he realize how precious love was? That jerk. That fool. That man!

Maybe it was time somebody had a talk with him. The courage of the rescue was with her once more, churning in her veins and making her heart brave.

"I'm going to miss dinner," Fiona announced.

"You leaving the cake?" Cassie asked.

Fiona rolled her eyes. Typical Cassie. "Yes."

"Good." Cassie started back to the house, then turned. "Say hi to Alex for me."

Fiona pounded on Alex's door again—harder this time—then peered in through his front window. There was no sound, no movement within. Damn. If that wasn't her luck. She kicked at his aluminum storm door. The sound was loud and satisfying, but only momentarily so.

She'd fumed the whole ride up, planning just how she was going to give him a piece of her mind. How could he just throw away her love? Did he really think she'd rather have a dead ancestor than a live lover? And now she had nothing.

She didn't even have the joy of yelling at Alex. Who knew where he was? He could be out of town on another job. He could have moved, for all she knew. She stomped up the steps to the sidewalk. It had started to rain—in bucketfuls, and her jacket wasn't waterproof. What had she expected?

"Hello?" a voice called down at her.

Fiona turned and looked up, squinting into the rain to see an old man looking out an upstairs window. A little ray of hope crept into her heart. If this old man was anything like Mr. Kaminsky, he knew everything that went on in the building.

"I'm looking for Alex Rhinehart," she called up to him.

"It's Mother's Day," the old man said. "He's a good son."

What did that mean? "Did he take his mother out to dinner?" she called out.

"To Bowers," the old man replied. "Very expensive. He's a good boy to be so nice to his mother."

"Thanks," she called up to the old man and hurried back to her car, splashing uncaringly through the puddles. She was drenched by the time she got in.

So he hadn't escaped her, after all. Just had chosen a different setting for their confrontation. It didn't matter to her. She just was not going to let one extra minute go by without getting this settled.

She wasn't sure how she remembered the way to the restaurant, since she'd been pretty much in a coma that first night here, but she did. Maybe it was the spirits of the swans helping. The thought bolstered her and she parked in the first available place, not even bothering to look if it was a legal spot, then raced into the restaurant.

"May I help you?" The tuxedoed maître d' stood in her way, his eyes raking down her in disapproval.

Fiona glared at him. She knew just what she looked like—soaked from being in the rain, grass stains down the leg of her jeans and mud all over her white shoes. And she knew they had dress standards here, but for once she didn't care. The hell with their rules!

"I need to see one of your patrons," she said, her voice just as haughty as his. "Alex Rhinehart."

"I am sorry," he said. His voice had turned to ice. "If you would care to wait outside, I will get him for you."

Wait outside—in the pouring rain where she'd eventually give up and go away? She didn't think so. "Look, bud. This isn't going to take long."

The "bud" caused his eyebrows to flicker, like a power surge had bypassed his circuit box. "I'm afraid I must ask you to leave."

She felt a sudden surge herself—of strength, of determination, of conviction. She wasn't some silly little woman to be brushed aside; she was a home-run kicker. She was a rescuer of swans. She was someone who could make the impossible happen. And if winning Alex back didn't rank with the impossible, she didn't know what did.

"Look, it's not like you don't have water, mud and green stuff in your silly little pretend forest already," she retorted. "I'm not going to contaminate anyone."

She had not helped matters. Obviously, she didn't quite have this fighting business down pat.

He seemed to grow to about ten feet tall. "If you are going to be difficult," he said, "I shall have you removed." He looked over her shoulder and flicked his finger at someone, calling for reinforcements, no doubt.

But Fiona was not about to be thrown out. She'd come all this way to see Alex, and see him she would. Darting under the maître d's arm, she fled into the dining room with its pretentious maze of trees and little arbors and babbling brook. Dirty as she was, she should blend in very well with the scenery and stay hidden for days. But then, hiding wasn't the objective.

"Alex?" she called out. "Alex Rhinehart!"

The people nearest her looked startled, pulling back as if something unknown and dangerous had entered their midst. She grinned at them, and hurried farther into the room. From the commotion behind her, she knew the cavalry had arrived and she'd better be quick.

"I know you're in here, Alex," she shouted. "You can't hide from me."

"Fiona?"

She spun and saw him standing by a table across the room, his confusion clear even at a distance. She was about to hurry down the aisle between the tables that would take her over to him when she saw a group of hefty-looking men bearing down on her. Damn.

Turning the other way, Fiona squeezed between a grove of potted trees. The posse was getting close and she hurried—with apologies—past a group of strolling violinists who were watching with more amusement than horror. Then it was through the brook—whose water was incredibly cold—and through another grove of trees.

"What the devil is going on?" Alex said. "Is something wrong? Is it Kate?" His eyes were a mixture of worry and annoyance. And just a flicker of pleasure at seeing her.

"Hi to you, too," she said.

"Fiona, what is going on?" Alex asked.

But Fiona just ignored him, and turned to the older woman seated at Alex's table. "You must be Mrs. Rhinehart." Fiona's brain suddenly caught up with her mouth. "Oh, no, you're not, are you? Well, anyway, I'm really sorry to be interrupting your dinner."

"Fiona!"

Alex's mother slid out from her side of the booth, her gaze on something behind Fiona. "Nonsense. This looks to be quite entertaining. Much more so than my son's dreary conversation."

"Thanks, Mom."

His mother was ignoring him as she gestured for Fiona to slide into the booth between her and Alex. "But perhaps you should join us."

With a glance over her shoulder at the approaching bouncers, Fiona did as she was told. No sense in getting thrown out before she had her chance to give Alex a piece of her mind.

"Now what is going on?" Alex snapped. "If it's not Kate, then what is this all about?"

Fiona watched the security force near the table, her courage wavering for a moment. But then she wiggled her toes in her wet shoes and knew she had to go on.

"It's your own fault," she told Alex. "You've been acting like a complete jerk."

The older woman patted Fiona's hand. "It won't have been the first time, I'm afraid."

But Fiona refused to take her eyes off Alex. His were flaring at her. He was getting impatient, but she didn't care.

"Well, it had better be the last," Fiona said.

"Sir." The head bouncer was frowning at Alex. "Sir, we must ask this young lady to leave."

Alex didn't just frown back. He glared; he almost snarled although he didn't make a sound. The head bouncer took a step back.

"The young lady is dining with us," Alex informed him. "Please see that a place setting and menu are brought over."

The man looked at Fiona, then at Alex. It was obvious he didn't want to let her stay, but it was also obvious that he didn't want to make any further fuss. She fought the urge to make a face at him and studied the basket of rolls on the table.

"Very good, sir."

Fiona made a face at his departing back. "This is not one of my favorite places," she announced.

"I don't recall you being invited," Alex retorted.

"Alex!" his mother scolded.

"Don't 'Alex!' me," he said. "She's the one who made the scene and told me I was a jerk."

"I didn't say you were a jerk," Fiona corrected. "I said you were acting like one. There's a difference."

"I fail to see it."

"You've failed to see a lot of things." A waiter brought over her place setting but she just waved away the menu. "I'd really like a cup of hot tea. I'm a little chilled."

Alex's mother touched her arm. "My dear, you're frozen."

Alex slipped out of his suit coat and put it around her shoulders. His eyes were tired as if this was a battle he didn't want to fight. "Can we get back to the issue at hand?"

"You don't have to worry about getting a cold," Fiona said.

His eyes looked confused. "I beg your pardon."

She slipped one sopping shoe off and held it up. "See. No need to risk your health. I walked through the water."

"What are you talking about?" He was reaching down and grabbed hold of one of her feet. "My God, they're like ice." He brought her feet up into his lap and began to massage the feeling back into them.

"I'm not sure this is a good idea," Fiona said. Heat was rushing over her at his touch. She was, after all, trying to behave and not cause any further scenes.

"What isn't? You barging in here? Calling people jerks? Or getting your feet warmed up?"

The waiter returned with her tea, and salads for Alex and his mother.

"Would you like some salad, my dear?" Alex's mother offered.

"She can have mine," Alex said and shoved his plate so that it was in front of her. "I'm waiting for her to answer my question."

"I didn't come here to eat your salad," she said, shoving the plate back in front of him. She poured herself a cup of tea and warmed her hands on the cup.

"I don't mean to pry," Alex's mother said with a gentle touch on Fiona's arm. "But how would Alex's health be risked if you didn't walk in the water?"

"A good question."

Fiona took a sip of her tea, then faced Alex. "You once told me that love meant walking through the puddles and not expecting you to put your coat down."

"I did not!" he snapped.

She glared back at him. "Well, it was something like that."

"He's usually more chivalrous than that," his mother said. "He's always wanted to be Sir Lancelot or King Arthur or someone like that."

"Mother."

She glared across Fiona at him. "Well, it's true. I can't remember how many swords you made out of cardboard and wood."

"Mother, Fiona's not interested in that."

"Well, actually I am," she admitted. "But it's not the reason I came to see him. I came because he lied to me."

Anger flared again. "I did not!"

"You lied when you said it wasn't working out between us," Fiona went on.

"It wasn't," Alex said.

She put her cup down, then pulled her feet from his lap, tucking them under her so that she could be in complete control. It was now or never. "You left because you found out Horace Waldo wasn't my great-great-grandfather."

If ever she needed confirmation, it was there in his face. He looked stunned. All the fight seemed to go out of him. "How did you find out?"

"Same way you did. I went down to Mentone." Her anger left, but not the determination to win.

"I didn't want you to find out."

She took his hands in hers. "Alex, how could you think I'd rather have a dead ancestor than a live you?"

"Who's Horace Waldo?" his mother asked.

Fiona glanced over her shoulder. "Not my great-great-grandfather."

"You relied on him," Alex reminded.

"I relied on you more."

"You talked about him all the time."

"All the time, Mr. Honesty?"

He shrugged. "All right, not all the time. But enough."

She'd had enough of this fudging around. "Just tell me one thing," she said. "Do you love me anywhere near as much as I love you?"

He stopped as if frozen, but then looked away. "That's not the issue," he said.

"Of course, it is. It's the only issue. If you love me, we can work out the differences. If you don't, then there's nothing to talk about."

"Fiona—"

"Mr. Honesty—"

He sighed and turned her hands so that he was holding them. "Why are you doing this?" he asked. "It was all settled."

"Nothing was settled," she argued. "Except that you were running away from love."

"I am not," he cried.

"Sounds to me like you are," his mother said.

"You are," Fiona assured him. "That's all this boils down to. You're caught up in your fear of commitment just like Juliet was caught in the garbage."

"Who's Juliet?" his mother asked.

"Her swan," Alex said, then turned back to Fiona. "And I suppose you're planning on rescuing me."

"I already have," she said. "I cut away at your feeble excuse just like Cassie cut away at that plastic strip. I've offered you my total, unconditional, 'forever' love. You just didn't realize you were free."

His eyes said he wanted to believe her, but his voice was filled with doubt and caution. "Fiona—"

"Is something the matter with your salads?" the waiter asked. He sounded worried, as if his pay depended on them cleaning their plates, but Fiona was on a roll.

"They're fine," she assured him. "But do go away. I'm about to propose."

"Fiona!"

"Oh, do accept, Alex," his mother urged.

The waiter glanced at Alex's face and must have seen the obstinacy that Fiona saw, and then at his mother and her open curiosity. Then he turned back to Fiona and she could tell he was taking in her wet, dirty clothes and disheveled hair. But his face softened and he turned, clapping his hands sharply. Within a moment, the violinists were there, filling the afternoon with sweet romantic music.

The waiter bowed slightly; then, with a wink at Fiona, he straightened. "Will there be anything else, ma'am?"

"No, thank you very much." She turned to Alex. "Well? Will you marry me and take a chance? Or are you going to hide away forever?"

Alex just looked at her and she could see everything flashing through his eyes. His worries and fears. His love and adoration. His hunger. His need. His hope that wishes could come true. The violins grew louder.

"Oh, Fiona," he said as he pulled her into his arms. His voice was loud as he competed with the violins. "This isn't like you. What happened?"

"I kicked a home run in kickball," she told him.

Alex started to laugh and all his worries, all the shadows fled from his eyes. He bent down to kiss her lips as the violinists grew even louder and his mother started to clap.

"So is this a 'yes'?" Fiona asked.

"Yes," he mumbled, his lips otherwise occupied.

"At last!" his mother cried.

Epilogue

"We've got a lot to figure out," Alex said as he sat on the edge of Fiona's bed to pull his shoes off. "I don't think either of us want a two-hour commute."

"Jeez, engaged four hours and thinking up problems," Fiona teased. "You certainly are a worrier."

"I figure I'll move here. Either we move into a bigger place with office space for me or I'll just rent some away from our home."

"Are you sure?" Fiona asked. "Don't you have clients in Chicago?"

He shrugged. "Lots of my work is done by phone and computer nowadays. I shouldn't lose too many."

"Yeah, but—" The phone rang and Fiona lay across the bed to reach it.

"Fiona? It's Kate. Hi."

"Kate?" Fiona felt all wobbly and sat up straight as if it would give her strength. "How are you? How are you feeling?"

"Great," the girl said. "The doctor says it's looking real good. He thinks I'm making new blood cells, but it's a little too early to be sure."

"That's wonderful news." Alex took her free hand in his, holding it tightly.

"Yeah. I might someday get outta this jail." But her voice was laughing.

"I bet it'll be soon."

"Anyway, I was calling to wish you a Happy Mother's Day," she said.

Fiona's heart stopped. "You what?" They wouldn't have told her.

"Mom and Dad and me were talking this morning about how you kinda gave me a new life with the transplant and how that kinda made you like my mother in a way."

"Your mother?" Fiona gasped.

Kate laughed and it was like spring bursting out all over. "You know. Mothers give life and that's what you did. So if you want, you can be my honorary mom."

Fiona's eyes filled with tears, her world turned blurry. "I'd like that very much," she said. "Thank you."

Somehow she made small talk for a few more minutes, then got off to fall into Alex's arms. What did she need Horace Waldo for, when she had everything the world could offer and then some?

She suddenly pulled away from Alex. "Oh, darn," she said. "I forgot to tell Kate about my home run."

"You mean there's someone in the world who doesn't know?" he teased, then kissed the tip of her nose. "Relax. You can tell her next time. Or the time after that."

She smiled. That was true. There would be time for all that and more.

*   *   *   *   *

He was all rebel—and he needed a bride...

Cal Whitaker would not be refused. What he wanted was Lindsay Hayes—but now that he had marriage on his mind, suddenly the prospective bride-to-be was thinking anything but!

Can three sisters tame the wild hearts of three Texas brothers?

Find out in

THE REBEL'S BRIDE (SE #1034, June)
by **Christine Flynn**

Only from Silhouette Special Edition!

INSTANT WIN 4228 SWEEPSTAKES

OFFICIAL RULES

1. NO PURCHASE NECESSARY. YOU ARE DEFINITELY A WINNER. FOR ELIGIBILITY, PLAY YOUR INSTANT WIN TICKET AND CLAIM YOUR PRIZE AS PER INSTRUCTIONS CONTAINED THEREON. IF YOUR "INSTANT WIN" TICKET IS MISSING OR YOU WISH ANOTHER, SEND A SELF-ADDRESSED STAMPED ENVELOPE (WA RESIDENTS NEED NOT AFFIX RETURN POSTAGE) TO: INSTANT WIN 4228 TICKET, P.O. BOX 9021, BUFFALO, NY 12469-9021. Only one (1) "Instant Win" ticket will be sent per outer mailing envelope. Requests received after 5/31/96 will not be honored.

2. Prize claims received after 6/15/96 will be deemed ineligible and will not be fulfilled. The exact prize value of each Instant Win ticket will be determined by comparing returned tickets with a prize value distribution list that has been pre-selected at random by computer. For each one million or part thereof tickets distributed, the following prizes will be made available: 1 at $2,500 cash; 1 at $1,000 cash; 3 at $250 cash each; 5 at $50 cash each; 10 at $25 cash each; 1,000 at $1 cash each; and the balance at 50¢ cash each. Unclaimed prizes will not be awarded.

3. Winner claims are subject to verification by D.L. Blair, Inc., an independent judging organization whose decisions on all matters relating to this sweepstakes are final. Any returned tickets that are mutilated, tampered with, illegible or contain printing or other errors will be deemed automatically void. No responsibility is assumed for lost, late or misdirected mail. Taxes are the sole responsibility of winners. Limit: One (1) prize to a family, household or organization.

4. Offer open only to residents of the U.S., 18 years of age or older, except employees of Harlequin Enterprises Limited, D.L. Blair, Inc., their agents and members of their immediate families. All federal, state and local laws and regulations apply. Offer void in Puerto Rico and wherever prohibited by law. All winners will receive their prize by mail. No substitution for prizes permitted. Major prize winners may be asked to sign and return an Affidavit of Eligibility within 30 days of notification. Noncompliance within this time or return of affidavit as undeliverable may result in disqualification, and prize may never be awarded. By acceptance of a prize, winners consent to the use of their names, photographs or other likenesses for purposes of advertising, trade and promotion on behalf of Harlequin Enterprises Limited without further compensation, unless prohibited by law.

5. For a list of major prize winners (available after 7/15/96), send a self-addressed, stamped envelope to: "Instant Win 4228 Sweepstakes" Major Prize Winners, P.O. Box 4200, Blair, NE 68009-4200.

SWP-T596

My three sons...

Single dad (and one-time lady-killer): Craig Haynes
Nanny (two parts sweetness, one part sin): Jill Bradford

Pint-size redheaded nanny Jill Bradford proved a wizard
with Craig Haynes's three rambunctious boys. Could
a houseful of Hayneses ambush her wary heart...and
make her a mother and wife?

Find out in

PART-TIME WIFE
(SE #1027)
by Susan Mallery

Don't miss **THAT SPECIAL WOMAN!** every other
month from some of your favorite authors and
Silhouette Special Edition!

This July, watch for the delivery of...

An exciting new miniseries that appears in a different Silhouette series each month. It's about love, marriage—and Daddy's unexpected need for a baby carriage!

Daddy Knows Last unites five of your favorite authors as they weave five connected stories about baby fever in New Hope, Texas.

- **THE BABY NOTION** by Dixie Browning
  (SD#1011, 7/96)

- **BABY IN A BASKET** by Helen R. Myers
  (SR#1169, 8/96)

- **MARRIED...WITH TWINS!**
  by Jennifer Mikels
  (SSE#1054, 9/96)

- **HOW TO HOOK A HUSBAND (AND A BABY)**
  by Carolyn Zane
  (YT#29, 10/96)

- **DISCOVERED: DADDY** by Marilyn Pappano
  (IM#746, 11/96)

Daddy Knows Last arrives in July...only from

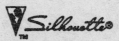

You're About to Become a *Privileged Woman*

Reap the rewards of fabulous free gifts and benefits with proofs-of-purchase from Silhouette and Harlequin books

Pages & Privileges™

It's our way of thanking you for buying our books at your favorite retail stores.

Harlequin and Silhouette—
the most privileged readers in the world!

For more information about Harlequin and Silhouette's PAGES & PRIVILEGES program call the Pages & Privileges Benefits Desk: 1-503-794-2499

Silhouette®

SSE-PP134